monsoonbooks

OPERATION HUNTER

Lt. Col. JP Cross is a retired British officer who served with Gurkha units for nearly forty years. He has been an Indian frontier soldier, jungle fighter, policeman, military attaché, Gurkha recruitment officer and a linguist researcher, and he is the author of twenty-four books. He has fought in Burma, Indo-China, Malaya and Borneo and served in India, Pakistan, Hong Kong, Laos and Nepal where he now lives. Nearing his century, he still walks several hours daily.

Operation Hunter is the ninth in a series of historical military novels set in Southeast Asia, including *Operation Black Rose*, *Operation Janus*, *Operation Red Tidings*, *Operation Blind Spot*, *Operation Stealth*, *Operation Four Rings*, *Operation Blowpipe* and *Operation Tipping Point*. The series features Gurkha military units, and the author draws on real events he witnessed and real people he fought alongside in various theatres of war in Southeast Asia and India.

'Nobody in the world is better qualified to tell the story
of the Gurkhas' deadly jungle battles against Communist
insurgency in Malaya in the 1950s. Cross spins his tale
with the eye of incomparable experience.'

John le Carré

'... a gripping adventure story ...
learn the ins and outs of jungle warfare from a true expert'

The Oldie (on *Operation Janus*)

Also by JP Cross

FICTION
The Throne of Stone
The Restless Quest
The Crown of Renown
The Fame of the Name
The Age of Rage
Operation Black Rose
Operation Janus
Operation Blind Spot
Operation Stealth
Operation Four Rings
Operation Red Tidings
Operation Blowpipe
Operation Tipping Point

NONFICTION
English For Gurkha Soldiers
Gurkha – The Legendary Soldier
Gurkhas
Gurkha Tales: From Peace and War
In Gurkha Company
It Happens with Gurkhas
Jungle Warfare: Experiences And Encounters
Whatabouts And Whereabouts In Asia

MEMOIRS
First In, Last Out:
An Unconventional British Officer In Indo-China

The Call Of Nepal:
A Personal Nepalese Odyssey In A Different Dimension

'A Face Like A Chicken's Backside':
An Unconventional Soldier In South-East Asia, 1948-1971

ORAL HISTORY
Gurkhas at War

OPERATION HUNTER

JP CROSS

monsoon

monsoonbooks

First published in 2024
by Monsoon Books Ltd
www.monsoonbooks.co.uk

No.1 The Lodge, Burrough Court,
Burrough on the Hill, Melton Mowbray LE14 2QS, UK

ISBN (paperback): 9781915310262
ISBN (ebook): 9781915310279

Cover design by Cover Kitchen.

A Cataloguing-in-Publication data record is available from the British
Library.

Printed and bound in Great Britain by Clays Ltd, Elcograf S.p.A.
26 25 24   1 2 3

List of Characters

Historical characters:

Ah Soo Chye, most senior guerrilla leader in north Malaya

Bongsu Helwood, chief Temiar in the east of Malaya

Chin Tiang, Deputy Head of the Malayan Communist Party's Central Propaganda Department

Lee An Tung, Head of the Malayan Communist Party's Central Propaganda Department

Lo See, a senior guerrilla in north Malaya

Mobarak, Ismail, Head of Special Branch, Seremban, known as 'Moby'

Tek Miu, a senior guerrilla leader in north Malaya

Too Chee Chew ('C C Too') brilliant propagandist, Special Branch, Malayan Police

Some of those below were real people, here disguised, and others only dwell in the author's imagination:

Ah Fat, police 'mole' and non-voting Politburo member, Malayan Communist Party

Ah Ho, name used by secret Malayan Communist Party courier

Chan Man Yee, Malayan Communist Party 'mole' in Police HQ, Kuala Lumpur

Chen Geng, Communist contact in Singapore

Cheng Fan Tek, a Hakka in Calcutta used as a cut-out to the Soviet consulate

Chen Man Yee, potential rapist and Communist operator

Chijbahadur Tamang, Sergeant, champion swimmer, 1/12 Gurkha Rifles

Chow Hoong Biu, fresh ration contractor for 1/12 Gurkha Rifles when Goh Ah Hok (q.v.) was absent

Danbahadur Rai, Gurkha Lieutenant, Platoon Commander, A Company, 1/12 Gurkha Rifles

Deng Bing Yi, uncle of Siu Tse (q.v.), who worked in a garage

Dow Gai Ngaan Yeh Yeh, Boss-eyed Grandfather

'Emissary' a.k.a. Meng Ru (q.v.), trusted member of Communist Party of China

Fong Chui Wan, a.k.a. Siu Tse, 'Little Miss' (q.v.), 'Little Sister' (q.v.) taxi-girl in the Yam Yam night club

Fong Heng Lit, bastard son of Fong Chui Wan (q.v.), sired by Hinlea (q.v.)

Forbes, Adrian, Lieutenant Colonel, Commanding Officer, 1/12 Gurkha Rifles

Foster, Dan, Captain, Auster pilot

Goh Ah Hok, fresh ration contractor for 1/12 Gurkha Rifles

Goh Ah Wa, surrendered guerrilla

Helbit, Norman, Director of Aborigines

Hemlal Rai, Rifleman, 1/12 Gurkha Rifles

Hinlea, Alan, Captain, renegade officer in 1/12 Gurkha Rifles

Jaslal Rai, Corporal, Light Machine Gunner, 1/12 Gurkha Rifles.

Jitbahadur Gurung, Rifleman, 1/12 Gurkha Rifles

Kwek Leng Ming, surrendered guerrilla

Kwek Leng Joo, barman at the Yam Yam night club

Kulbahadur Limbu, Rifleman, 1/12 Gurkha Rifles

Law Chu Hoi, ex-Purser of SS Eastern Queen

Lin Soong, guerrilla leader in central Malaya

Liu Yew Kui, purser of SS Princess of the Orient

{Little Miss, nickname for Fong Chui Wan (q.v.)

{Little Sister, nickname for Fong Chui Wan (q.v.)

Manbahadur Rai, CQMS, 1/12 Gurkha Rifls and one-time Havildar (Sergeant equivant in 3/2 Gurkha Rifles)

Mangalsing Tamang, Intelligence Corporal, 1/12 Gurkha Rifles

Mason, James, Colonel, Director of Intelligence, HQ Malaya Command

Meng Ru, Communist Party of China emissary, a.k.a. 'Emissary'

Ngai Hiu Ching, one-time schoolmaster in Mantin

Rance, Jason, officer in 1/12 Gurkha Rifles

Siderov, Sergey, MGB 'eyes' in Soviet consulate, Calcutta

Sik Long, Lustful Wolf, nickname of Hinlea (q.v.)

Siu Tse, taxi-girl in the Yam Yam night club, a.k.a. Fong Chui Wan (q.v.)

Sobolev, Leonid Pavlovich, MGB representative in Soviet consulate, Calcutta

Tay Wang Teik, Deputy Head of Special Branch, Seremban

Tsarkov, Dmitri, Deputy MGB representative in Soviet consulate, Calcutta

Wang Ming, a.k.a. 'Bear'. Hung Lo, deputy to Ah Fat (q.v.)

Wong Kek Fui, Hakka in Calcutta used as a cut-out to the Soviet consulate

Yap Cheng Wu, manager of the Yam Yam night club

Yeh Gwai Tsai, uncomplimentary nickname of Fong Heng Lit (q.v.) wild little devil

Abbreviations

2 ic	Second-in-Command
ADC	Aide de camp, personal staff officer to a senior officer
Air OP	Air Observation Post
'chopper'	helicopter
CO	Commanding Officer (of major units)
CQMS	Company Quartermaster Sergeant
CSM	Company Sergeant Major
CT	Communist Terrorist, 'Charlie Tare' in radio jargon of that time
ETA	estimated time of arrival
GOC	General Officer Commanding, a two star, **, officer
GR	Gurkha Rifles: grid reference
HQ	headquarters
IO	Intelligence Officer
KL	Kuala Lumpur
LMG	light machine gun
LP	landing point
MA	Military Assistant
MCP	Malayan Communist Party
MGB,	Soviet Ministry of State Security, Ministerstvo Gosudarstvennoi Besopasnosti, from 1946 to 1954 only
MRLA	Malayan Races Liberation Army
MTO	Mechanical Transport Officer
NCO	non-commissioned officer: ranks up to CQMS (q.v.)
NTR	nothing to report
OC	Office Commanding (of minor units)
OCPD	Officer in Charge Police District
'O' Group	'Orders Group', sub-commanders for whom any orders are relevant

QGO	Queen's Gurkha Officer
QM	Quartermaster
RAF	Royal Air Force
RV	rendezvous, previously arranged meeting place
SEP	Surrendered Enemy Personnel
sitrep	situation report
WO	warrant officer

Signals jargon

Acorn	Intelligence officer
Roger	message received
Starlight	senior medical practitioner
Strength 4	ability to receive messages from strength 5, 'loud and clear' down to strength 1, 'virtually unreadable'
Sunray	senior officer of unit contacted
Sunray minor	next senior officer of unit contacted
Wilco	will comply

Glossary

Chinese

I sincerely thank Mr Bernard C C Chan, MBE, AMN, for his unstinting help in matters Chinese.

char sui	crispy roast pork belly
boo long gei gain cueing	light machine gun
cheongsam	long, tight-fitting dress with slit sides
Dow Gai Ngaan Yeh Yeh	Boss-eyed Grandfather
Goo K'a bing	Gurkha soldiers
gwailo	foreign devil, European
loi pai yi wa	Nepali
Min Yuen	Masses Movement
ngau gok cheung	cattle horn weapon, Bren gun, from the shape of the magazine
Sinsaang	Mr, sir
t'o yan	'earth man', aborigine
tung chi	equal thinkers

Malay

anak	child
bomoh	medicine man
bukit	hill
gunong	mountain
ikan bilis	dried prawns
inche / encik	Mr
ipoh	a poisonous tree, Antiaaris toxis
ladang	an aboriginal settlement
orang	man
orang asli	aborigine
puteh	white
saka	'ancestral property', here used to describe aboriginal chief's hereditary area

sungei	river
tabek	welcome (from a junior to a senior)
tahu	know
taptibau	great-eared nightjar, Lyncornis temminckii
Tuan	sir, mode of address to someone senior

Nepali

ayo	come
chha	is
Cheena	Chinese
daku	(lit 'dacoit'), guerrilla
dushman	enemy
guru / guru-ji	a teacher, a non-commissioned officer
keta	lad
Sarkar	word used for Government and to royalty
ustad	a teacher, a non-commissioned officer

Russian

maskirovka	military deception, camouflage, deception

Temiar

One of the groups of orang asli or indigenous people of peninsular Malaysia, speaking their own language.

iwoh	rice harvest
rakid	raft
Senoi Praaq	fighting men, a quasi-military lightly armed recce force
tata	old man, term of respect
tongoq	headman

Note: place names in the book are spelt as they were at the time being written about.

Malayan Peninsula

PART ONE

PART ONE

1

The Anglo-Chinese bastard baby never knew his father. No one can ever say if his life would have been better or worse had he ever known him; probably not, as he was the result of a political gambit rather than of any procedure more normally followed between man and woman. His English father was killed in the jungle on Thursday 28 August 1952, some four months before he was born. His mother, Fong Chui Wan, better known as Siu Tse, 'Little Miss', did know who the father was and, to begin with, she had accepted his advances as 'part of the job'. She was a taxi-girl who worked in the Yam Yam, a sleazy nightclub in Seremban, Negri Sembilan, Malaya. The taxi-girls were all Chinese, delicately attractive in their long, tight-fitting, slit-sided *cheongsam*. Their work was to dance with, chiefly, sweaty red-faced Europeans, certainly in the early 1950s, who, once back at their tables, were then inveigled to buy drinks, always at inflated prices, while the girl they had danced with sipped lemonade. Unaccompanied girls either sat silently in small groups waiting to be picked up or else danced with one another. Not official whores – never would the British colonial administration have allowed such! But money was money, wasn't it? – especially for girls from poor families, 'squatters' living, mostly, in rudimentary shacks, without any legal tenure, in the waste land between the rubber estates and the jungle, or from the poorer end of town.

Like other similar places, during working hours lights were dim and there was no cooling system. At weekends the one room became over-crowded and the noise loud, with the atmosphere malodorous with sweaty bodies, cheap powder, cigarette smoke and alcohol fumes poisoning the air. A small band played and a man, bawling into a microphone, sang the local hits, *Rose, Rose I love you*, *A slow boat to China* and *Terang Bulan – Bright Moon* – over and over again. He seemed to know no other songs.

Most of the Europeans who frequented the place were junior British Army soldiers and, especially at weekends, junior planters from neighbouring rubber estates. Senior planters, British administrators – police and civil – and military officers relaxed at the Sungei Ujong Club, reserved solely for Europeans. Malays, Chinese and Indians had their separate places; that is how everybody liked it and everybody was used to it – each to his, fewer her, own.

The Japanese invasion of Southeast Asia during 1942 was like an unstoppable flood that very nearly but not quite wiped out all traces of pre-war colonialism. What it most certainly did achieve was a shift in the mindset of all Asians – and indeed Europeans – to such an extent that nothing was quite the same ever again. In Malaya, incipient communism started in 1928 when Communist agents from China established a South Seas Communist Party in Singapore, although the Malayan Communist Party, MCP, itself dates from 1930. The Japanese invasion of Malaya saw Chinese Communists join forces with British Army stay-behind groups but once the Japanese surrender had taken effect, Chinese Communists and the British went their separate, indeed opposite, ways.

Communist cells were found in a number of organisations, trade unions, drama groups and school boards being some of them. Others were found in places like the Yam Yam where the manager, Yap Cheng Wu, and the senior barman, Kwek Leng Joo, were card-carrying communists, the latter a member of the *Min Yuen*, the Masses Movement. Most squatters belonged to the *Min Yuen*, willingly sometimes, fatalistically always, such people's unspoken motto being 'Anything for a quiet life'. Almost every *Min Yuen* and guerrilla was Chinese so bonded together more easily than with any colonial master. Survival in Asia is to bend; not to bend is to break and anyone recalcitrant was easily bullied by the local strongmen. In this way they provided food, shelter and information to the communist terrorists (CTs) as by this time the guerrillas were officially designated.

The Yam Yam's senior barman, Comrade Kwek Leng Joo, was a messenger for the nearest guerrilla camp where the Negri Sembilan Regional Committee, the political wing of the MCP, lived. This was situated in a flat space surrounded by thick jungle not far from the summit of Bukit Beremban, 3293 feet high, itself overshadowed by the even higher feature, Gunong Telapak, at 3914 feet. It was guarded by elements of the Malayan Races Liberation Army, MRLA. The camp of the resident Gurkha battalion, 1/12 Gurkha Rifles, GR, could be seen from the guerrilla camp. Kwek Leng Joo did not go there often, only when there when he had news of special importance. Besides being a dangerous journey, it was unwise to establish anything like a pattern of movement that Special Branch might the more easily find out about. By 1952 Special Branch work was something the Brits were good at; they suspected both manager and barman but seemed happy to keep a 'weather eye' on them. In any case, until a communist victory, both men had to work surreptitiously.

Kwek Leng Joo had a good working knowledge of English so could normally understand what the 'bar proppers' were talking about, even though at times he found their accents and slang beyond him. He was normally able to pick up much useful information from loose-tongued and over-garrulous British soldiery, unaware of their indiscretions as they gossiped in his hearing, and occasionally of sufficient importance to make one of his infrequent journeys to the Regional Commissar in the jungle. When asked about his own politics, which was seldom, he always gave an 'I'm-not-interested' type of answer.

One frequent visitor was, unusually, a commissioned officer serving in 1/12 GR, a Captain Alan Hinlea. His childhood was moulded by nineteenth-century conditions found on the margin of society in a coal mining community. He had been a communist for as long as he could remember and his background was basic enough to make being a communist an obvious choice. It was one more than unlikely to make him a commissioned officer as he had come from a dirt-poor background in a coal-mining village in Nottinghamshire and had never lost the edge of his working-class accent. His father, a card-carrying and devoted communist who had visited Moscow and been 'initiated', passed on all his teaching to his son. The family of six lived in a small square room that served as kitchen, living room, eating place and, once a week, bathroom, the water used by two or three people before being changed, with a privy in the backyard and candlelight in the shared bedroom. He was culturally unsuited to any other type of society. His parents often went hungry to give their four children enough to eat and he grew into a big, strong lad, standing at five feet ten. His arrogant, haughty features were topped by an unwavering scowl, a permanent sneer and the pupils of his muddy brown eyes, always a-flicker, did not appear quite in the centre but rather high up, so always looking over ones' head. He was prone to making derogatory remarks that caused much embarrassment. He tried hard at the local school and, as would be expected in such a pre-war area, developed a hatred for his despised social superiors.

In those days government schooling was not of a high standard so his parents, knowing the use of education for any advancement, skimped and scraped enough money to better their only son. Never having any chance to play games other than kicking a ball in the street, he became a body-builder fanatic. He liked learning and was successful but such were the local feelings against anyone 'bookish', that other boys started to bully him when he was small – but he always won out – and by the time he was due to leave school he was strong enough to become the local gang leader.

His father had been a party member from an early age. 'You're dedicated all right, lad,' he told his son, 'but you'll fail in life unless you can convince those plutocratic swine who rule us that you're with them until you get the chance properly to do them down. There are two worlds with two views, "theirs" and "ours". When I was in Moscow I was taught about *maskirovka*, a trick to manipulate "them" into looking the other way and not for a moment guessing your real aim. I once learnt that the word January comes from Janus, meaning "looking both forward and back", almost "two-faced". Imagine that you're on a permanent military operation, let's say you give it the code-name "Operation Janus",[1] so that you are always making "them" look at your good record in the past and never guessing your real purpose in life for the future.'

Those words had stayed engraved in Hinlea's mind. During his formative years he had developed a capacity for total resentment against "them" that had never left him.

During the 1939-1945 war, everybody in Great Britain not in a reserved occupation, such as learning how to become a doctor or, for instance, an expert on a factory bench making fighter plane engines, had to enlist as a private soldier when he was two and half months short of eighteen.[2] After basic training, anyone who showed any spark of initiative and had passed his School Certificate Examination was seen as potential material for a commission. It was a travesty that Hinlea was ever considered good enough to be commissioned but by 1944 the War Office in London had to 'scrape the barrel' to get the numbers required. His peers looked on him as an over-educated nonentity. Around that time heavy casualties were expected – the invasion of the continent followed by the struggle against the Japanese. Had those two atomic bombs not been dropped and forced the Japanese to

1 See *Operation Janus*.
2 As happened in your author's case.

surrender, allied casualties would have had stupendous, most likely unacceptable.

Hinlea passed the War Office Selection Board and was sent to India for officer training. Having been a Gunner he was posted to an Indian Gunner regiment as a Second Lieutenant with a Short Service Commission. He was now one of 'them'. He thought that the British officers, the sahibs, behaved in a contemptible and supercilious manner with Indians and that appalled him. His own approach to the Indian sepoys was much too familiar for discipline but the normal relationship between officers and men, accepted for many, many years, was accepted by all as correct. Hinlea's Indian CO thought that he was a 'bad type' and was delighted to get rid of him at Independence in 1947.

Although Hinlea was unsuccessful in changing the Indian soldiers' views he still had that as a secret aim, so he was cunning, cautious and very, very careful as he waited for any opportunity to 'do the Brits down' before he left the army. He had no clear-cut plan, just an instinctive urge to stop being one of 'them', do and be his own 'thing' and in some inchoate manner 'make Indians happier than they were'. He was as impervious to reason and that uncommon faculty of common sense as are all communists, the party seeming to enshrine the worst of its followers and bring low even the more sensible of its members. Communism permits no doubt and says that belief can be implanted like a conditioned reflex and which answers to questions – and the questions are always there: Whence? Where? Why?

He kept his long-term thoughts inside as much as he could but made no secret of how happy he was when India got its independence, so could now get rid of all the British colonialists. Learning that four Gurkha battalions were leaving the Indian Army to join the British Army he felt distressed. He would like to see Gurkha battalions no more officered by British officers but by the Gurkhas themselves who should command their own men. When he heard that the two battalions of the 12th Gurkhas were to be made into a Gunner regiment he saw his chance of seeing what he could do to get rid of British officers, so he requested a posting to one of the battalions. He was posted to 1/12 GR in early 1948 and joined them in Seremban, Malaya. The communists started the shooting war in June of that year, which would become the Malayan Emergency.

Hinlea prided himself on being a woman's man, hence his frequenting the place where even to clutch a woman was an outlet for his frustration. Clutching merely being 'stage one' and so lascivious was he, he was given the name of Lustful Wolf, *Sik Long*, by the taxi-girls. During the intervals between dances he would go to the bar and over the months he was unwittingly and easily induced to talk about his dislike of the colonial system and British class arrogance, the barman taking full note of everything said although only appearing indifferently sympathetic.

Apart from absorbing a hatred of the class system he had had a personal grudge ever since being prevented from becoming a temporary member of the Darjeeling Club when talking to the secretary his Party membership card had slipped out onto the table, with the following oral drubbing causing him shame and offence; and again before the Emergency started when invited to a Mess Night by 2/12 GR in their tented lines in Wardieburn

Camp, Kuala Lumpur. He had managed to save up some money to buy a second-hand Singer Roadster, an open-hooded car, safe in the knowledge that the British Treasury was taxing officers in Gurkha units at Malayan not British rates because their long-term service was in Malaya, not Britain. He had driven up to camp after booking into a hotel. At dinner he had drunk too much and become offensively and openly anti-British. As a punishment, some of the subalterns kept him drinking after the meal while others jacked up both rear wheels of his car.

After warning the others and the Mess staff to get out of the way, they escorted Hinlea to his car. He got in, put it in gear and let out the clutch, waving good bye as he did. It didn't 'click' he wasn't moving forward as he changed gear and pressed the accelerator hard, waving goodbye once more. The car, vibrating violently, fell off the jacks, 'dived' into the by-now empty Mess tent, hit one of the upright poles thereby bringing the tent down over it. Luckily the engine stalled and a badly frightened and sobered Hinlea crept out.

As he put himself to rights, one of the subalterns leant over to him and whispered, 'Never come back with your party line. You may destroy the tent but you can never destroy our Gurkha regiments by your filthy propaganda.' Hinlea, furious, vowed he never would and those two incidents soured him even more – and irrevocably.

Sensing a 'catch', the communist manager and bartender of the Yam Yam hatched a plan to make Hinlea commit himself, initially, of only being open to blackmail. To keep him talking, Siu Tse was 'given' to him as his own for no extra charge and the two of them were lent a room at the back of the building. The lure for the penurious girl of a steady income, even in 'enemy' England – hunger knows no political loyalty – attracted her sufficiently to give herself to him to give her a better life. However, she was not his first priority, politics was. Even so, she, with rudimentary English – he did not know any Malay or Chinese to say more than a few words – ensured he never lost his interest in her.

Tongue loosened by drink, Hinlea started talking against the colonial British when propping up the bar. As he was not contradicted he opened his heart more and more about his real views to a sympathetic barman, who now realised that there was no need to think anymore of blackmail so, after a couple of months, the barman quietly suggested telling the manager, Yap Cheng Wu, of the Lustful Wolf's desire to joining the MCP. Siu Tse was ordered to play her part and so drifted into pregnancy more as a duty than a desire. Party policy and tactics were never to be gainsaid.

The Gurkhas never liked him; they saw he was not a 'proper Saheb' so somehow resented him. His Nepali language was primitive, mixed with Urdu from his Indian Army days, and the men obeyed him even if he was apt to be too familiar. He saw them as illiterate peasants who were being exploited. He didn't like their being under colonial Brits and he could not understand that Nepal had never been part of the British Empire and, for Gurkhas, service in the army was the only honourable job, with a pension at the end of it, that was open to them. Gurkhas were pragmatic enough to accept foreign leadership, especially when the officers saw them as individual men rather than cumbersome peasants as was the case in their own country, when pay and pension were of paramount importance.

1/12 GR had been made infantry **again** in early 1949 but even so Hinlea, despite being a gunner and not infantry trained, asked to stay on to finish his three-year tour before discharge. Until then he would pretend to be anti-communist – *my own* maskirovka! – but all the while secretly plotting to join the MCP, using the undercover comrades in the Yam Yam to help him lay his plans. With the manager's help this was initiated but took a long time to eventuate. During this phase of his metamorphosis the only officer in 1/12 GR with whom he liked to pass the time and ask questions about Gurkhas and Malaya was a Captain Jason Rance. Radiating health and self-assurance, taut as a strung bow and as active as a hunting leopard when on operations, Rance was nearly six feet tall and just over ten stone, with fair hair, a resolute face and clear blue eyes that had the ability to penetrate and probe into another's. His gaze was steady and non-committal until provoked, which was not often. The breadth of his shoulders, the long muscular neck and the convex lines of his chest were evidence of a body honed to physical precision and strength. He was slender but not thin, his was the tautness that comes with discipline, training and a fully active life. Crosshatching of fine wrinkles at the corner of his eye sockets bespoke time spent in the Asian sun. This was because Rance had been born there, in 1922, so knew more about Malaya than did any other officer.

Hinlea never hinted of his plans to join the MCP and, in turn, Rance never told Hinlea that he had been brought up with a

Chinese lad, Ah Fat, of his own age, and was bilingual in Chinese, knowing enough characters for simple reading and writing, nearly as fluent in Malay and that he was a ventriloquist. He never talked about his Chinese 'brother' Ah Fat who had joined the communist guerrillas fighting against the Japanese and, so convincing had he been, the MCP had accepted him and he had risen to the heights of being a non-voting Politburo member – but as a police 'mole'.

The Negri Sembilan Regional Committee based near the top of Bukit Beremban was told of Hinlea's wish to join the MCP by Kwek Leng Joo who, using his usual guile, reached the base unobserved. It so happened he got there during a visit by two senior officers of the Politburo, one being the mole Ah Fat, who had been sent south to investigate a possible 'leak' in the armed struggle. One thing led to another and, for the first time since Jason Rance left Malaya in 1938 to go to school in England, he and Ah Fat, both using the most careful tradecraft, secretly met up in Seremban. It was then that Ah Fat alerted Jason Rance to Hinlea's secret – oh, how secret! – plans to try and join the MCP Politburo and the very few people it was essential to be told about it, the 1/12 GR CO and the Officer in Charge Police District, the OCPD. Accordingly, they were briefed. Had that not been the case Hinlea's disappearance would never have been traced, nor, most likely, would he have been killed.

With the manager's help, Hinlea eventually disappeared and started on his long, arduous and dangerous journey. It took much time to arrange but happen it did. By that time Siu Tse was pregnant; she never did know if her Alan knew that she was. Hinlea secretly left the battalion to join the guerrillas over a weekend so had a two-day head start. No one knew where he had gone. He was escorted to the Regional Committee camp prior to onward despatch to HQ MCP in north Malaya. There he was introduced to Ah Fat, the comrade from the Central Committee, responsible for taking him north. Hinlea could never know that Captain Rance knew Ah Fat. A few days after they had started off, Hinlea correctly suspected Ah Fat of planting a gizmo in the radio set that the Political Commissar of the Negri Sembilan Regional Committee, who was in charge of the escort party taking him on the first 'leg' of his journey, was linked to a tracking Auster aircraft. He was also ignorant until just before he was killed in the jungle that Rance was bilingual in Chinese and a proficient ventriloquist, so he never passed that on to his anticipated future wife. She too did not know about those attributes, did not know Rance's name nor did she recognise him.

The operation to re-capture Hinlea had only been the total success it was because of some brilliant detective work by Captain Jason Rance, who, by using his Chinese language skills, had discovered his till-then secret destination and equally brilliant work when he and a four-man team, with superb tracking and fieldcraft skills, had successfully caught up with the absconding guerrilla group taking him to the Central Committee, a few week's hazardous journey away in north Malaya. After a fierce fire fight Hinlea and several guerrillas had been killed. Those remaining had surrendered to Rance, saying they were ready to serve under him against other guerrillas if he so wished them to.

The forward elements of the guerrilla escort group, clearing the way for Hinlea and his escort, had been ambushed by the main part of the battalion farther on. In all it was an operation perfectly carried out. The fact that Captain Jason Rance and his four-man follow-up team were responsible for Hinlea's death – it was actually Rifleman Kulbahadur Limbu who had shot and killed Hinlea when he had been about to kill Rance – was thought to be a watertight secret. But what secret is watertight forever?

The taxi-girl Hinlea most used for pleasure, Fong Chui Wan, better known as Siu Tse, was born in 1920 in a squatter area behind Bhutan Estate, not all that far southwest from Seremban. Her childhood was the same as in many other poor Chinese families, a struggle to make ends meet. Her father had come from south China to work on the rubber estates but during the '20s and '30s the price of rubber had fallen through the floor; life was so bad he cursed himself for ever leaving China but he could not go back. He was lucky to find work in a timber concession in a government forest reserve so made ends meet – just. He even managed to get his children some basic schooling. His favourite daughter was Fong Chui Wan. As she grew up she became pert, petite and pretty enough to be attractive to young men. One of the things she found she loved and was good at was climbing trees. When she played 'hide and seek' with her playmates she often hid up trees which meant she was never found. It was that that gave her a taste for winning and confidence to walk where trees were. There were a lot in the area where she lived.

By April 1938, at 18 years of age, she knew she was ripe

enough to have to be careful of straying too far from home by herself. Daytime was considered safe enough but nights, never. There was talk of some bad men who 'did things' to young girls they came across in the jungle. There was, apparently, one particularly savage one who was recognised by having one eyebrow higher than the other, a face that looked almost like a pig's, with a sour mouth and who was known for his perpetual bad breath. In the police books, rudimentary as they were, he was listed as Chen Man Yee.

One day Chui Wan was sent on an errand by her mother, 'you have to be quick as this is important so go the short route through that corner of jungle. There'll be no risk as it is daylight and if you see any wild animal you can always climb a tree. You're so good at that aren't you?'

'Yes I am,' she said, but even so she hesitated to obey her mother, something most unusual. 'Mother, I am worried by those bad men I've heard about.'

'Nonsense, child. That's girls' talk. You'll be quite safe as it is daylight and there's a track.'

Off she went, not really convinced, but her mother had somewhat mollified her. She was about halfway down the narrow track running through thick jungle when suddenly she was grabbed by two men. Before she could scream a hand clamped her mouth, the ring on one finger scratching her cheek and drawing blood. The men dragged her away to the edge of a patch of open ground where someone had, a long time ago, built a small shrine by a well, now dried out, with crumbling side walls. She managed to get her mouth free by biting the hand over it and screamed shrilly as she resisted as bitterly as she could – but to no avail. *If I had known and had time enough I'd have hidden up a tree* flashed though her mind in the middle of her abject fear. She was wearing a *samfoo*, comprising a brown cotton top and pyjama-type trousers, also coloured brown, and one of the men lifted her legs and easily pulled them down before he tried to mount her. She kept her legs tightly closed but he was rough with her. The thongs she wore on her feet slipped off. To keep her quiet the second man sat on her head.

That very same day a 16-year-old good-looking English boy with fair hair and blue eyes named Jason Rance had gone to Bhutan Estate to visit a Gurkha friend he had met in the previous school holidays. Jason lived about sixty miles or so away in Kuala Lumpur and, with his Chinese friend, Ah Fat, used to go to Sepang, a village to the southwest of Seremban, and then on to Bhutan Estate which had a Nepali labour force, during the holidays. There just the pair of them or with the Nepali boys from Bhutan Estate, they went and tracked each other through the jungle. On this occasion Ah Fat could not go with him so Jason was allowed to go on his own. He met up with his friend with whom he was to spend the night and they went to see a shaman who had come from Darjeeling,[3] armed with some unhusked rice and a ten-dollar note. The shaman was old, rheumy-eyed and long-haired with a wispy grey beard and exuded an aura of authority. Jason was shown a board, not much bigger that a child's school slate

---

3   See *Operation Black Rose*.

and now wiped clean from the last occurrence, and the shaman covered it with fine dust. Jason was told where to put the rice on it. He also placed his ten Straits dollars on the ground beside the board and was bidden to sit. The old man started by putting his liver-spotted, grave-marked hands in the rice, feeling it, lifting some and letting it fall, and gently kneading it. He asked Jason his name and age, all the while staring hard at the young English boy, forcing eye contact. Picking up a stick he started drawing lines on the heaped rice, seemingly at random, scrutinising the grains carefully.

This shaman told young Jason that seven men would try to kill him, but not all at once and over a period of a few years. That worried him so the two boys left and the Gurkha invited Jason back home. 'I'd like to think over what I was told,' he said. 'Let me go for a walk by myself to clear my thoughts.'

'Fine by me. Come back before dark as you might lose your way.' Just as Jason was about to set off his friend said, 'take my khukri; never know when you might meet a leopard. He looked up at the sky and saw some menacing dark clouds. 'Here, take my umbrella too,' and he went into the house, brought it out and handed it over. It was the wax-covered canvas Malayan type with wooden rods.

Jason gratefully took them both, thanking his friend for his forethought, carrying the umbrella in one hand. Wearing a white shirt and grey slacks, with a pair of canvas shoes on his feet, he walked slowly towards the jungle. He made his way to where he knew it was quiet and he could mull over what he had been told earlier on, to a patch of open ground where someone had, a long time ago, built a small shrine by a well. As he was nearing it he heard shrill screams and a man's voice, followed by the sound of a heavy smack. Without a second thought he quickly and quietly went to investigate. What he saw on the far side of the clearing, not far from the edge, were two Chinese men, dressed like any worker on a rubber estate and a young Chinese woman. One man slapped her hard in the face, threw her to the ground and sat on her head, muffling her cries while the other groped at her underwear.

The instinct for survival, on the girl's behalf, overwhelmed him. *I simply must save her, come what may.* It was the first time ever he had witnessed such brutality and it instinctively overwhelmed him.

Before deciding quite what to do and while still out of sight he saw a third Chinese man, armed with a crowbar, emerge from the far side of the small clearing, unobserved by either man engaged with the girl. Creeping up behind the man sitting on the girl's head the new arrival smashed his crowbar down on his skull. The man collapsed, sprinkling blood over the other one and knocking him off the girl. The second perpetrator managed to get up, pushed the attacker to one side and closed with him to prevent any more swinging arm movement. The attacker was quicker and deftly slipped a knife out of his pocket and stabbed his adversary in the throat. Blood gushed over the dead man lying on the girl, not on the girl herself. The man with the knife looked around and saw nobody. He went over to the man he had first killed and, lifting him up over his shoulder, took him to the well and dropped him inside. He came back and did the same to the other corpse. By then his clothes were truly blood-stained.

During this time Jason made a quick detour through the trees to get as near the girl as possible. The killer had left his knife near the well, came back empty-handed and, grinning fiendishly, took down his trousers, ready to lower his rampant self onto the girl.

Chui Wan, already paralysed by fear, looked up and saw an ugly, wicked, pig-like face looming over her. It had one eyebrow higher than the other giving it a sardonic and quizzical leer. His bad breath overpowered her. She fainted.

Jason, hidden and unseen, remembered the most vicious curse in Chinese that Ah Fat had taught him and, making his voice come from behind the man's head, he spat out 'Get away from that girl. *Ch'uan jia chan!*' – may your entire family be wiped out. In ancient days a punished man's entire family would be wiped out and even in modern times hearing it induced such fear that often no counter-reaction was shown.

The man, almost stunned by shock, looked behind him but saw no one. Jason repeated the oath and it really did seem that the voice came from one of the men he had killed but whose corpse was no longer there. From the undergrowth Jason saw the man's ugly face clearly. *Easy to recognise again!* The man, stood up, tried to move forward and fell over, bursting his nose on the ground, having forgotten to do up his trousers. He stood up again, shakily, and re-arranged his trousers properly. As if without thinking, he muttered 'ghosts, ghosts, I must get away and never come back.' He scuttled away though the jungle, Jason listening until silence replaced the noise.

Going over to the girl, he saw her eyes flutter open so he

gently lifted her up to put her undergarments and trousers back on. Still thinking she was about to be raped, she squirmed helplessly, moaning, 'no, no.' He saw that her face was red where it had been brutally slapped and a ring on the slapper's finger had scratched her cheek and drawn blood.

'I'm a friend. I am rescuing you,' Jason, answered softly in Chinese as he gently helped her to his feet. He gently patted the dirt off her back and buttocks with his hand. She thanked him, not having realised how dirty she had been from lying on the ground, luckily dry enough to be easily brushed off.

'Oh, my face hurts.' She put her hand up to it, touched her cheek and winced. She withdrew her hand and saw blood on it.

Jason carefully dabbed the blood off her cheek with his handkerchief. It was rimmed in blue, a fad of his mother's who did not like sharing handkerchiefs. Hers had a green rim and her husband's were red. The girl flinched. 'Sorry if I hurt you,' he crooned consolingly. 'When we get to a stream I'll help you wash your face clean.' He had no intention of letting her find out what was in the well.

She looked at him, eyes brimming with tears of gratitude now she knew she was with someone ready to look after her kindly. Her heart was too full to say anything. She was still unbalanced by her sudden rescue – and by such a good-looking lad.

'Let's get away from this place. Can you walk? I'll help you. If so, let's move off, slowly, and find a stream to wash your face.' Jason smiled as he encouraged her.

Before they moved off the girl tried to tidy herself and Jason went to retrieve his umbrella.

She took a couple of hesitant steps then stopped. She had not been raped, only roughly handled but nevertheless it was painful for her to walk, even slowly.

'Yes, with your help I can manage,' she whimpered, pointing out the way she wanted to go. She said nothing as she bit by bit came back to her senses.

They slowly moved off, Jason with one arm round her shoulders and her hand in his. When they came to a stream they stopped and he carefully bathed her cheek for her with his handkerchief. 'Hold the handkerchief against your face for a bit. It will stop it bleeding.'

'Where did those dreadful men go to?' she asked, looking behind her as though they were following her.

'I severely cursed them and they ran away,' he dissembled. She did not ask him what his curse was. In any case what he was saying hardly made sense to her in her disturbed state of mind. Jason did not elaborate.

'Will they come back again?' she asked with a shudder.

'No, there's no worry about that.'

They reached the edge of the jungle. She stopped. 'I must sit down a while,' she said.

Jason let go of her hand, took his arm from round her shoulder and said, 'let's sit on that log under that big tree for as long as it takes for you to get your strength back.'

'If I had known what was going to happen to me I'd have climbed a tree,' she said, looking at him as they sat down. 'I'm a good tree climber.'

That struck him as an unusual activity for any girl. 'I am sure you are. Good, now let's be good log-sitters,' he grinned back at her as they wriggled themselves comfortable. It started to rain. Jason opened his umbrella over both of them, thanking his friend's foresight. Malayan umbrellas are not wide so they had to sit close together not to get wet. Putting his free arm around her to keep her as dry as possible as well as calming her nerves, he looked down at her face as she looked up at his. Warm smiles matched each other. He decided to sing her a song he'd learnt from Ah Fat, based on the lullaby, *Bright Moonlight*, changing the words from boy to girl and improvising where necessary. Looking into her eyes, he sang:

> *The sun shines its bright light on the hill,*
> *Bright Virtue, be good and go back home to bed,*
> *For tomorrow morning mummy has to rush to plant seedlings,*
> *And grandpa has to go up the hills to tend cattle.*
> *Bright Virtue, will you grow up quickly,*
> *To help grandpa tend cattle and sheep?*
> *The sun shines its bright light on the hill,*
> *Bright Virtue, be good and go back home.*

It was a virtuoso performance, something she had never expected nor ever heard before. Returning his gaze she hugged him tightly, head nestling into his chest, her breath shortening as tears gushed. Jason, having no sisters so not used to such behaviour, reacted by cuddling her as his mother had cuddled him when he had been hurt as a small boy. He took his handkerchief out of her hand and dabbed her eyes with one dry corner of it.

'You called me Bright Virtue,' she said, smiling shyly as she looked at him and saw someone she couldn't take her eyes off. There was something compelling in his youthful good looks. *If only I was able to get to know him better and, who knows ...* The thought of what hateful thing had nearly but not quite happened to her earlier on was overtaken by its opposite, so taken was she. She was still not quite herself but happily cuddled up to him, putting one arm around him. Saying nothing as the rain was noisy on the umbrella, they sat silent till the rain eased off. Then she turned fully towards him and, taking his face in both hands, kissed him, slowly at first, then fervently. Jason had no option but to respond likewise, natural for both youngsters.

'Tell me your name,' she asked him shyly.

Instinct came to Jason's rescue. 'Just call me Shandong P'aau' – Southern Mountain Cannon – 'as I was strong enough to rescue you. And tell me yours.'

'I never use my name so people call me Siu Tse.' Siu Tse, Little Miss.

'Siu Tse, are you strong enough to go back home by yourself?'

Yes, she was. 'Where will you go, Shandong P'aau?'

'Oh, Bright Virtue, I'll find somewhere.'

She seemed to have forgotten why she had gone to the jungle in the first place. 'Will you take me home?' she asked shyly, not really wanting him to leave her.

Jason, without hesitation but kindly, told her he would not have the time to go so far.

'Will we meet again?'

Jason answered by quoting a short Chinese saying to her: '*Yau*

T'in pat yau yan' – It's up to heaven, not up to man. 'The rain has stopped and we'd better make a move.' She seemed unaware that an English (whom she presumed he was) man was talking Chinese to her. 'Go home now and don't come this way again by yourself.'

'Can I keep this handkerchief as a lucky charm? As a keepsake?'

He did not answer immediately.

'Oh please, please.'

'Very well then, if that's what you want,' he said helping her to her feet.

She smiled her thanks. 'I have nothing to give to you.'

'Oh, there's no need to worry about that.'

They parted. Once she looked back at him, heart heavy and feelings mixed. She wondered what her mother would say about her bruised cheek. She washed the blood-stained handkerchief before she reached home, knowing blood stained quickly but the stain could be got out with cold water. In fact she was unable to completely take the stains out but only then did its blue border strike her. As handkerchiefs were not part of her or her mother's belongings she had not seen that sort before. *My keepsake!* There and then she decided that only if she kept it with her would she be safe as her mother would be too inquisitive if she showed it to her.

Her mother saw her swollen and cut cheek and asked what had happened. Her daughter took a side step from the truth and said that a stranger had hit her when he had met her on the path through the jungle and tried to be 'familiar with me so I kicked him hard on the shin and in return I got this in my face. I came straight back home as I was afraid to go any farther alone.' Had she mentioned any fumbling 'down there' her mother would suspect that she had lost her virginity and problems galore would follow. She had expected her mother to say that it had taken a long time to come back home just for that but luckily no such query was asked.

Her mother accepted her tale, shaking her head at such a narrow escape. She went to lie down on her bed, looking back in her mind's eye the whole ghastly few minutes before that good-looking young saviour came. *I'll never be able to thank him properly. Will I ever meet him again?* she thought with a little prickle of lust 'down below' as she drifted off to sleep.

On his return, Jason gave the khukri and the by-now dry brolly back to the owner. 'I didn't need to use the khukri but the umbrella came in very useful.'

'Enjoy your walk?' his friend asked him.

'Yes, it gave me a lot to think about.' His friend, thinking he was talking about the shaman's prophesy, did not want to probe so asked for no details. Jason was glad to get on the bus on the morrow and even gladder to get back home in Kuala Lumpur later in the day.

'Did you have an enjoyable time?' his parents asked him. 'You look just a little bit tired for only one night away.'

He took his time to answer. 'No mother, not tired. My stay was more fascinating than enjoyable, you might say, yet I am glad I went. I wouldn't have missed it for anything.'

'That's good, dear. Go and have a shower before your tea,' said his mother with a smile. He was glad she had not asked him where his handkerchief was. As he lay in bed before dropping off to sleep he played the whole business over in his mind, as he had also done in his friend's house. *I doubt I'll ever forget what happened … yes, she did seem grateful for what I managed to do for her … I doubt I'll ever forget her … I wonder for how long she'll remember me?*

Red ants, with huge nests in the banyan tree by the once-wet well and attracted by the smell of blood had eaten so much flesh within twenty-four hours the two corpses were unrecognisable; it took the clothes longer to rot so when the two ragged skeletons were eventually found many years later nobody bothered to report the matter to the police so they could still be there. Certainly neither Jason Rance nor Fong Chui Wan ever mentioned it again, for different but obvious reasons.

2

Fong Chui Wan's mother worried that her daughter needed something to keep her occupied so she would be safer than being at her mother's beck and call, however inconvenient that be. She therefore decided her daughter, who knew how to cook, should find a suitable place not so far away and work there.

It happened that not far from their house there was a shop that served food so cooking took place there and help was always needed. It was owned and run by a friend of Chui Wan's father and as the owner's eyes had a heavy squint they were known as 'fighting cock' eyes and the man as Dow Gai Ngaan Yeh Yeh, Boss-eyed Grandfather. Fong Chui Wan's father owed him a debt and as he had no money to spare he sent her to help out instead. Boss-eyed Grandfather was famous for his breakfast *cha siu bao*, dumplings filled with barbecued pork, and his specialities were *dai bao*, twice as big and filled with hardboiled egg, chicken meat and mushroom, to say nothing of his *char siu*, crispy roast pork belly. The shop also sold items the local Chinese needed, mainly rice, dried fish, spices, vegetables such as brinjal (aubergine), beans, bitter gourd and pumpkin, mostly brought in from the squatter area, as well as basic household articles, including cheap clothes, local medicines and condensed milk that Chinese mothers gave their babies. Chui Wan, or Siu Tse as she was more commonly addressed, was of great use to Boss-eyed Grandfather, especially when he was selling stuff and his wife was busy with his young family. She paid off her father's debt and stayed there until the Japanese invaded Malaya. That was bad news for everybody. She didn't think it would affect her, nor did it until the Japanese put the shopkeeper to working on the land and took Siu Tse away to work at a new nightclub, named Yam Yam, the Japanese commander had ordered to be opened in Seremban. There, with a number of other girls, the Japanese used them for more than dancing. One night in the autumn of 1943 Siu Tse was taken outside and raped. Although she once more screamed as loudly as she could there was no saviour like that last time.

In 1944 when obviously pregnant, the Japanese threw Siu Tse out of Yam Yam so she had to return home to the squatters' area where she gave birth to a son. She stayed there as long as was needed to give him milk but the little creature seemed doomed from birth with ill health and died before he was eighteen months old. The baby's mother was torn: the birth of her baby, however ill-conceived he had been, was a severe blow to her happiness.

By then the war had ended and the Japanese troops had withdrawn from Malaya and gone back to Japan. Her pre-war saviour was but a distant albeit happy memory, sadly not on hand to deliver her from similar troubles, and, when feeling down in the dumps, she'd take 'that' handkerchief out and look at it. It had not been properly washed after he had given it to her and there was still a stain near one corner. But that did not matter; it was a constant and happy memory for her. She often looked at returning

British military in the vain hope of seeing him but she never did; in fact she never really expected to meet him again especially after a dream – from which she had woken in tears – which had caused her to believe he had been killed in the war. She gave up all hope of ever meeting him again. But the last part of the dream, mixed with real life, remained, him turning around and waving before disappearing into a mist.

'I need money,' her father complained, so Fong Chui Wan went back to Seremban to see if the Yam Yam was still functioning. It was, just, but came properly alive again in early 1948 when a British Army HQ, a Gurkha battalion, an Army Air Corps flight of Auster aircraft, and supporting troops – for example medical, provost, transport and supply – were posted in to counter the increasing guerrilla activity. British troops liked the place but the Gurkhas never did, it was not their 'thing' and, even had it been, strictures on what they were allowed to wear when out of the lines and a lack of money made their presence there a complete non-starter.

That was when her Alan Hinlea entered her life, changed it by hinting of marriage and by making her pregnant before disappearing. She thought she would be sent for. She knew it would take quite a time, several months maybe, before he could arrive at the Central Committee. First the request had to be taken by hand, then discussed, then the answer brought back before he himself could make the journey – if they said yes – which was much more than a month's walk away. When she knew she was pregnant she realised that her man would not have known but as she firmly believed they would meet up in his new place, it did not worry her. But after several months with no news at all she became seriously worried. The baby was born, an unwanted embarrassment to her family, a shame and a burden to his mother with no firm news and a problem to the village society. Still not knowing that the father was dead, she gave him a name sounding like Hinlea, Fong, her family name, Heng, prosper, and Lit, strong. This was a sentimental gesture to her future husband – she still thought he was alive. It made no difference in any kindness shown to their – *not only my* – son, if anything the opposite for those who realised why those two names had been given. In any case it was always a problem to be a poor native in a British colony, though she would never know that it was worse in a French and Dutch one. It was also hard to be a Chinese in Malaya, especially later after it had gained independence, harder still to be a bastard of mixed blood, Chinese and English.

However, the baby was her son and she came to love him. She nursed him in her home in the squatter area and her parents accepted what had happened. The manager of the Yam Yam told his senior barman to make a journey to the Regional Committee camp to try and get confirmation that *Sik Long* (always *Sik Long* as they did not like Hinlea) had safely reached the HQ of the MCP, to see if there was any news of her joining him, to let them know about the boy also to try to arrange for some financial help for the mother on the promise that, in effect, the boy would be theirs to train and use when older. She was told about it and held her breath in readiness for a delayed answer for both of them – she was tired of waiting.

Barman Kwek Leng Joo made his way as usual. Wearing

nondescript clothing, he got on a bus going along the road from the town towards the camp and getting off it a way back from where he entered the jungle. He waited, tying up a loose shoelace to see if anyone was in watching distance, till there was no one to see him and he stepped off the road. After the usual time it took to reach the other ring of defence posts had elapsed he picked up a stick and beat a tree in the usual code, three, two then three shots. No answer. He waited five minutes – *can't be too careful* – then did that again. Once more no answer. He moved off to the inner ring, recognised the place he normally stopped at and made the frog noise of recognition. No answer. Another pause. Again. For the third time no answer. *Is something amiss?* he wondered. Moving with deliberate caution he reached the bottom of the slope on the top of which was the Regional Committee's camp. Under the long grass, hidden from casual eyesight, was a rope woven of grasses that a lower sentry would pull to alert the upper one. *I'll pull it and having got the answer go up anyway.* But there was no rope. He clambered up the slope and was flabbergasted to find the camp deserted and not all that recently, either. Tidy bed spaces were overgrown and the stores kept in a small cave had all been destroyed. He sniffed and smelt a faint smell of explosive as though a grenade had exploded inside. He shook his head in disbelief. *What has happened? And who could have done it?* he asked himself. Of course there was no answer. He searched around, found no clues to tell him any more than he knew so went back and reported it to the manager of the Yam Yam who, likewise, was dumbstruck. Nothing about any attack on the camp, nothing about any incident concerning a British officer, nothing untoward militarily had, since Hinlea had left on his journey, been broadcast or published. Did that mean that he had achieved a clean get-away or not? Hinlea had spent the last night before escaping with the battalion's fresh ration contractor, Goh Ah Hok, and the Yam Yam manager himself had driven him to the place where he entered the jungle to join the guerrillas. There had been no one on the road to see Hinlea get into the car and drive off in the dawn. It was a mystery.

Rumours, both of the disaster at Regional HQ and of the deaths of a group of guerrillas eventually started to spread. By the time it reached Siu Tse the talk included the death of an officer in 1/12 GR that was caused by another officer by the name of Rance, a Captain Jason Rance. Siu Tse had never understood military names – her Alan's English was not easy to follow – but it rang a bell with what her Alan had told her. The new name, Rance, was pronounced slowly for her as she had never heard it before so it was new to her but it meant that he was responsible for her Alan's death. As it was the first time such a rumour with her Alan's name had reached her the 'bottom of her world' fell out. But was it true or only a rumour?

Sadly it really did seem to be the truth because surely firm news of his arrival at the other end and her joining him would have reached her by now. She had to go and ask someone and that someone could only be the manager of the Yam Yam. She just had to go and ask him to find out one way or another. Leaving her baby and some extra condensed milk with her mother, she went to meet him to see how he could help her with a firm answer. All he could do was to say that there was nothing definite either way but Hinlea was probably dead otherwise how could that camp have been destroyed?

'Which camp?' she asked.

'The camp he first went to at the start of his long journey.'

'But that would have happened after he had left it, wouldn't it?' she asked. 'If anyone had gone after him from here and attacked the camp, news would have spread surely?'

Yam Yam's manager Yap Cheng Wu felt the same. Had there been an attack by the Gurkhas, they might not have heard the firing but most certainly would have heard about it from talk around the bar. He shrugged and said nothing, not quite knowing what to say and not wanting to lose face with a vacuous reply.

'So, what can I do now?' she asked him, trepidation in her voice. 'If it is true I must get my revenge. I don't know this Rance, never met him so would not recognise him if I did. But he needs killing. I'll need help for that as I can't do it myself but how, how, how?'

Indeed, what could she do? The manager was at a loss, sorry for her but, frankly, not all that concerned. After all, *Sik Long* was a colonial, wasn't he, despite all his talk. *I can't just dismiss her, can I?* No. 'I am sorry, Little Sister, but there is nothing I can do. Let me think. Come back next week when I might have an idea.'

Bitterly angry, she left him and on her way home tried to imagine how she could, in fact, 'get her own back'. Despite any proof that this Rance person was in any way to blame, as he seemed to be in Alan's battalion he was as good a target as anyone else – so why not take revenge for her baby's missing father by killing him? As she did not know what her new enemy looked like, nor was she a guerrilla with the training to despatch him if she met him, somehow or other she'd have to leave recognition and method to others. Such a man would be the opposite of that nice lad who'd rescued her from being raped, who'd sung that lovely song and spoken perfect Chinese – her heart fluttered as she thought of him – it always did when he came to mind. He was different from her Alan who really was an animal the way he ravished her, which that … yes, Shandong P'aau, never tried, but now revenge was worth it for her future prospects, *wasn't it?* she asked herself as she waited for the manager's answer. In her mind's eye she had formed a picture of this Rance; an evil man, medium-sized, slack-jawed, pinched-faced, short-sighted and balding with close-cropped, black hair. She somehow felt she could recognise him on sight.

By the time she went back to see the manager, Yap, he had found out that her third uncle, Deng Bing Yi, worked in a garage that serviced the cars among which were those of the officers of the Gurkha battalion. Yap told the frantic woman about it so she went to see her uncle and said she wanted his help He took her to a private corner and she blurted the whole story out to him. He was sympathetic but said he was not in the business of tracking people. 'Can't you find anyone else to help you?'

'There is no one else and,' she added pointedly, 'you are family. If you can think of anything to help me, please do.'

Her uncle wanted to get on with his work and to get rid of her but she was so persistent he sat and tried to think of an answer.

An idea did not come immediately but, as he thought back at what he had done to Japanese vehicles during the occupation, he said 'I think I can help you out.'

What he had just thought of, desperate though the gambit was, was to try and sabotage Rance's own car, which indeed he did service. His niece obviously wanted an answer so he said, 'Tell you what. I'll sabotage this Rance's car when he next brings it in and it will explode and kill him when he drives away.'[4]

'Really and truly?' she queried.

'Yes, for you I will do it.'

His niece was delighted and went away happy for the first time in ages. Her uncle did work on sabotaging the car but the Fates were against him and the one he put the explosives in belonged to someone else who was killed when it blew up. Deng Bing Yi kept mum about it, for obvious reasons. When his niece went to ask him about it, saying she had heard nothing he was too ashamed to admit his mistake and told her a lie about the owner of the car not yet having brought his car in for servicing. 'Have patience,' he counselled.

Frustrated at the delay, she once more visited the manager of the Yam Yam who said 'you won't be happy whilst you are doing nothing positive. I have an idea … ' His voice trailed off as he thought it out.

She waited patiently. She knew it was no good trying to hurry him.

'If you can't get anyone to kill the man you want dead how

4 See *Operation Blowpipe*.

about assuaging your anger by joining the guerrillas in the jungle and getting your own back against the colonialists by killing as many white men as you can. If that's what suits you I can take you to someone who can arrange it.'

A revolutionary idea that can only be successful! 'Yes, please.'

Yap Cheng Wu took Siu Tse with him by local bus, sitting in different seats, to Mantin – an early attempt to say 'tin mine' – ten miles or so north up the main road to Kuala Lumpur where a senior party member lived. He was a one-time schoolmaster, now elderly, bespectacled with a white wispy beard, named Ngai Hiu Ching. He lived openly in the village, which was a clandestine communist centre. Many semi-fugitives hid in that area as indeed they had during the Japanese occupation. *Sinsaang* Ngai was a centre of information and advice, coordinating matters that needed retaliatory action by the MCP.

His two visitors waited till there was no one on the road outside his house, set back in an orchard grove, before venturing towards the front door. It opened as they reached it and Ngai Hiu Ching invited them in. He and Yap Cheng Wu had known each other for many years. 'Come inside,' he said with a smile, and in they went.

Once in a back room with curtains drawn – *never too careful!* – 'and who is this young lady you have brought to meet me?' He bade them to sit down and clapped his hands for the man who looked after him, his wife having died many moons previously, and told him to brew some tea. 'We can talk better with some hot green tea inside us.'

The two men exchanged pleasantries until the brew was brought in and they sipped silently, not wanting to lose any of the aroma of the green tea, which is so good for a person's health.

'So, how can I help you?' Ngai Hiu Ching asked his friend. 'Tell me all, slowly so my creaking brain can understand it without my asking too many questions.'

The Yam Yam manager told Siu Tse to start from the beginning, so she did, leaving out the more intimate bits which weren't necessary to the narrative. At the end *Sinsaang* Ngai told his friend to add to the story, giving background details as yet untold but which were necessary for full understanding.

It had taken nearly an hour for both parts of the story to be told. 'Let me think of my answer and as I do, a bowl of gruel each won't go wasted and it helps me think.' He clapped his hands once more and gave the order. 'While it is being prepared, you two stay here and I'll stroll in my orchard. I find it easier to think when I move about by myself than when I sit.' Out he went and came back when told that the meal was ready.

Silence reigned till the bowls were empty. The servant came in with three hand towels and took the bowls out. 'I think I have the best answer for her. The girl is a cook as well as a dedicated worker for the Party. One of her advantages is that she has had so much contact with the British she could also be useful to the propaganda people in the Politburo. She also needs indoctrination in Party policy as well as some military training. The best way forward will be to start off listening to what the labour force in Jemima Estate, farther to our south, not far from Lukut village, has to tell her. This will be for a deeper indoctrination of Party policy than she already has. Her cooking skill will also be of great use. Then she will have to join the unit nearest Lukut for transfer to a deeper camp for some sort of military training. I will give her a written introduction and you, Yap *sinsaang*, can take her down there.' He looked at the girl. 'Do you agree with my plan?'

'Oh yes, grandfather, I do and, although I don't know anyone there nor have I ever been there, learning more about the Party will be of great help.'

'While you are under instruction I will send a message to the Politburo of the MCP – yes, I can do that – suggesting that your use for propaganda purposes must be exploited. By then you will be out of my hands.'

Purely out of interest the Yam Yam manager asked the one-time schoolmaster why, particularly, that estate, not that he had any reason not to accept his choice.

'On that estate all the workers and are anti-European so will help anyone like our little sister. Why more anti than others? It happened like this: the European manager had been in the army during the war and thought himself a weapons expert. He had what he called an "aiming disc". This is a small, round piece of metal, white on the top half, black on the lower, with a small hole in the middle. A rifle being pointed at a man with an aiming disc can be seen as "on target" or not. He tested the Malay police jungle squad he had to guard him that way. One day he told a man to take the aiming disc and he, the planter, would point the rifle at him. That way his aim could be improved. So the rifle was handed over. Both took the lying position and the policeman put the aiming disc to his eye. The planter took aim. He had not looked to see if the magazine was loaded. It was, so when he drew the rifle bolt back then pushed it forward, he automatically loaded it. At five yards range a bullet does a lot of damage. He was taken in front of a judge but was not found guilty of taking the person's life but of a lesser charge. The Malays, Indians and Chinese all thought that was too great an act of favouritism and had it happened the other way round the Asian man would have been hanged for murder.[5]

He paused for breath and let those details sink in before continuing, 'So you can see they will help you their utmost, especially when you tell them the reason for your wanting revenge.' He looked at her and let what he had said sink in. Then an idea struck him: 'You will be a guerrilla soldier on operations. All operations need code words and, as you will be hunting for your target, this man named Rance who you say killed your son's father, let us call it "Operation Hunter".'

She had never thought of anything like that before and it struck her as good. 'I understand and will call my work that, Grandfather Ngai Hiu Ching. I think my son's father would have approved. I thank you for all your help.'

Before the two of them returned to Seremban, Ngai Hiu Ching told them it would take time to contact 'those who can authorise matters' and an equal time to get the answer back. 'Be patient till you hear from me – hear you will.'

In due course the necessary Party approval was brought by

---

5 Your author visited the estate a few days before accident happened, saw such training taking place and remembers worrying what would be the result if anything went wrong.

courier and the necessary arrangements for Siu Tse's initiation to become a guerrilla were made.

After Jason Rance and his team had returned from their successful venture of preventing the renegade officer Hinlea's attempt to join the MCP, Jason decided to get his company together and give every man a description of what went right and why it did in case others had to do something like that in the future.

It was during his extended briefing that he mentioned about what they had decided to take as rations. 'Normal rations take quite a time to prepare, and more than five days' worth are heavy to carry. We needed to be as light as possible so we could move more quickly than normal. That meant taking three days' rations and eking them out for five, as well as biscuits and chocolate from some Compo ration packs. These need no cooking, are light and give you strength and they were of the greatest use when we were so near the enemy group our smoke and smell might easily have given us away.'

Compo rations, which some soldiers objected to, composed of hard tack and pre-packaged, ready-to-eat meals. There was a British type of Compo rations and a Gurkha type catering to the different dietary preferences of the soldier, and Rance presumed also a Malay type. They were less popular by far than fresh rations but higher formation had ordered all units to keep a stock of them and they had to be eaten before their expiry date, emergency or not, to prevent waste.

Then he had an idea. He knew that his Company Quartermaster Sergeant (CQMS), Manbahadur Rai, a much older man soon to go on pension, had been a Chindit[6] and knew what hunger was. He sent for him and asked him to tell how he had suffered hunger when, miles into Burma, they had to make their own way back to India.

'I know we don't have all that time, Manbahadur, so if you could just tell us what it was like when you had to return to India from the middle of Burma, when you were by yourself with no rations. How did you manage?'

'It was difficult on the way into Burma but the way back still haunts me. I still get nightmares and wake up thinking I am still starving when of course I am no longer like that. Eventually our ammunition finished and there was no resupply. We were told to make our own way back to India. It was an unpleasant situation. We were surrounded by Japanese, had been for three months. So we moved off towards the west. With no issue rations we searched for jungle produce, especially yams to eat. We tried to buy food in Burmese villages with "king's money" that had been dropped to us with the earlier rations. There were mosquitoes everywhere.

---

6   The Chindits, officially Long Range Penetration Groups, were special operations units of the British and Indian armies which saw action in 1943–1944 behind Japanese lines. Their use has always been controversial. One story written in *Gurkhas at War*, edited by JP Cross and Buddhiman Gurung has a Chindit story on pages 66–68 of the first edition, given by Colour Sergeant Harkaraj Gurung. At the end of his interview your author asked him if he would like his regards paid to the officer who was with him on the Chindit operation. 'Yes.' This was done and when the officer, now a retired colonel with a heart condition, started reading the letter, still so incensed was he at having to leave men behind that he had a fatal heart attack before reaching the bottom on the first page. Your author learnt this from his widow.

Our clothes were in rags, footwear was worn out and our feet were in a bad state. Our hair hung down to our shoulders. Those who were too sick to move were left with some money near Burmese villages or left to die. That was very hard for all of us.'

To those of the company who knew nothing of the Chindits that sounded unthinkable.

'I, a machine gunner, was with two Gurkha officers. We dumped our weapons. The Gurkha Officers wanted to surrender but I said, "No, let's escape or die. If we stay alive we'll meet in India; if we die, we'll die here." We separated. I reached the Irrawaddy' and here he was asked to say how wide and fast the river was 'and the problem was how to cross over. Just short of the near bank in the jungle I met one of our majors who had a biscuit in one hand and a life jacket in the other. He asked me where I had come from, where the Subedar and the other Gurkha Officers were and where was my machine gun. I told him I didn't know where the Gurkha Officers were. He said "what's gone has gone. You and I have to cross the river. Let's go together. If we live we live, if we die we die." He was so weak he could not swim so I went to look for a boatman. It was evening. I went to a house and all inside were very scared. I pulled one man out and took him back. He trembled a lot. The major put his pistol to the Burman's head and told him either to take us across in his boat "or I'll kill you here." That made the Burman even more scared. He put us in his boat and started rowing us across. There was enough moonlight to see a bit. We finished up on the other side exactly opposite a Japanese post. They opened fire and killed the major. I was unhurt. It was around one o'clock and I started walking. I stopped when I was at the top of a hill covered in bamboo. I was worried: the major was dead. I was by myself. We had come 700 miles from India: how was I to go back the same distance? I had a compass. At Mandalay we had been told that if we had to escape we were to march on a bearing of 300° to reach Manipur. I started on 300° and moved between 300° and 310°. Three months after that I reached Manipur.'

The Company 2 ic had, thoughtfully, ordered a drink of tea and it was brought to the CQMS at this stage of his talk. He smiled, gratefully, sipping it before putting the mug to one side before carrying on with his tale.

'That night it was moonlit and I sat down to rest under a tree and got covered in red ants. Did they bite! A large herd of elephants, fifty to sixty, came my way and smelt me. They started looking for me but I avoided them. I had to avoid the Burmans also as they would have speared me to death. They had already killed many of us that way as I had seen for myself.

'I was afraid of being captured by the Japanese but only once was afraid of one animal, a ferocious type of deer that was big, red and horned. I knew it would attack any human it smelled. I was only once attacked by one and I escaped by hiding under a large, fallen tree. I saw many tigers, singly or in groups, all potentially man eaters. The first one I saw did frighten me and I managed to jump into a river and swim across. I nearly bumped into a group of Burmese, who were all smoking. They didn't see me but they would have killed me had they caught me.

'When I came across tigers they took no notice of me. I put that down to the fact that my body smell was different then. They do not have a particularly good sense of smell but have good eyesight. Bears, on the other hand, have dim sight but a good sense of smell. I only saw the red-nosed type, not the black-nosed type we have in Nepal. Once, trying to cross a broken railway bridge, I came across a group of Japanese riding on elephants and I hid from them. One evening I was fascinated by finding myself in the middle of a large herd of deer.'

He took up his mug of tea and drank a few more gulps before continuing. Everyone looked at the speaker with the greatest respect, some tut-tutting, others shaking their head in wonderment.

'I was always hungry. One river I started fishing with my hands and caught some prawns which I ate alive as I did two fish I caught in a teeming pool formed by the monsoon rain at the side of another river. I scooped some out and ate them alive also. There was no salt but they were good. I once came across a nest of twelve eggs of jungle fowl. I ate six straightaway and kept the other six for later. I came across a nest of two young doves. I killed one, plucked it and ate it raw – I had no method of making fire – and kept the other for later.'

Hearing this tale of tenacity, the soldiers who had not fought in Burma sat, listening spellbound. Jason and his four-man team realised that this was something monumentally different which demanded much more stamina and willpower than anyone had previously guessed would be needed and for much, much longer, all by oneself.

'After one spell of three or four days without any food I came across a Burmese village. The Burmans were afraid of me and ran away. I found some dried maize and carried as much as I could away with me. The Burmans were very scared of the Japanese. The Japanese would come and check on such things as the number of chickens or eggs and if the amount was inexplicably fewer punishments were meted out. Some were extra work and others were death. Women suffered badly: gang rapes and then stabbed to death.

'I was happy to find wood apples which were most sustaining. They kept hunger away for up to three days. The fruit of the ebony tree kept hunger away for twelve hours.

'One day I came across three boxes of cigarettes that had been dropped from an aircraft so I knew I was on the correct way out. Three months after I started back I saw a Gurkha post on the far bank of the Chindwin, with artillery nearby. 1/8 GR was to a flank. They knew about our column. A British captain aimed his weapon at me as I approached the near bank. I waved a leaf at him hoping he'd take that as a recognition sign. He signalled to me to stay there and a boat came over to fetch me. In great haste I got into the boat and when we reached midstream firing broke out from both sides of the river, British and Japanese. I felt I was finished. I almost collapsed when I reached the bank and the captain sahib pulled me into safety in dead ground. He gave me a drink of rum from his water bottle. I drank it. I was told to hide there and food and drink would be brought to me.'

Jason could sense the relief felt by the listeners. *My, but what terrific guts!*

'I stayed in a trench. The saheb spoke good Nepali and gave me a towel. My morale soared. I had not had a rice meal for three months so when some was brought I ate four mess tins of it. I then fell asleep for the rest of the day. That evening the captain came to see how I was and woke me up. He told me he had contacted my battalion HQ and I had to report there. It might be difficult as reports from an agent had been received indicating an enemy attack.

'But I knew then that I was destined to live.'

The men automatically clapped their approval and Jason stood up from the chair he was sitting on. 'Ustad, I think I owe you an apology for not having asked you your story before and to congratulate you.' The OC turned to his men and demanded three cheers for the Quarter Master Sergeant ustad. Such was the noise that birds in nearby trees flew away. There were no more grumbles about eating Compo rations afterwards.

Captain Rance thought he ought to sum up so he stood and said: 'What we have heard is the difference in fighting against a major enemy in a war when outnumbered, far from base, with no radio communication and no salt rather than here and now fighting against guerrillas with everything we need for success. What comes out of the Quartermaster ustad's story is the art of survival when you are alone and your morale cannot be high so your view of affairs is different from ours here in Malaya where we have every support for our task. The former's view of life, and indeed death, must be different from ours: two views, almost a world apart in one way, yet the same in another.'

The men nodded. 'Before we go I want to make two points: having heard that story I want to hear no more mumbling and grumbling about Compo rations and that basically as Gurkhas, in my view you are the finest soldiers anywhere so I know all of you could manage to survive because you are Gurkhas.' He looked around. 'Many men like our Quartermaster Sergeant ustad died on the way back: far too many. It is those we must especially remember when once a year we parade with a poppy in our hat. I salute them,' and he stood to attention and made a salute, an unusual gesture that the men took as their OC remembered how many times he himself had brushed Jemaraj, the Angel of Death.

Silence as the men thought about what their Company Commander had said. Some wanted to ask if the CQMS had been given a bravery award for what he did. In fact, no one was decorated merely for survival.

The OC looked at his watch. 'Just one more thing to say: if such wonderful soldiering had not happened in Burma, Africa and Italy we could well not have been chosen for the British Army and if that had been so, the daku would probably have already won here in Malaya. Fall out the officers. Major Ba, dismiss the men.'

It was seldom, if ever, that any such lecture on events in the Second World War came over as a lecture, although senior ranks often talked about their experiences when the occasion arose. A few days later the Company 2 ic, a Captain (QGO), came into his OC's office, saluted and said 'Saheb, the men would like to hear any war stories about your service you have to tell them,

Jason grinned back at him and said 'Saheb, what an undertaking that would be. I think it would take too long and distract them.'

His Gurkha Captain asked him why. 'Because then it was a war against a first-class enemy, both sides using many more assets than the different type of war we are engaged it here.'

'Couldn't you tell them why and how you are still alive?' If they can do what you did it will increase their morale a bit, even if everybody has complete faith in how you operate.'

Jason turned that over in his mind. 'Yes, Saheb, in Burma I was the Recce Platoon Commander for 4/1 GR and a sniper instructor to a battalion of the Nepalese Contingent so would go forward to help the snipers I had instructed to find good positions.'

That was news to the Gurkha but, typically, nothing showed on his face.

'In fact I have always acted carefully whenever moving in the jungle.' He thought for a moment. 'Saheb, I'll leave the lecture for a while but I'll write out the movement points and issue them to platoons which can then practice, not that they don't know all about it already.'

'Thank you Saheb, especially if that will save lives now the daku are getting more canny.'

Jason took a piece of paper from the desk drawer, picked up a pencil and thought about both sides of jungle warfare, the hunter and the hunted. This is what he wrote; 'If the hunter carelessly leaves a footprint, he probably only misses a contact: if the hunted does, his probable fate will be death or capture. I know because I have been both. But I am still alive because when moving I never cut what I can break naturally: I never break naturally what I can bend; I never bend what I can move; I never move that which I can get through without moving; I never tread on anything that

I can step over; I never step on soft ground when I can tread on something hard; where possible I tread in water so get my feet wet; where possible I move backwards over soft ground. I never do anything needlessly.'

He then re-wrote it in Nepali.

3

The MCP Politburo, worried that the campaign to topple the government was not going as they had planned and that Gurkha successes had reached a tipping point, voted to try and get help from a still-secret MGB unit presumed to be in Calcutta. It was decided to send 'Comrade' Ah Fat by boat to try and discover it and, if successful, ask for help.[7]

By one of those unplanned coincidences, the boat he sailed in had a Gurkha leave party on board and the OC Troops was his boyhood friend, by-now Captain Jason Rance. Once in Calcutta Ah Fat was taken to the Soviet consulate where the MGB 'Rezident', Leonid Pavlovich Sobolev, and his Assistant, Dmitri Tsarkov, were masquerading as normal diplomats. At the meeting the reaction of Sobolev to a Chinese man was so offensive that Ah Fat hit on the idea of getting his own back for such blatant and intentional rudeness by saying that he had a friend with him who was an undercover card-carrying companion and it was agreed to bring him to the consulate. When asked the friend's name Ah Fat replied that his friend only gave his 'working' name as Captain Jason Rance.

---

7   See *Operation Tipping Point.*

After Rance and Ah Fat returned together a later-arriving Indian comrade's English had been imitated by Jason, using his ventriloquist ability, which made the drunken MGB representative think that the Indian had offended him, so causing a most undiplomatic scene. The Rezident became so drunkenly angry that he threw a glass of vodka at the Indian, bending his nose and cutting his cheek. The Russian then fell on the floor in a stupor. At that, Jason demanded transport to go back to the boat that was tied up in the harbour. After a suspicious delay a vehicle was ready. Just before they left, a Russian who had merely stood nearby not speaking but listening, Sergey Siderov, gave Ah Fat a letter for Law Chu Hoi, the purser of the boat, SS *Eastern Queen*, the one on which Ah Fat and Jason had come on from Singapore and were on it going back to Singapore. Sergey Siderov was the 'secret eyes' of another MGB department whose task was to check up on people like the Rezident. Neither Ah Far nor Jason knew his name which was not divulged, the letter having been signed by Dmitri Tsarkov.

In the consulate car taking the pair of them back to the docks neither man had spoken, both well aware of possible 'bugs'. Once on board, Ah Fat took the letter out of his pocket and when he looked at the envelope he saw that the ink was smudged and the envelope badly stuck. It looked as if it had been written in a great hurry and most Indian envelopes had no 'sticky'. 'Jason, there is something wrong here. I am suspicious: I feel it in my bones. Shall I open it just in case? If it is above board we can always stick the envelope shut again.'

'Yes, it won't hurt. We'll open it and read it then make up

our minds.' So saying, he filled and heated the coffee pot in Ah Fat's cabin and steamed the envelope open, giving the letter to his Chinese friend. At Fat read it with a sharp intake of breath then handed it to his friend. Jason noticed it had been hastily written in English and read that the purser was ordered to get both of them thrown overboard with no one else knowing about it. 'Essential for the Party. Don't ask questions. You will be rewarded.'

On disembarkation Jason gave the letter to the ship's captain who, having read it, sent for his purser. In that the letter never reached him, Law Chu Hoi could not have known anything about it. Even so, he admitted he was a secret comrade and was dismissed there and then so found himself out of a job.

Sergey Siderov knew the dates of the boat's reaching Rangoon and Singapore so kept a keen watch on any news bulletins that would announce the death at sea of two passengers of the SS *Eastern Queen*. Nothing. He was satisfied that Leonid Pavlovich Sobolev and Dmitri Tsarkov would be succinctly dealt with and that he could control the Indian – he was wrong there – but without the deaths of those two visitors from the boat, nasty rumours of the secret MGB set-up could spell serious external disgrace, possibly amounting to disaster. Sergey Siderov searched for the notebook that Sobolev used, looked up a name and number, found what he was looking for and, hoping that his security would not be breached, rang the number of Chen Geng in Singapore, on an open line. It took three phone calls to get his man and, in desperation, throwing caution to the winds, asked him if he knew whether someone named Ah Fat had returned on the *Eastern Queen*. It happened that Chen Geng did know that he had and told Sergey Siderov so.

'Thank you,' was all that came over the line from Calcutta, which was much less than what was churning around in his mind. *Now what to do?* He thought hard for five minutes then he contacted Chen Geng again. 'I am sending you a priority registered airmail letter as soon as I ring off. Act on it and tell the man I write about also to act on it without fail.'

After Ah Fat got back to the Central Committee's hide-out he pleaded for time to rest after his arduous journey – not that the sea journey had been arduous at all but the journey into the jungle with a small escort, avoiding Security Forces, was always tiring – but he had yet to make up his mind exactly what to report to the full Plenum about any help he had managed to get from the MGB. 'Yes I did make contact and I'll tell you all about it after I've rested.' Great excitement ensued and all members of the Politburo rubbed their hands in anticipation of learning how to gain victory after so many tribulations.

He had been sent 'openly' to Calcutta – a first and at great risk to MCP security. The fact that he was a police 'mole' was the tightest of tightest secrets. The reason he had been sent was that, as it was feared that Gurkha successes in the jungle fight had reached a tipping point, a secret Soviet MGB, Soviet Ministry of State Security, office somewhere in Calcutta, was controlling all communist activity in Southeast Asia, could, somehow or other, arrange for serving Gurkhas to be converted to communism and so be disbanded as unwanted by the British Army, or sent to Sarawak to quell some Sarawak United Peoples Party's anti-government machinations. Both failed but Ah Fat was asked for help in the former, not the latter.

Before setting out on his unusual journey, the three-man 'chain of information' to get him from Singapore to Calcutta was clearly laid down – that was where the unfortunate purser came into the plot, he was the middle man – and without it Ah Fat would never have reached the MGB office. His problem now was what to tell the Politburo: one, to say 'not to worry as the MGB was helping all it could so put it out of your minds and carry on as usual'; two, to tell the truth that the meeting ended in fiasco with, probably, the 'Rezident' being returned to Moscow for harsh punishment and so it were better to ignore the Soviets; or three, to somehow have an amalgam of the two. As he had a copy of the letter that got the purser the sack he decided on course two. But he had a copy of that letter with Jason Rance's name on: *show it or not? If so be convincing about his friend.*

After a laudatory welcome, the Secretary General of the MCP, Ong Boon Hwa, better known as Chin Peng, almost deferentially asked non-voting Comrade Ah Fat to tell them everything about his journey. This was impossible as he had visited his 'home team' in Kuala Lumpur and in Singapore so he had to give a truncated, albeit true, version of events, how he had met the contacts to set him on the three stages of his journey, how the OC Troops of a Gurkha leave party had been friendly 'and, unbelievably told me he was really a deep card-carrying party member. I shrugged that off. I was just an ordinary passenger.'

'So, all was a success,' asked, rhetorically, Chin Tiang, Chin

Peng's chief confidant and Lee An Tung, Head of the Central Propaganda Department, almost in the same breath.

Ah Fat mustered his most doleful expression and, to everybody's dismay, shook his head. 'Alas, not … '

He was interrupted by cries of reproach and such remarks as 'how come?', 'why not?' and 'so your journey was wasted'.

When all was, relatively, quiet once more he continued, noting that everyone would try and find fault with anything they did not understand, by asking an unexpected question, 'Have any of you ever met a Russian, ever spoken to one?'

No, nobody had.

'I saw he was the worse for drink. As I came into the room he said "another slit eye?" … '

'So, what did you do?' someone asked, horror in his voice.

'I turned to my guide and said "Stand up and make for the door. I'll follow you."

'"Where are you going?" called out the startled Russian.'

Heads nodded at such a move. *Quite right!* came into every mind.

'I spun round and spat out "I have made an uncomfortable and long and lonely journey to report to you as I was told to by the Politburo of the Malayan Communist Party about your helping us and I do not expect to be insulted and spoken to as a piece of shit. I'll go back and tell them you are nothing but a fraud" and, reaching the door, turned the handle.

'The Russian was surprised and told me and the guide to come back and talk as friends, so went back and sat down. "You say you come from where?" he asked me.

'When I had told him once more he did not quite know where Malaya was. I then asked him if he had an Indian member who could help get the Gurkhas to abscond from Malaya. He didn't seem interested in helping us, which upset me.'

'Quite right and most sensible,' muttered Lee An Tung.

'Yes, he had so I was to go back there in two day's time. I was so upset by the way I was referred to as a "slit eye" and a "Chinaman" rather than "Chinese" that I felt I had to take one tremendous gamble. Russians, I now knew, are not good with Asians and do not like collaborating with them or telling them anything secret unless they really, really know them. They would, I thought, talk to a European: no "colour bar". I had to confirm that this Indian would help and that, were I to take this deep-cover British comrade with me, he could very well get much more out of the Russian than could I.'

'You took him back with you on your return visit? Was that wise?' asked the General Secretary, dubiously.

Supreme effort needed. 'Comrades, having come so far how could I come back not having done all you asked me to without taking a risk when a completely unforeseen situation was met with? To have done anything else would have been too risky.'

A vote had to be taken to approve this or not. All in favour! 'Proceed. Then what happened?'

'All was going just as I hoped; the Englishman showed his card' – not true but ... – 'when this Indian came in. Then,' shaking his head glumly, Ah Fat dramatically hesitated, 'the Russian and he had such a quarrel that the "Soviet spider" said he wanted nothing more to do with Gurkhas or the Indian and threw his glass of vodka at him. Broke his nose and badly cut his cheek.'

More gasps of horror.

'The Soviet then passed out, fell down unconscious and medical treatment was given to the Indian, in other words, consternation. This Englishman, using the name Jason Rance, asked for a vehicle to take both of us back to the ship. There was a surprising delay and as we left an envelope was put into my hand and I was told to give it to the ship's purser, Law Chu Hoi. I was suspicious and only opened it once back in my cabin.' He stopped short, again dramatically. *Let them wonder what was in it.*

'What did the letter have in it?' Chin Tiang asked, 'or did you destroy it?'

'I did not want the signature of one of the Soviet staff to be known so destroy it I did but,' he put up his hand to ward off any questions, 'I made a copy.' He put his hand into his pocket and pulled out a piece of paper. 'Now, listen to this,' he said harshly and make your own mind up about it. "Comrade Law Chu Hoi, you are ordered to get both men thrown overboard with no one else knowing about it. Essential for the Party. Don't ask questions. You will be rewarded." Both men meant me and the Englishman.'

As he went over to give the piece of paper to the Secretary General the only noises to be heard were insects in the trees around them as his audience digested this amazing display of party antagonism.

Then people started to talk once more. A debate among them was proposed and officialdom prevailed. The Secretary General opened the session: 'I will ask our non-voting member to give his advice than we will pass a motion on it. If anyone disagrees, we will hear him.'

That sounded sensible so heads nodded.

'Comrade Ah Fat,' began Chin Peng. 'You have been industrious, brave, rash and, all told, have reacted to an unprecedented and completely unforeseeable situation. What do you recommend we, as a Politburo, do from now on?'

'Forget the Soviets and look towards the Communist Party of China for help,' and sat down.

'But the Gurkhas being made into communists and those who are kept on in the army being sent to Sarawak so we can have a chance of settling matters here?'

'For the former you might think of my liaising with this man who calls himself Jason Rance – I never asked him his real name and even if I had he would not have told me – and as for Sarawak, that was not in your orders to me. For the latter I believe there is nothing further any of us can do.'

The final vote was that, only if ordered, would Comrade Ah Fat try to meet up with the Englishman and, if nothing could be done to diminish the Gurkha presence, matters would, presumably, be as they had been before what the Central Committee had blandly and blithely termed 'Operation Tipping Point'. Ah Fat was also told he would not be sent south until and unless the purser chasing him was somehow 'permanently dissuaded'. The Secretary General also determined to send a courier to Singapore to warn Chen Geng but it somehow slipped his mind and he never did.

As Ah Fat went to sleep that night he congratulated himself of mixing glib guile with appropriate aplomb for significant success.

It was only to himself that he allowed his fluent English to be practised.

The Brigadier who had recently come to take command one of the brigades deployed against the guerrillas had fought his war in Europe, nor had he ever served anywhere east of Suez. He had an over-opinionated impression of his superiority and, from what little he had seen of the troops in Malaya, thought them slack. He had arranged a familiarisation flight over the jungle, in the mistaken idea that flying over a place was nearly as good as walking over it.

Without his hat on, his hairless skull glistened as though it had been basted with oil. It always shone hence his nickname 'Moon Face', a soubriquet which his subordinates used only when they were absolutely sure he was not in earshot.

When he met his pilot at the Army Air Corps base near Kuala Lumpur he did not like the look of him at all. Looked seedy. Trying to appear condescending to a junior he asked: 'All right are we for our flight? Flight plan registered? Compass working? What, what.'

'Yes, sir. We are chiefly flying over Selangor and Negri Sembilan.'

'Show me on your map.'

This the pilot did, sensing that his passenger was not all that interested. He also felt unhappy with his passenger's attitude but was resigned to senior officers' caprices. Today he was the only pilot available for duty. He really ought to have reported sick with the gnawing pain in his chest but he dared not. Once he was out of a job he would be unable to repay debts from his spendthrift wife's expensive shopping forays. But if the pain inside him grew any worse than it was today, he supposed he'd have no alternative but to report sick. 'Everything is okay, sir. Please get in, with your aide in the back seat, fasten your seat belt and I'll carry on as normal.'

He had been told by a senior officer in HQ where to take the brigadier, 'over all typical tropical rain forest terrain' so had made out a journey on a full tank, to arrive back at 'empty tank minus thirty minutes'.

They became airborne without any difficulty. The Brigadier had an elder brother who had been commissioned into the Indian Army's 1st Gurkha Rifles and posted to the 2nd battalion. Along with two other Gurkha battalions, milked of NCOs to raise a 3rd and a 4th battalion, the brigade had gone to Bombay destined for the Middle East before being told no, Malaya is your destination. Vehicles were repainted from yellow to green and off they sailed. Shortages of kit, lack of inspiring senior officers and an inspired enemy spelled disaster. The Brigadier's brother was never heard of again. As the plane flew over the jungle the new commander looked disdainfully down on what looked to him like an impenetrable see of vast cabbages. *How did those short-sighted, spectacle-wearing, yellow-dwarfs manage to beat the Indian Army so easily, I wonder,* he thought to himself as he dismally looked below him.

They flew over a broad, brown river. *No bridges: why couldn't our men have made a stand at such places? Why didn't they get across somehow and prevent the Japanese from following? What a useless, bloody country this is and I doubt if the native troops are any better now than they were.* He grunted in disgust and took out his pocket notebook and started to write a list of points he'd damned well make sure everyone, white, black, khaki in his brigade would have to do. *None of those sloppy jungle boots for instance: proper boots that good soldiers wore on parade.* He scribbled fast and furiously, starting to hate Malaya more than he had so far.

Twenty minutes' flying time away the pilot saw the bad weather in front of them. Over his head-set he said 'the weather is bad. I must divert or return to base. I don't like the look of the storm in front of us.'

The Brigadier looked at his watch. 'No time to change plans. Get on with it' and relapsed into silence. *Even this damned pilot has no guts, no discipline. I'll fix him when we get back.*

The pilot said nothing but felt aggrieved so he changed course without informing his passenger or the relevant control tower as he did. *I'm my own boss!* Without any warning they were engulfed in thick cloud and the plane was jolted harshly from side to side. As the pilot tried his best to control his machine the pain inside him overwhelmed him and he lost consciousness.

The plane, now completely out of control, plunged towards a ravine, the wind turning it sideways and, in a one-in-a-thousand chance, no, many-thousands chances, it slipped sideways on without the wings breaking in its fall. It landed just above the level of the water at the bottom of a five-hundred-foot cliff without any easily seen trace.

The next courier who came with mail for the Politburo brought a letter from Ngai Hiu Ching, the one-time schoolmaster living in Mantin. He was known to everybody from wartime days and was greatly respected. The letter was filed then handed over to Comrade Lee An Tung, Head of the Central Propaganda Department, as he seemed the correct person to read it. It concerned the woman who had hoped to be the wife of the *gwailo* Hinlea, *Sik Long*, the Lustful Wolf. *Yes, everybody remembered waiting for him and use him against their colonial enemy but he never arrived.* She was the mother of his son and felt she could be of some use instead of her baby's father, who she had heard was dead.

Lee An Tung called Ah Fat over and asked him if he knew anything about this person, whose name was, he looked at the letter again, Fong Chui Wan. 'No, I can't recall ever meeting the woman and I don't know anyone of that name,' was Ah Fat's answer. Lee took the letter over to the Secretary General and showed it to him. A meeting was to be called and a decision, to let her come or not, would be voted on.

The vote was in favour and arrangements were put in train to bring her up, but this time ensuring that nothing untoward happen on the journey. The plan was the same as it had been in the case of *Sik Long*, the Lustful Wolf, namely that a member of the MCP's military staff, properly escorted, would move south by stages to collect the woman. This was not as quickly put into effect as it sounded because the woman's group in the south would have to be notified before such a process could start. An outline programme was made and a courier was sent back to Mantin who, in turn, had to pass on the Politburo's instructions to the girl's group with the necessary details for her journey north – it all took time.

The letter from Sergei Siderov to Chen Geng was a model of brevity: 'Get Liu Yew Kui, the purser of SS *Princess of the Orient*, to kill Law Chu Hoi as soon and as securely as possible, telling him beforehand it is because he disobeyed party orders. If hunting him first needs funds, pay for any help needed; repayment will be made on killing completed.'

I'm no more a secret communist than a pig has wings Captain Jason Rance said to himself as he returned to his battalion after being OC Troops to Calcutta. His mind turned over as he thought how he had managed to confuse, totally and irrevocably, the Indian who was talking to the drink-sodden Rezident; by deft ventriloquism he had inflamed both men that resulted in the glass of vodka being thrown at the Indian and hitting him in the face. It was this uncomradely behaviour that had made the third Russian present, so far a silent watcher of the Rezident's disgraceful conduct. He had been so shocked at two outside people witnessing what had happened that he decided they both had to be got rid of on their return voyage. He had dictated the letter to the Deputy MGB representative, Dmitri Tsarkov, and made him sign it.

Sergey Siderov was also duty bound to report the whole disgraceful incident to his own HQ and what he had done in 'damage limitation' by getting the two visitors being secretly thrown overboard on their return journey to Singapore. He sent it under most secret cover to his office in number 1 Derzhenskii

Square, resulting in the soon-to-be-ex-Rezident's sojourn in the prison in the Lubyanka building, where Leonid Pavlovich Sobolev found himself not long afterwards. Dmitri Tsarkov was more fortunate: he was posted to the MGB HQ where he could be kept under observation, pending another report on his conduct. It was not knowing about this change of personnel that made Law Chu Hoi's 'hunt' to find the one – *or is it two?* – people he had to dispose of all the more indeterminate and difficult.

Unconcerned about and ignorant of the rumpus his previously unthought-of initiative at the Calcutta Soviet consulate had caused, Captain Rance happily returned to his battalion and early in January 1953 operations against the military wing of the MCP, the Malaya Races Liberation Army, MRLA, guerrillas started again – but badly.

News of a missing aircraft carrying a senior officer and his aide was taken seriously by most people, especially the Security Forces, but gladly by units of the MRLA who, if they did not have their own portable wireless would soon hear from someone who had either read about it in the papers or heard it on Radio Malaya. Each Regional Committee decided to search for it in the hope of capturing a senior officer at best – even finding official papers that could help them in their struggle could reap benefits otherwise unavailable.

Both sides in the struggle intensified their efforts to find the missing plane. The Security Forces concerned were told of the intended flight path so could plan where, in their area of operations, it was best to search. How it was lost was debated at all levels – when the plane was flying over some particularly rugged jungle-covered terrain had a fierce storm suddenly engulfed it? Were the pilot and his two passengers dead or badly injured? Had they managed to get out whole, with their jungle survival kit and started making for the nearest road? If they didn't know where they were did they know to follow the flow of water which eventually would lead to a bridge or a road? Sadly probably not.

No one had the answers so all other operations were brought to a halt and a hunt was set in motion, codenamed 'Operation Hunter' for troops hunting for both men and plane. 1/12 GR was detailed to search over such a wide area that troops were thinly spread. As platoons were to work on their own, company commanders were ordered to stay back in base and direct movement from the rear link as and how information came in. Only A Company, Captain Rance's, kept a platoon in base as a reserve.

The majority of troops were sent to both sides of the line of flight as shown in the flight plan. After a week of intensive searching, during which all troops were re-rationed, either by road or airdrop, nothing had been found. HQ Malaya Command began to worry if the search area was, somehow, not the one they expected to find the lost plane: had the engine failed and the surging wind blown the uncontrollable plane a long way off its intended path? Had the compass failed? Had the pilot had a fainting fit? The search, always slower than it might have been because it was felt that the guerrillas would also be searching for it – albeit for different reasons – was widened. There were no more troops to send into the enlarged area and so that meant troops were farther apart than before and a number of airdrops for resupply were a constant. After ten days of hunting for the plane no trace of it or its passengers had been found.

Three months earlier, Jason Rance's A Company had gone by rail up the Blowpipe Express to Kelantan. Halfway on their journey a bomb, laid by some guerrillas, was detonated and the train had been brought to a stop. The guerrillas opened heavy fire; previously Jason had given orders of what to do if the train was ambushed so within a very short time his 1 Platoon had engaged the enemy, killing three and wounding two. A Gurkha soldier had gone to examine one of the corpses and a wounded guerrilla had violently slashed his back, causing serious injuries. Another Gurkha immediately shot him; the other wounded man also died so there was only one casualty, the Gurkha, to look after. [See *Operation Tipping Point*.] He was sent to the local hospital and had returned to the lines just before his Company Commander set off with the leave parties to Calcutta.

After Rance had returned to normal duties he sent for the man, Rifleman Jitbahadur Gurung, to come to his room that evening and, over a glass of beer, tell him how he was now. Seated, with a glass of beer in both man's hand, Rance said 'Cheers! When I left you were getting better. How are you now?

'Almost completely better, Hajur, but the scar on my back does not yet let me carry a full heavy pack.'

'Does is still hurt?'

There was a dubious look on the man's face before he answered. 'When you weren't here, Saheb, and the Major from England was commanding the company, I could not get rid of the pain. One of the Malay civil workers in the camp advised me to see a *bomoh*, named Yasin, who was, so he told me, the fourth generation of a family that could cure body aches. He lives not far from the lines. So, as the medicine the battalion Doctor saheb was giving me didn't help, I went to him.'

'And did he?'

'Oh yes, he did,' and Jitbahadur smiled. 'I told him what had happened to me. He … ' and then he stopped talking and looked slightly ashamed.

'Tell me more,' Jason urged. 'Tell me what he did. I'm sure I'll understand.'

'It was half like a doctor and half like one of our shamans,' Jitbahadur began, glad that his Rance saheb seemed interested. 'He made me put a little water in a glass, drink it and put the glass back on the table, upside down. He then made me take off my shirt and, with some strange-smelling oil on the tips of his fingers, he probed all around the scar.'

'Why?'

'He said he wanted to make sure that no bones had been touched when the parang struck me.'

'And had it?'

'Yes, just a little.'

'So, what did he do?'

'Massaged it to the limit of my bearing the pain. I went to his place every evening.'

'Did it get any better?'

'Not until he said that I had a good heart and that he would transfer my injury into a chicken.'

By now Rance was fully interested but he looked at his watch. 'Time to take the radio calls from the platoons searching for the lost plane. I'll be back after I spoken to all three platoons.'

After he had returned, the soldier continued with his story. 'He told me to get six ten-dollar bills, twelve one-cent pieces, betel nut and lime, nutmeg, a clean handkerchief, a plate, a healthy chicken and five rust-free nails.'

'Did you?'

'Yes, I managed to. I took them to him. When all was ready, I drank an inch of water and put the glass upside down, like I did every time I went to him for treatment. Yasin tied the chicken to the leg of the chair, and he started his prayers, blowing over my back as he did. He then vigorously massaged me, again till I nearly cried out in pain. Yasin was sweating by then. He stopped, ate the betel nut, lime and nutmeg, placing the handkerchief over the glass and took the money. Payment. He did not touch the nails which I have kept for good luck.' Jitbahadur shook his head as he came to that point and smiled before continuing. 'The chicken was unwound from the chair, prayed over, blown over and its claw drawn around the hurt area of my back three times, waved around my head three times and, likewise thrice, spat on by me.'

Rance interrupted the soldier's flow. 'How did it react?'

Jitbahadur had not considered that before. He thought back to that moment before replying. 'It seemed surprised, Saheb, but it didn't try and get away. Yasin tied it up outside. He then told me only to come back in three days' time.

'The next three days saw no lessening of pain in my back but, when I went over to Yasin's place that evening as bidden,

Yasin's face was happy. He told me that I would soon be pain free because the chicken had, until that morning behaved no differently from normal. But suddenly, around midday, it had mysteriously developed a stiff back which had prevented normal movement and had caused it to go round and round in circles. Two hours later it died. My pain had been transferred to the chicken and four days later my back stopped hurting.'[8]

Rance filled up both glasses. 'That was wonderful. I am so glad for you.'

'Yes, Saheb, I am a lucky man.' He drank some of his beer and said, 'Saheb that is not all. He knew about the lost aeroplane and told me he knew where it was.'

Rance bolted upright. 'He really did, did he?'

'Yes, he really did.'

'How did he know? Where is it?'

'Saheb, this is what he said. I wrote it down. Here it is,' and took a bit of paper out of his pocket and gave it to Rance.

Rance read it, saying nothing, then repeated what was written: 'Follow the river upstream until another river, a smaller one, flows in from the west. Cross that and walk uphill. It is very steep, almost a cliff. At the top go north along the ridge until you find a tall, single *belimbing hutan*.' He looked at his list of Malay jungle trees to confirm it was a 'red-flowered spindle tree'.

Jason sat down and continued reading. 'The tallest stands

_____

8 A bomoh named Yasin cured your author's right shoulder, damaged in a parachute landing, in the same fashion. The top of the chicken's right leg refused to move normally four days after Yasin's 'ceremony' when he had drawn the chicken's right leg over the injured shoulder. Full use of the shoulder came one week later.

at a deep and very narrow precipice. If you climb up it you can probably see the plane that lies at the bottom of the precipice.' *How utterly weird but with such a man as Yasin, could it be true?* He thanked the soldier who stood up, then to attention and, as he was not in uniform, tilted forward on his toes and left.

How many people would believe such a story? Jason wondered. *Is it worth telling my CO?* He decided to sleep on it and next morning decided yes, it was his duty to do so. He told the Adjutant that he wanted to tell the CO that he had a clue as to where the missing plane was.

'Jason, you are rum one. Who else would ever think of anything like that? Have you been having bad dreams from too much hooch or what?' He robbed any malice from his question with a smile. 'All right, I'll talk to the CO. All he need say is "Captain Rance, dismiss."'

'I'd like the Gurkha Major to be present if possible and if he believes what I say maybe the CO will too.'

The CO well knew that his OC A Company was, what? Not really maverick but certainly with a mind of his own and had experienced affairs many others had not – he still remembered the answer to his question 'have you a personal credo?' Captain Rance had and the question was answered without thought: 'Yes sir. Stand up and be counted, we are our own shop window and react to the unexpected.' *That should work well in peace and war* the CO considered. He was an unusually understanding man and, remembering how Jason got the best out of his men, especially on Operation Janus, said to the Adjutant, 'yes, sometimes that man almost frightens me with what he produces. You also come in.

And while you're about it bring the IO, Intelligence Officer, and the Gurkha Major saheb along with you.'

They met in the CO's office that had a large map of the battalion area on one wall so anything Jason said could easily be related to features on the map. Jason told his story as he had heard it, using Nepali as the Gurkha Major's English was not good enough to understand it. The note the *bomoh* had given Jitbahadur Gurung was also produced. The CO's decision was to ask the Gurkha Major whether he thought it genuine enough to take action on. Jason felt that was unnecessary but was glad he had thought to bring the senior Gurkha in the battalion into the matter.

The CO looked at Jason. 'Rance, fine as far as it goes but is that far enough? Higher command will never believe this. I'll send you with a small team to have a look-see if you can find it on the aerial photo I have of the area. Take it to the IO's office and have a good look at it then, if you can find it, let me know.'

Jason saluted him, went to the other office, put the aerial photograph on a long table and unrolled it, putting something heavy on each corner to keep it flat. He asked the Intelligence Corporal, Mangalsing Tamang, for the stereoscope. Jason had been on a course on how to use them at the very end of the war in Rangoon; it was when the first of the two atomic bombs were dropped on Japan and so he could always remember the time even if the details of using the eye things were rusty.

Although the IO, a recently joined subaltern, had been given a copy of the flight plan of the lost aircraft it was not easy to plot accurately on a map as it was so circuitous. They carefully picked it out as best they could both on an ordnance survey map and the photograph, the former to see where contours marked high ground which, of course, the photograph did not show. In quite a few places the map showed 'cloud' which would be of less than any use to those on the ground even though they had been given map co-ordinates of their areas with the strictest orders not to go into others' areas. And indeed, even on the photograph there were patches of cloud obscuring details. Yet, even so, there did not seem any such place as the *bomoh* had described.

The CO came into the room at that moment. 'Any luck?' he asked and was not particularly surprised at the gloomy looks on all three faces. 'So, what is the snag?'

Jason told him. 'Cloud marked on the map and shown on the photo makes precisely locating the place difficult, sir.'

'So you think your *bomoh* fellow is wrong?'

'Sir, my gut feeling is, no, he is not wrong. Is it just possible that the plane's compass was faulty, either because the plane flew over some hidden loadstone – or worst case, both?'

The CO sucked his lips. He, too, was torn. *Even if there is the smallest chance we can't let it go, can we?* 'So, what do you suggest, Jason?' he asked.

Jason looked up at him and smiled, 'You'll probably think this unrealistic, sir, but I'll go and talk to the *bomoh* as my Malay is better than Jitbahadur's. I'll see if I can get any more definite clues. If I do and we feel it's worthwhile let me go up in an Auster for a recce. Having got a picture of what the *bomoh* has said there may be a chance of spotting it from the air. I'll take the Int corporal with me as another pair of eyes.'

The GM had an idea: 'Saheb, our pundit is also a shaman. I suggest that I ask him to see what he can find by using his skills. If they agree with the *bomoh* then it could be taken as confirmation.'

While the CO was considering that Jason saw that Jitbahadur was itching to say something. 'Out with it, *keta*, what is it you want to say?'

Jitbahadur hesitated before answering obliquely, 'Saheb have you heard about the local Tamil schoolmaster's son? The younger of the two, the one about twelve years old?'

'No, never. Why do you ask?'

'Because whenever there's a problem with no answer, his father puts him in a trance and he writes the answer on a piece of paper before being revived. I have been told that he has never been wrong.'

'What are you two talking about?' grumbled the CO.

'Jitbahadur has suggested getting the younger son of the local Tamil schoolmaster, sir, putting him into a trance and getting an answer to our question. Apparently the young boy is never wrong or should I say, so far he has always given a correct answer.'

The CO blenched at hearing that. *Is it ethical?* 'Why not?' Then, with a touch of levity, 'Like playing liar dice, three of a kind is better than a pair.'

4

Law Chu Hoi was a thin rake of a man, balding, with a pock-marked face, deep-set eyes and thick eyebrows. Middle-aged and standing around five and half feet, his face had an air of subtlety about it, making him look dangerous. Now it was plain angry and tight-lipped as though he had a problem he couldn't solve but wanted to.

He had been the purser on the SS *Eastern Queen*, Captain Lam Wai Lim, of the Indo-China Steam Navigation Co. Ltd., registered in Hong Kong. It was a job he had had for several years. He always tried to appear anti-communist but he was, in fact, a hardcore, card-carrying member of the Hong Kong Communist Party. Apart from his 'day' job his secret one was to be bearer of any news, orally, never written, to any comrade he had been told would be travelling to Calcutta, from Hong Kong, Singapore or Rangoon but chiefly from Hong Kong. Although he did not know any details other than what message he had to pass on and to whom, he knew it was of great importance to help the cause. As it was against the colonial masters in Asia and as he hated all Europeans, he was content to be an important link in an important chain between 'outposts' and the next link, which was a leather tannery in Tangra Chinatown in the east of Calcutta.

He did not know that that was the last link to the secret office of the Soviet MGB, the Ministry of State Security, that was in 'clear sight' in the Soviet consulate in Calcutta as there was no need for him to know about it. Security in the Soviet world was of paramount importance, often outweighing an individual's own innate abilities.

He had a system of inconspicuous code words he could send to MGB helpers, locals in the countries his boat visited, sometimes to meet him on board or at other times to ask if any Party passenger needed a cabin. His contact for any comrade travelling from Singapore was one Chen Geng, who worked openly at 47 Pedder Street as a normal trader.

In mid-November 1952 the SS *Eastern Queen* unusually took a leave party of Gurkha soldiers from Singapore and Penang to Calcutta, whose OC was Captain Jason Rance.[9] On board was a comrade he had been told to brief, one Ah Fat. The purser had no need to know that he was a non-voting member of the Politburo of the MCP, travelling as a normal passenger, only that he was 'one of us' so needed the usual briefing for any further activity once he had arrived in Calcutta. On board, Jason and Ah Fat never spoke to one another when in sight of anyone. Tradecraft: how did either know that were they seen laughing and talking together it might get back to the HQ MCP to Ah Fat's disadvantage?

Once in Calcutta the purser had taken 'Comrade' Ah Fat to the next link in the chain, either of two senior men in the Tangra Chinatown leather works, Wong Kek Fui or Cheng Fan Tek. These

---

9   See *Operation Tipping Point*.

people, Hakkas, had been there since before the British arrived in India. One of them was the last link in the chain to take a visitor to the MGB set-up where he would hand him over to one of the staff. Neither Hakka knew that the MGB representative was in charge of anti-colonial matters in Asia as there was no need to. Before Wong Kek Fui took Ah Fat to meet the person in the Soviet Consulate in Alipore Park Road, he warned him about his dislike of Asians. Ah Fat's anger made him tell the Rezident that he had an undercover agent to meet him.

Before Ah Fat and Jason Rance went to meet the Rezident there was time to visit the tanneries. There Ah Fat took Jason to meet the second 'link' man, Cheng Fan Tek, and told him that Jason was, in fact, a dedicated communist working from within.

In Cheng's office, Ah Fat was asked what nationality was that ugly man with him, not knowing that Jason could talk Chinese. 'Looking at this ugly lout I would be happy to see him drown himself in drink, better still in rat's piss.' Jason's unexpected answer: 'Why not pig's piss. Better if you were drowned in it but not with me. You uncouth *Fei Toh*' – bandit – completely bemused him and, not having expected two comrades, later rang the purser of the SS *Eastern Queen,* to enquire if there was any Chinese-speaking *gwailo*, foreigner, on board. *I told him 'no' and now I am without a job.* He was at a loss what to do: find a job or get his revenge but with a nagging wife, a shrew even normally, his life was in crisis. Luckily he had saved some of his pay, so he was not destitute. He decided to take what gold ornaments he had given his wife without her knowing and blame a thief if he felt short of money. But the other problem was who could he ask for advice? Even 'fellow travellers' in Hong Kong were in danger if seen talking in earnest to anyone. Law Chu Hoi did not think he was on any police list of suspects but ... *There always is a 'but'* he thought miserably. The more he thought it over the more it worried him: Cheng Fan Tek had phoned him in his purser's office on board and had said that the *gwailo* was a secret card-carrying comrade but ... but was he really one? The thought nagged him: if he was not one then he was certainly a consummate actor but the way he answered back Law's barbs in his Tangra office showed hostility to a fellow comrade that was quite out of character and intentionally hostile. If the latter was the case then his next move was sure: track him down and get his revenge. But was that practicable. And if so, how?

He had his own special place where he used to go to think things out. It was not far from his house in *San Kai*, the New Territories, and he needed to stretch his legs. It was late evening and as he wanted to go unseen he dawdled till it was dark then set out. His destination was a small sandy plateau, not far from the border with the mainland. It was said to be haunted by the souls of Nationalist soldiers who were chased over the frontier at the end of the civil war and were massacred to a man. Some people said that you could still hear communist soldiers going back to cross the border to the mainland. He only half believed it, never himself having heard anything when he visited the place on one pretext or another. *Tonight, even if I hear nothing, I might think of an answer to my problem* was a comforting thought as he made his way there, with a torch in his pocket. He sat down on one side and tried to think of an answer to his pressing problem.

By now it was late December and he had an overcoat on to keep him warm. After an hour or so it was getting cold and he was just about to get up to go back when he heard a definite *shuff, shuff, shuff* of moving feet. *Men moving! How many?* He shone his torch. No one was there. He turned it off but still he heard *shuff, shuff, shuff*. 'Who's there?' he called.[10]

No answer but the *shuff, shuff, shuff* got fainter till he heard it no longer. He stood up and, shining his torch once again, went over to where he had heard the footsteps crossing the sandy surface. He shone it all around. No footsteps were to be seen – *but would there be any in soft sand?* He shook his head to clear his mind and slowly went back home to a late meal, put on the table by his niggling wife. He went to bed early and woke up in the small hours. *Yes. It was a sign for me! The footsteps were comrades returning after killing the Nationalists.* His breathing quickened as the message became clear.

Next morning he knew he had a definite aim to find out why he had to kill the two men; now the plan ... *but for the* gwailo *only or for both men?*

The *gwailo* was a military man and he had heard that they gave fancy names before going to battle or even to find comrades fighting against them in the jungle. He grinned to himself. *They call them 'operations' don't they? I'll give my work a name like that.* He wondered what name to give his operation. *They say they hunt us so I'll hunt the* gwailo. He grinned sardonically. *I'll*

10 Your author has also heard those same shuff, shuff, shuff sounds. He was not answered when he asked who was walking there nor could he see anyone.

call my work Operation Hunter. He felt, intuitively, that speed in starting his operation was of the essence.

He was never to know that the *shuff, shuff, shuff* sounds were not those of returning comrades but of defeated Nationalists unable to get back home, so would not bring him the extra good luck he craved even though he was now even more sure he'd get another sign to tell him whether his prey would be one or two. One thing he did know was that his main adversary, the long-nosed, running dog, was his priority whatever clue was shown him. That meant he had to go to Malaya to search him out, to hunt for him. Law Chu Hoi had no idea at all about matters military but he presumed that all officers stayed in their base and never went into the jungle so it would be comparatively easy to find him. So first stop Singapore where his one contact, Chen Geng, would be the person to contact.

Before Siu Tse went to Lukut she had contacted the fresh-ration contractor for 1/12 GR, Goh Ah Hok. She knew that her Alan had spent his first night away from the battalion in his house and that her manager, Yap Cheng Wu, had gone there early next morning in his car to take him on the first stage of his long journey. Anything that Yap had been ready to tell her, which wasn't much at all, had already been told so maybe she could find out something definite about her Alan this way; it was certainly worth trying. In any case, Goh Ah Hok was a useful man to talk to as he had met Captain Rance – that evil man she saw as medium-sized, balding, slack-jawed, pinched-faced, short-sighted and close-cropped, black hair – met him many times and might, just, give her a clue about him to make her task a bit easier. Her thoughts turned to the boy who had saved her so many years ago: *now, if I were to meet him, he would give me some good advice, of that I am sure* and she took the handkerchief out of her pocket to look at and to feel, to give her strength in her task, her heart skipping a beat as it always did when she thought of him.

She went to see Goh Ah Hok but, to her disappointment, she could get nothing out of him. She was shocked rather than dismayed. He just clammed up harshly telling her he knew nothing about what she was asking. She did manage to talk to his daughter who said she had taken some gruel to, she didn't know his name, his bedroom before he disappeared but somehow or other, her father had been different from that day on. No, she didn't know why so. 'You know I can't ask him and even if I did I'd get no answer and probably be punished.' A disappointed Siu Tse thanked her and left the house. *What could be the matter with him?* she asked herself – in vain.

By her asking Goh about that time vividly brought back to him the unexpected horror of a visit Jason had made: '*Sinsaang Goh Ah Hok*,' he had begun, 'I know that you know where the main camp of the guerrillas is,' naming the two senior ones as he did. 'You will get out your van and take me to the place you get out to go to it then lead me and my men to the guerrillas' camp, *now*.'

I was totally overwhelmed to be addressed in fluent Cantonese, he recalled, violently denying any knowledge of what was being talked about. *I was flabbergasted that the* gwailo *officer could know anything about that side of my affairs.*

He played back in his mind that fateful day: 'Don't fool about and tell lies,' the British officer had spat out angrily. 'I'm in a hurry to get there with my *Goo K'a* soldiers. I also accuse you of having had the man you call *Sik Long* here last night. True or false?' Goh did not know that he had said that because he had smelt the type of cigarettes Hinlea smoked.

Again I denied any knowledge of anything. But how could he know the Lustful Wolf was here last night and, another terrible thought, *how does he know that nickname,* Sik Long?

Goh remembered how the angry officer had leant over towards him and, coldly, distinctly and forcibly, 'You are a liar. Listen to this' and he then cursed me in the oldest and most virulent curse all Chinese know: '*Ch'uan jia chan*', and I could see he meant it.

Of course I know what the curse means: *May your entire clan be wiped out* and, in days gone-by in China, that was literally meant, no sibling, kith or kin remaining alive.

Before I could remonstrate what else had he said? He knew I spoke *Loi Pai Yi Wa* but I was lost until he translated it back into my own language: 'I will curse you with a curse which, if broken, will result in leprosy in your entire family for seven generations.' He then added '*ngok yau, ngok bo*', evil has its recompense.

I dare not open my mouth to Siu Tse as I fear the curse and if 'he' hears about it I may well lose my fresh-ration contract.

He never mentioned the subject again, nor ever forgot it.

So, Siu Tse had learnt nothing firm before leaving Seremban, only guessing that this *gwailo* might be a powerful and difficult man to track down and contact. Her life was now completely different, in one way certainly, than it had been before in that now she felt she was working for the Party's good in an active sense rather than as was the case before; yet in another way it was the same, living in a marginalised community where nothing was easy and without her baby. She often felt torn about leaving him behind but as an active Party member doing what she was doing was her duty – or so she told herself.

She had gone to Lukut by bus as an ordinary civilian and looked for the place that had been warned to receive her. She wandered around and found where Jemima Estate was. She had been told to dress as a rubber tapper did and had been kitted out by Grandfather Ngai Hiu Ching, so when she visited the labour lines she caused no interest to the tappers. It was only after working hours that day had she met the leader of the Chinese rubber tappers, a middle-aged man whose vituperative language both thrilled and horrified her. He snarled rather than talked in a normal voice and, as he had a stammer, was difficult to follow. He told her to fetch her belongings from the hotel she had spent the last night at and report to him. After letting her feed, he asked her why she wanted to be so active in the Party and, once she had fully understood him, her answer intrigued him. 'I want to kill a *gwailo*.'

'We all do, not one but many,' he rumbled back at her, trying to sound pleasant.

'There is one I particularly want to kill. He commands *Goo K'a* soldiers and is based in Seremban.'

'Why him in particular when there are so many easier targets?'

'He killed the father of my baby boy,' she said with a snuffle she could not control.

Her questioner looked at her for a long moment. 'Then you'll be happier in the jungle with an active unit than with us here.'

'Yes, I think I will be.'

'Leave it with me. I will send a report to the Schoolmaster Grandfather who will, I am sure, fix it for you. Can't promise but as you are genuine I expect you will be acceptable.'

While she waited for an answer one way or the other she learnt how to be a rubber tapper. She had never realised how skilful one had to be to take the minimum sliver of bark off the tree trunk with a small knife. She found the work tiring, the ever-present mosquitoes a curse, and the coarse tongue of her immediate overseer hard to bear when he cursed her for what he saw as careless work. After the first two days her wrist hurt because of having to hold the knife at a certain angle the whole time. Also the hours of work, out at dawn when the sap rose, back after her task had been completed, a meal she sometimes had to cook herself, then back again with a bucket to tip the latex that had dripped into the little bowls tied round the tree. And the smell of the latex processing factory! She had a headache in no time.

Her overseer saw that she was too clumsy as a novice and that the owner of the estate would get into a rage if and when he saw such rough 'tapping' so she was taken off that job and put into the factory that took the latex and turned it into flat sheets of rubber. There was less for her to damage here, especially as she was put on the most basic jobs, lifting and carrying various bits and pieces from one place to another. The smell in a latex factory is one which some people can never get used to and she hated it. She felt dispirited and vowed that the longest she could stay working on a rubber estate was two months; if nothing came she'd have to go back to Seremban and find some other way of assuaging her wrath at her Alan's death.

Luckily it was only after one month not two when, one night, one of the estate workers came to take her away in a taxi. They drove in silence for some way before she was led into a house and hidden there before the taxi reached the first police checkpoint. On the morrow the estate worker took her to a lorry that was taking some bananas to market before leaving her. She hid in it, until oh so carefully, with no witnesses, she was transferred to another vehicle which at last light dropped her off on the jungle edge. She was told to get out with her bag of clothes and almost at once a squad of five armed and uniformed men came out of the jungle to fetch her. After they had had a meal which they cooked so the fire could not be seen from the road, off they went along a narrow path.

The guerrilla foot soldiers who came to escort their new recruit were a plucky and hard-living lot of men whose continuous life in the jungle had given them an almost animal sixth sense of danger and a seemingly telepathic ability to communicate between themselves which allowed them to stay alive where 'softer', European-bred soldiers would have wilted so become harmless. Although Siu Tse had, by living in a 'squatter' area, visited the local jungle from time to time as a girl, the jungle she found herself in was 'grown up' compared with what she knew; under the high tree-top canopy she saw that a green world jostled to find a space to catch the sun's rays, so was thick. She immediately saw how much, she searched for a word to compare it with what she had ventured in before but could not describe it to herself but instantly that youthful encounter with her saviour came into her mind. She smiled to herself: *now, he would never have killed my Alan, would he?*

In this new jungle it was never silent. Until she got used to it her sleep was disturbed by cries, whistles, screams, muffled roars and croaks; this litany of sounds was caused by myriads of birds and insects producing the cacophony of an out-of-tune orchestra, as well as sounds of a wild animal, disturbed by the presence of people, rustling away to safety. It was then that she was taught various noises, easy to imitate, and easier still for a woman, clicking the tongue a certain way. Another was croaking like a frog to announce an unseen presence and to answer similarly. One particular bird call, the *taptibau* – great-eared nightjar – was also used to keep contact. In fact it only ever made its distinctive cry at dawn and dusk but the guerrillas reckoned it was no risk to use it by day as it was presumed none of the Security Forces they might come up against would know that.

A library of sights also greeted her: vast spiders' webs, large ants' nests, the occasional monkey up a tree. Their own progress was quiet, as damp soil and a mulch of fallen leaves cushioned their movements. They retained the tracks of her guard's footsteps on their way to fetch her.

Towards the end of their journey the Squad Leader, Lin Soong, saw his new recruit was struggling. He put up hand as a silent signal to halt, went up to her and, smiling, said, 'You have guts beyond your size and experience. Let us rest here awhile.'

Oh, how grateful she was!

Comrade Lin Soong made the others move a few yards and face outwards, to hear any noise of a possible follow-up. Five minutes later, with all quiet, he took off his pack and rummaged around. He produced a packet of biscuits and a small flask, took off the cork and handed it to her. 'First drink, little sister, then share a biscuit with me.'

She put the flask to her lips and, to her surprise, tasted the guerrillas' favourite drink: Ovaltine. She drank as much as she dared before handing it back to him. She thanked him before he took a long drink before putting the cork back on and the flask back into his pack.

After eating their biscuits, he said 'Little sister, this next and last part is quite stiff as the ground rises steadily but the jungle becomes thinner so walking becomes easier.' Off they set and eventually came to an abrupt, almost perpendicular slope, at the bottom of which were two armed and uniformed guerrillas. The elder saluted the Squad Commander, looked at Siu Tse and said, 'Welcome, Comrade. We are glad to have you join us.'

That first night she slept better than she had for a long, long time. She had really, really started on her hunt for her enemy – and it must have been the jungle that let her see her youthful saviour of so many years ago in her dreams.

It was only much later that she found out that a retentive memory along with a cool head were the main requisites of knowing where one probably was; the direction of stream flow, a rise or fall in contours were normally the only aids in featureless terrain to work out one's position if lost. The depth of a stream, the thickness of undergrowth, the flight of the birds, the age of a track and many other signs are always there to be read like a book by the initiated and turned to his advantage when, to most others with senses deadened and mind dulled by a depressing and endless similarity, the jungle takes over as a master who cannot be bettered. She never did learn that the Security Forces said that the jungle was neutral but an armed neutrality that should never be taken for granted.

Tactical precautions normally restricted movement to about a thousand yards an hour, while in swamp it could be as slow as a hundred. Under the canopy of tall trees visibility was also heavily restricted, often being no more than a few yards in any one direction, so the ears had to take over from the eyes. Her Alan never told her that jungle movement and fighting had the characteristics of night work as he, only ever gunner-trained, never learnt otherwise.

He had found out on the way to the MCP HQ, as he had thought of his target, never dreaming for a moment it would be the last journey he'd ever make in his life, that the jungle was a world of its own, to some frightening, to some a sanctuary, to most a place to keep out of and only to a few a place to respect, come to terms with, almost revere. As Hinlea had left the flattish ground near Seremban he soon became lost in the close-horizon, all-pervading, never-ending green of trees, vines, creepers and undergrowth. Not a gap in the tangle; it rose from the ground, trunk by trunk and stem by stem, each one crowding upon and striving to outgrow the other, and tied and netted together with the snake arms of creepers into a closely woven web. Aerial roots and liana-nooses hung from high above. Leaves laid themselves out in vast terraces, fantastic umbels descended in cascades and creepers united in stout, tightly-wound, spiral columns. Vegetation teemed in the steamy twilight; great fronds broken under their own weight, ropes which had neither end nor beginning, plants with fat, sticky leaves or with hairy or scaly stems, or stems that opened out like buttresses and some with large, luxuriant flowers, exuding a strange and deathly scent. It was also swampy in places and leeches prolific and squashy in his shoes and itchy and uncomfortable elsewhere. He had felt overwhelmed even before he had really started. Like him, the mother of his son thought similarly: *I just can't imagine getting used to this, but I must if I want to be successful in my quest for revenge.* It showed remarkable spirit that she never once regretted her impulse. Her military leader spoke with the Political Commissar and they decided she should be issued with a pistol, a Smith and Weston .38, that had been captured during the war, and six rounds of ammunition.

Dismissed purser Law Chu Hoi was no fool, so he realised that his task required both a sensible plan and someone to help him – he knew it was too much to take on by himself. He had no real idea of just where either comrade was that he had been ordered to dispose of except 'somewhere in deep jungle', if what radio and newspaper reports he had come across were true, which they probably were. He knew that he was no jungle man nor had any training in how to use such terrain to his benefit. He saw, therefore, that there had to be some scheme to persuade either or both to come out and meet him somewhere he could use a hired 'hit' man to perform his allotted task. *But where and how?* plagued him. *Who can I turn to?*

After the ship's captain had called him to his cabin and dismissed him, he still had certain residual rights, receipt of any pay yet to be sent to his bank account to include any paid leave he was still entitled to and, by terms of his contract, a gratuity at the end of his service. Yet, the captain was so angry and he himself so upset that he meekly let himself be taken to his cabin to pack his clothes before being escorted off the ship. He was not allowed to go to his office; the captain would get a company auditor to check all the accounts and, if anything was found to be missing, he would get the magistrate to allow the police to go to the purser's house and collect him for questioning.

He had a good memory and as his training had stressed 'never to leave any evidence to do with his secret job, possibly incriminating or otherwise, anywhere it could be found were he not there to hide it' he was not worried at leaving his office unvisited. In fact, his accounts were correct and as much cash was in his petty cash box as was reflected in the account, so he had no worry on that score either.

Back home, shutting his ears to his nagging wife who was pestering him to know why he was not going back to his office on board – 'I'm on shore leave' – he thought out the phone numbers and addresses of the contacts he had in Singapore, Rangoon and Calcutta. As the two people he had to get to grips with were in Malaya, the communist contact in Singapore was the one to approach first. *Yes … Chen Geng at 47 Pedder Street.* He remembered the phone number and decided to go to the main office of Cable & Wireless and book a call.

Without telling his wife where he was off to, on the morrow he went to the cable office and booked a call. He was lucky and contacted Chen after the first few rings. He used the code words he had always used before, so Chen knew that something unusual was afoot. The talk was casual to start with for who knew how much any overseas call was tapped?

'Do you travel in your business?' Lau asked a rather bewildered Chen.

'No, I don't. I am not senior enough. The white Tuans do that. Why do you ask?'

'I'd have liked to have met you were you coming to Hong Kong."

'A nice thought but no. Any chance of your coming my way?'

'Not at the moment. I'm due a holiday and the idea of visiting Singapore and spending more than a rushed visit from my purser's office attracts me.'

'Fine. Tell you what. Drop me a line and I'll see what I can fit in. Maybe if it's not too dangerous we could take a trip to Malaya.'

Lau's eyes lit up at that suggestion. 'Forget the letter bit. Once I've got dates I'll give you another bell and see which ones suit you. I'll ring off as this is not all that cheap.' He put the phone down.

Chen Geng looked at the silent phone in his hand. *Most unusual!* He shrugged, put the phone back and was about to get on with his work when a postman delivered a registered letter that needed a signed receipt. *If it's not one thing it's another* ... He shook his head in utter disbelief as he read the unsigned letter, written on paper he knew had been bought in India: 'Get Liu Yew Kui, the current purser of SS *Princess of the Orient,* to have SS *Eastern Queen* ex-purser Law Chu Hoi killed as soon and as safely as possible, telling him beforehand it is because he disobeyed Party orders. If hunting him first needs funds, pay for any help needed: repayment will be made on killing completed.'

There are three types of Nepali shamans, one that goes into a trance, talks in a different tone of voice to a voice only heard by him and, having asked whatever questions necessary either gets the advice wanted or nothing at all. The second type is given a pound of unhusked rice and, putting it in a pile, strokes it with his right hand as he inwardly prays until he is told the answer to his queries. The third type almost does likewise but whose fingers make lines on sand which he then interprets. The 1/12 GR pundit was of the second type; as a 12-year-old he had become stuck up to his waist in mud and not been rescued for thirty-six hours. By the time he was rescued he had somehow obtained the gift of both hindsight and the future. He willingly undertook the GM's request, 'try to find out where a plane carrying a brigadier and a captain has crashed', being twenty Malayan dollars the richer for his pains.

When he had finished he looked up at the GM and said, 'I can't tell if this helps, GM saheb, but what you asked is not where other people think it is.' This the GM reported back to the CO who happened to be with his OC A Company at the time.

'Curiouser and curiouser' was the CO's only comment as he digested the meaning of the message.

The CO and Jason, both wearing plain clothes, were present at noon when the Tamil schoolmaster led his son into Jitbahadur's empty barrack room and sat the boy cross-legged on the floor in front of a table he had previously asked for, a piece of paper and a pencil ready for use. The father stood over his son, crooning softly in Tamil. After some five minutes the boy started trembling. His father put his son's hands on the table, picked up the pencil and put it between the thumb and index finger of the boy's right hand, crooning the while. The boy leant forward and all the three observers could see was line after wavy line, no writing as such. Not knowing the script none of them could tell if there was any message to be deciphered or not. When the lad reached the bottom of the page he slumped forward, his head on the table.[11] All three watchers looked on aghast.

His father leant forwards, took the boy's head in his hands, smoothed it and spoke softly into his right ear. Gradually the boy responded, looked around him, eyes unfocussed and his father helped him to his feet, and the boy, groggily swaying, was led outside. There was handed over to someone the others did not see. The father came back, scrutinised the squiggles and said, 'My

_____

11 Your author has seen exactly the like enacted when a young Tamil boy was asked about a thief in his unit lines. The lines on the paper were like a seismograph but the boy's father read 'Under the bed' somewhere along the lines. The stolen stuff was found in a box beneath one of the soldier's beds. When he asked the soldier why he had stolen the stuff his answer was 'my father was a thief. What do you expect me to do?'

son has written "what you asked is not where other people think it is". I hope that helps you, sir,' to the Colonel.

'I am sure it will. Thank you, Headmaster,' and, so saying, the CO gave him a one-hundred dollar note.

Back in the officer both Colonel and Captain shook their head at this most curious of coincidences. 'It's too uncanny to be an accident,' said the senior of the two. Jitbahadur came in and, having thrown up the necessary preliminary salute, said 'Rance saheb, Yasin says he'd like to meet you.'

'You'd better go Jason,' the CO said. 'We might be given a helpful clue to this most strange situation.'

Jitbahadur took Jason to meet Yasin and he introduced himself, saying that he, too, had been born in Malaya, not in Seremban but in Kuala Lumpur. Yasin told Jason that he had tried to join up as a Special Constable but was told he was too old … and after the obligatory time on non-essentials was over Jason broached his subject: could Yasin expand on what he had told the Gurkha?

'Tuan, not much but I suppose it is that what you asked is not where others think it is.'

Jason thanked him, gave him some sweets for his children and the two men returned to the lines.

The CO, Adjutant, Captain Rance, the IO, the Gurkha Major, Corporal Mangalsing Tamang and Rifleman Jitbahadur Gurung gathered in the CO's office, an unusual mixture of ranks. By the time they had heard the message 'what you asked is not where other people think it is' three times in uncanny repetition, there was little else to do but once again search both map and photo for a last look. So, Jason and Mangalsing once more studied the aerial photo for all the high ground not near the flight plan. 'I have a hunch, Ustad. Look at the area around at Gunong Rajah, near Bentong in Pahang.'

They did and saw that the map hinted at what the *bomoh* had pointed out – in Pahang, not in Selangor or Negri Sembilan – and on checking with the sitreps they saw that there were no troops in that area. Did this explain why every sitrep was NTR, Nothing To Report?

Jason asked the CO to ask the OC Flight 'to find out if he doesn't know already the direction of any storm on the day the plane disappeared.'

'Does it matter?'

'It may well. At the moment it is just a thought. In any case I think the OC Flight will need some persuading to fly towards Gunong Raja.'

'Why so?'

'It is so far off anywhere anyone has thought to look he might jib at flying there a waste of time.'

The Adjutant rang Flight HQ and the CO spoke to the Major in charge. He said he felt that another aerial recce was needed because Captain Rance's knowledge of photographic interpretation as well as his experience on the ground had given clues that the plane had crashed somewhere in the Gunong Rajah area of Bentong.' It was a tactful request.

The CO heard what sounded like a smothered sigh before a weary answer 'Very well, sir, the day after tomorrow in my lines for a 1000 hours take-off. Just him or is there another passenger?'

'One more, my Int Corporal. No stores, except normal escape kit.'

'Only two stipulations, Colonel. No flying under five hundred feet or if bad weather prevails.'

'That goes without saying. And have you any details of the direction of the wind of any storm during the flight, even at the suspected time of the crash?'

'As we don't know the time of the crash, sir, that is hard to say. However, I did ask the met people and, generally, it was from north to south but once over the mountains the plane was trying to cross it was circular. The mountains make their own weather.'

The CO thanked him as he rang off and told Jason what he had been told. It was only to himself that Jason quoted a Nepali proverb, 'the goat has been made to shiver before being sacrificed: now all that is needed is for something to go wrong.'

5

Liu Yew Kui, purser of SS *Princess of the Orient*, was as different a character from Law Chu Hoi, ex-purser of SS *Eastern Queen* as could be. Out-going and ebullient, he was a model of cheery welcome to all his passengers. Like his opposite number of the SS *Eastern Queen*, he was also a serious link in the chain between Hong Kong and the MGB office in Calcutta. Unlike his 'oppo', whom he only occasionally met as sailing schedules precluded easy meetings – not often in Hong Kong but more often these were when the boats crossed halfway between journeys, normally at Rangoon – he was a cantankerous character. He was in his early forties and a happy family man. His manner with European and Asian passengers alike made him equally approachable. He was of middle height, had a round face, a mouth creased by smiles, an incipient 'pot belly' and, altogether, a pleasing example of Chinese middle-aged manhood. *The very last sort of person I can get to kill Law Chu Hoi* mused Chen Keng. *He should be in Singapore docks any day now and I have Law Chu Hoi coming here the day after tomorrow.* He put his elbows on his desk, his head in his hands and thought deeply.

'Got a hangover, have you?' came a cheery voice from the door which he had not shut.

Chen gave him a bleak smile, 'Not so much a hangover but more of a hang-up, a problem that does not seem to have an easy answer so I'm just giving it some of my infallible brain power.'

'Don't bother, that'll make it even more difficult to solve,' was the reassuring answer as the other man turned away.

Chen Geng had the grace to grin to himself as he got up and shut the door. Returning to his desk he realised, as indeed he had done in the past, that he was not the killing sort of person, nor was what he knew of Liu Yew Kui – far from it, strong-arm tactics repelled him. But he had to realise that others could 'strong arm' him. What little he had heard about methods from meetings with the Tangra Hakkas, Cheng Fan Tek or Wong Kek Fui, in Calcutta, acting on some sort of orders, was not pleasant. And his orders were the opposite of pleasant; just suppose both pursers, Law Chu Hoi and Liu Yew Kui, did meet in his office and – here another thought struck him, what weapon would Law Chu Hoi use once he knew his orders? – and, having been shown the Soviet letter, 'Get Liu Yew Kui, the purser of SS *Princess of the Orient*, to kill Law Chu Hoi as soon and as securely as possible, telling him beforehand it is because he disobeyed party orders. If hunting him first needs funds, pay for any help needed: repayment will be made on killing completed.' Chen Geng felt that last bit was unnecessarily flamboyant and rather wished he could show the message without it, but no, that was not possible. *So be it.*

Siu Tse did not know where she was, nor did she particularly care. It was in deep jungle and, in fact, not far from the path Alan Hinlea had taken, finding the going far harder than he had ever expected.

It was the Negri Sembilan Regional Committee, the political wing of the MCP at Gunong Telapak, at 3914 feet, the highest feature in the area. It had been reconstituted there after Captain Rance and his small team had destroyed the previous one on Bukit Beremban. It was there she was issued with the .38 pistol and six rounds of ammunition. She had been allowed a few extra rounds for target practice and been told that, as she would never find herself on her own, always being escorted by a member of the MRLA, it was more for self-protection than a killer of enemies, unless circumstances dictated otherwise.

She also helped out in the cooking and her skills were especially welcomed when any game had been shot or trapped and brought in. It was then that what she had learnt when helping Grandfather 'fighting cock' eyes came in so handy. She sometimes fretted that life, while wholly different from what she had been used to and had a different flavour to it, was not turning out quite as she envisaged it. But wisely she kept her thoughts to herself – being the only woman in camp there was no one to share them with.

One day a courier and his escort came into the camp. She had yet to learn that the system was that any Politburo policy orders that needed promulgation or messages taken to other committees in the country would have a courier from the Central Committee in the main MCP camp with his own escort and then taken on, stage by stage, escorted by Regional Committee escorts who knew the lie of the land which, somewhat naturally, the Central

Committee lot would know nothing about.

After the mail had been given to the Political Commissar, the courier and his men would be allowed to rest and freshen up as much as circumstances allowed before the next move. This time one of the letters concerned Siu Tse. Apparently the Politburo thought her knowledge of the *gwailo*, what affected them adversely, what sapped their morale and how best to achieve any propaganda victory was needed.

'That is a great honour, Little Sister' she was told on the morrow.

'Quite what will happen to me now?' she asked.

The Political Commissar, along with the Military Commander, called the Central Committee courier and the leader of the squad that brought him down from the last hand-over place over so they could be introduced to their charge. Both men saw that she would not be able to move as quickly or be as tactically reliant as a trained man would be so would need especial care. Normally any single woman in charge of a squad of men was treated well – adverse behaviour with the opposite sex was heavily frowned upon at all levels and was heavily punished if found out.

'Little Sister, we will go in easy stages. You need have no worry about not being defended properly if we meet the enemy. One man will always be responsible for your safety.'

She smiled. 'Thank you, Comrade. I am sure I will be safe.'

'How well do you know the country?' she was asked.

'Not at all outside where I was born and worked,' she replied. 'That is in the Sepang and Seremban areas.'

'The journey will take some time,' said the local commander.

'I will take you as far as Gunong Rajah, in the Bentong area of Perak, where I'll hand you over to the next squad. Before we go let us listen to the news broadcast from Radio Malaya. One never knows what useful tip will be given us for nothing.'

The headline news that morning was about a missing plane containing a senior British Army officer and his aide: it had failed to make contact during a storm 'somewhere in a large area southeast of Kuala Lumpur. Security Forces were being sent out to find it, hunting for clues on the ground as none had been seen from the air.'

The Central Committee of the MCP had its strict routine, one aspect of which was listening to the early morning news broadcast of Radio Malaya on its Chinese-language channel. All comrades were keenly interested and taken aback by the announcement of the missing aeroplane with a senior British officer and his aide the passengers. It sent a frisson of excitement through them as they listened.

At the end of the bulletin the Head of Central Propaganda Department, Lee An Tung, a man with a worried look on his face and a perpetual frown, said to his deputy, Chin Tiang, a squat man who looked at everyone suspiciously, said 'from our point of view let's hope the passenger is dead so he cannot inflict any harm against us.'

All the comrades agreed with this as, indeed, farther south it also caused much excitement: the *gwailo* probably killing themselves, some said – but, on hearing it, Lin Soong pursed his lips. 'That is good in one way but bad in another.'

His listeners knew better than to interrupt while their leader was contemplating about a forthcoming move. 'Good, because that means one less senior officer to threaten us and good that the troops won't be taking normal precautions as their attention will be for the hunt for the plane and any survivor. Also, good because there probably won't be any enemy anywhere else but where they're searching. Bad, because there will be more of the enemy milling around than normal. We will keep to our high standards as a matter of our survival.' He looked around and saw that faces were grimmer than usual.

He cracked a joke and said, 'On our way' and strode off. The others followed as fast as they could, and it was only outside their camp area that they started to move tactically. On their third day they reached Bahau to the southeast of that feature.

They hid on the very edge of Bahau and, with the help of some people who lived on the outskirts of the town, were brought rations for the next stage of their journey as well as some highly appreciated rice gruel before being led around the northern end of the town into the jungle once more. They were soon in the flat country north of the Ladang Geddes rubber estate. They heard much air activity. One of the group climbed a tree and saw parachutes dropping. Making his right hand into a narrow viewer and looking through it so seeing everything much more clearly than otherwise he looked around, searching for any parachute with a body hanging underneath it, but only saw packets: airdrops of stores. He stayed as long as he could bear the stings of the red ants and counted five different places where parachutes were dropping stores. Once on the ground he reported that the drops were all to the north of their intended journey, which was to the northeast.

After he had taken all the red ants off his body, the group continued, cautiously, on its way.

Law Chu Hoi easily remembered the way to 47 Pedder Street. When he was still a purser, there had always been just enough time when the SS *Eastern Queen* was in port for a short visit there as the ship's captain had let him hand over to his assistant once the disembarking passengers were off and before the new lot was scheduled to arrive. On this occasion he was made welcome by Chen Geng who was ignorant about the ex-purser's dismissal.

'When are you due to sail? How long have you got with me?'

'As long as you care to have me. I need to pick your brains,' he answered, with an unusual leer. He had a cold and his voice croaked.

Chen Geng tried to hide his surprise. 'In that case I'll order a meal.' He spoke into his telephone then asked 'Pick my brains? What about?'

'I need to kill two people.'

The Singaporean looked at him, stunned. This was quite the opposite of what he had expected. He gritted his teeth in vexation.

'May I ask who or is it a secret?' As far as Chen Geng knew there might have been some kind of in-fighting between the staff of the SS *Eastern Queen* and her sister ship the SS *Princess of the Orient*. 'You surely don't mean Liu Yew Kui do you?'

It was now Law Chu Hui's turn to look stunned. 'No, no. Of course not. How could that ever be?'

It was a question Chen Geng declined to answer and Law

carried on. 'As you are a comrade with a safe pair of lips I'll tell you. They are two comrades who have to be got rid of on orders of the senior MGB man in the area, Calcutta I think.'

'Who and where are they?'

'One is a Comrade Ah Fat –'

'Surely not. I know him. He is a solid man. Nothing wrong with him at all.'

'And the other is a *gwailo*, a deep-cover comrade working as a British officer in a Gurkha unit.'

That completely beat his questioner who merely shook his head in wonder. 'But how does this maniac, no, I mustn't call him that, in Calcutta know about that and surely that is a plus not a minus to our side.'

Law Chu Hoi sighed deeply. Matters were not going at all how he thought they would. 'I have been told to kill both of them … ' and out came the story of a letter the captain of his ship had shown his and his subsequent dismissal.

As he finished off they heard a knock on the door. 'Come in,' called Chen Geng, thinking it could be meal he'd ordered. In walked Liu Yew Kui who stopped short with obvious pleasure when he saw Law Chu Hoi.

Chen Geng hid his embarrassment by lifting the phone and asking for another portion to be added to the meal he had ordered.

The two others were obviously happy in so unexpectedly meeting up. It was, Chen saw, a situation he just did not know how to react to. Another knock, another 'come in' and the door opened and two portions were brought in from outside. Chen Geng told his two guests to eat while his own was being prepared.

'But before you start let's drink a toast to our happy meeting.' He produced a brandy bottle, a bottle of water and three glasses. He poured out generous amounts and, with the minimum of water, glasses were raised, and a toast to friendship was drunk.

The other two started on their meal and the other portion was brought in just after they had started. They ate in silence.

After their meal Chen Geng decided another toast was needed while he tried to make up his mind what to do about Law Chu Hoi not being the hunter but the hunted. No idea came so he poured out another generous lot for both of them – *lucky I have two bottles of this stuff* – and let's have a toast to friendship. They drank to it.

The telephone rang and Chen Geng answered it. It was another businessman asking about some invoice he had requested. 'I have it in my desk drawer. I'll get it out for you.' He held the phone in one hand and opened the drawer with the other. He looked inside, 'Yes, I have it. I'll send it around later on today. I have guests with me now.'

Not looking at the drawer to take out the invoice lest he forget it, he picked out the letter he had had from Sergey Siderov instead and, not being fully sober, threw it on the table where it lay for both his guests to read – which they did, with wide-open eyes and a horrified expression on both faces. Silence.

Liu Yew Kui broke it. 'I am to kill Law Chu Hoi?' and to the great surprise of both others broke out in roars of laughter, spluttering, 'k k kill my friend?' His laughter was so infectious that his target, Law Chu Hoi, also broke out in whooping laughter, something so rare it surprised him as he rocked back and forth on his chair, coughing as he did.

The infection spread to Chen Geng who, relieved of the burden that had been worrying him for the past few days of how to break the news, relaxed and joined in the mirth.

Someone came in from the next office to complain of the noise. He was told either to get the hell out or sit down and have a brandy with them. He joined the party and, without knowing why, also started laughing.

Eventually Liu Yew Kui looked at his watch and said. 'I'll have to leave in a few minutes.' By then the man from the other office had left. Chen Geng got out a piece of paper and wrote. 'Job done. It cost killer one thousand Malayan dollars. Send remittance now' and gave it to the purser of the SS *Princess of the Orient*. 'When you get to Calcutta, call your contact and give it to him. Tell him to give it to the Russian in the consulate. If he doesn't give you the money then tell him you'll collect it next time.'

Liu Yew Kui took it and left, slightly bemused by such unexpected happenings but happy he did not have to be an executioner. Later his thoughts turned to the Soviet type of communism and he felt that the Chinese type was more preferable. After he had docked in Calcutta he went to Tangra, met his Hakka contact and gave him the letter for 'onward despatch'. No money was available then but he did get it eventually and used it to educate his children. After that contact with Calcutta was never restored.

After Liu Yew Kui had gone, Law Chu Hoi and Chen Cheng spoke about the quest of getting recompense from the two men who had ruined his career. He did not say 'get his own back on' or mention the word 'kill', feeling it safer for both of them.

'All I can advise is to wait until a courier from Kuala Lumpur comes and meets me, as he does from time to time. There is never any advance information of when he might come. If you are happy to wait around till he comes I'll hand you over. He usually uses the name Ah Ho.'

Law Chu Hoi thought about that. 'I could do it but I'd have to find some work until that happened as I will soon be out of money.'

Chen Geng, feeling that, as a comrade, he should help, said, 'I was advertising for someone to help me out in the office. If you're willing to work under me under my terms until the courier comes I'm willing to employ you.'

They shook hands on that proposal and waited ... and waited.

Jason Rance and the Int Corporal, Mangalsing Tamang, each drew a rifle and fifty rounds of .303 ammunition from the armoury and dressed in operational jungle green uniform and wearing 'skeleton' equipment, put a tin of emergency rations and the universal 'first field dressing' into their pouches. They always wore their identity discs, one for the corpse and one to return, as a matter of course. Jason also carried a map, a pair of binoculars and a compass. They got into the Land Rover to go the few miles to the quaintly named, as Jason thought, Air OP Auster flight. He presumed, though did not know, that the Austers had originally been designed and used as 'spotter' planes for artillery targets rather than for ferrying passengers.

They reached the Flight HQ, dismissed the vehicle, telling the driver they would ring the MTO for being fetched, and reported into the briefing room. There was Captain Dan Foster, the pilot detailed for their flight. Jason introduced the Int Corporal, who understood a modicum of English, to him – he and Dan had flown together before.

'Jason, point out on the map just where you want me to take you. It seems far too far from all accepted search areas. It's not just a joyride you are wanting is it?' A ghost of a smile robbed the remark of any unintended sting.

'Far from it, Dan. Certainly my source, or rather sources, are not the usual ones used for any recce but, after considerable discussion with all concerned, we have come to the opinion this area might, just, be what we want.'

Dan Foster knew that Jason had an uncanny method of knowing where guerrillas operated so did not ask what the sources were. 'Show me on the map on the wall just what and where you have in mind.' The three men went over to the map and, taking the piece of paper that had what the *bomoh* had told Jitbahadur from his pocket he read out: 'Follow the river upstream until another river, a smaller one, flows in from the west. Cross that and walk uphill. It is very steep, almost a cliff. At the top go north along the ridge until you find a tall, single *belimbing hutan*. That is a red-flowered spindle tree. The tallest stands at a deep and very narrow precipice. If you climb up it you can probably see the plane that lies at the bottom of the precipice.' He glanced at the pilot who was staring at him with a puzzled frown and before he could say anything, added, 'The Int Corporal and I thoroughly searched both the map for high ground and then the air photo for clues. I have done an air photography interpretation course' – he omitted to say when – 'and, certainly without the tree-climbing bit, reckoned our most likely target area is Gunong Rajah, near Bentong in Pahang.' He once more glanced at the pilot who was nodding his head slowly and said, 'and here I need your knowledge, do you think it possible that the pilot's compass became unserviceable, that the pilot decided to fly south to southeast of the storm and, lastly but almost unprecedentedly, had a heart attack?'

After another silence, Dan Foster, not answering the questions, merely said, 'Okay, let's go and have a look. But no flying under five hundred feet.'

After registering his flight plan they trooped out to the aircraft, Jason and Mangalsing got in, Jason in the co-pilot's seat and the Int Corporal behind – the small windows either side vastly restricting vision – and fastened their seat belt while the pilot did his final checks, a ground-staff soldier helping him. When all was ready, the pilot got in, fastened his seat belt and taxied to the end of the laterite runway. He was given clearance for take-off, tested his engine with the brakes full on and in a singsong voice, crooned 'Roger rolling' into his microphone, let the plane speed along the runway until it lifted off. The day was fine, no clouds and no wind so conditions for a recce were well-nigh perfect.

As the group taking Siu Tse through the jungle neared the area of Gunong Rajah they met a small group of people that the new recruit did not recognise. They were *orang asli*, Jah Hut in fact, but the guerrillas would never have known that name. They were known as *t'o yan*, earth men, a name given to all aborigines as indigenous people were then known. They cultivated by the slash and burn technique, although the Department of Aborigines was trying to limit this activity and settle them. Some of the elders spoke simple Malay, and Lin Soong naturally asked for news of any Security Force activity. At first he was not understood so he resorted to imitation by taking his weapon and pointing, making firing noises, then putting it back over his shoulder and made a ring of index finger and thumb round his eyes – 'round-eyes' – meaning British troops.

As only Gurkhas had ever operated in that general area and now were nowhere near, the elders showed that the area was 'empty'. However, the man who was obviously chief of the group was certainly excited about something. He, too, had to make a pantomime of what he wanted to say, so he pointed to the sky, put out his arms, bent forward and made a loud noise. He then went to the base of the nearest tree and made as if to climb it. From other gestures it seemed he was referring to something quite a distance off. The guerrilla group immediately realised that the *t'o yan* elder did not know the Malay for 'plane' so he was describing the crash but none of them understood what was meant by the clutching of the tree.

'Can you take us there?'

'One day reach.'

As it was late they decided to make camp and move off next morning. A stream ran alongside one of the *t'o yan*'s 'slash and burn' tapioca cultivations.[Pre-war the government tried to keep sowing tapioca in the same place to once in seven years. An intake of 40 pounds in one day gives the calories needed for a normal diet. This is more than a cow will eat in one day.] They decided that camping at the edge would get them any breeze there might be: a refreshing difference to what they had come used to. After they had cooked their meal and before they went to sleep it was decided that not all the group should go as it probably meant a detour. And a rest would do some of the less strong of them good.

'Why did he clutch the tree?' someone asked.

They tossed that around among themselves but came to no answer until Siu Tse suddenly remembered her childhood tree-climbing and said, 'I think I know. It will be to climb a tree and look around for signs.' A sudden thought struck her, 'and, if the plane has fallen down a precipice the tree climber might be able to see it.'

Yes, that made sense. 'Why did you think of that?'

Rather bashfully she replied, 'I used to climb trees when I was a small girl.'

'Then you will come with me and one gunman tomorrow,' said Lin Soong.

That night they stayed with the *t'o yan* and were asked by sign language if they were hungry and indicated that, yes, they were. The head man beckoned to a woman and said something to her. She turned and brought two bamboo cylinders and some tapioca tubers out of her hovel. She took both bamboo cylinders to the nearby stream and, bent over with legs apart and sarong above her knees, filled them with water. Someone had already made a small fire at the side of the hovel to bake the tapioca but first she had to prepare the tubers for cooking. She peeled them, squatting down, holding a bamboo container between her knees lest it spill. As each piece of tapioca was ready for washing, she tilted the container up to her mouth, took a swig, replaced the bamboo between her knees and picked up the piece of tapioca, holding it a little away from her. She then squirted the water out of her mouth, jet-like, onto the tapioca, deftly cleaning it before her supply ran dry. It was then put into the ashes to roast, with a slight dowsing of the flame until it dried off. When the fire had done its job she neatly flicked each tuber out, put it on a large leaf and beckoned one of the guerrillas to come and take it. One by one each man fed and was replete.

Luckily Lin Soong had some spare tobacco on him and hospitality was repaid by giving it to the *t'o yan* headman.

'Is there any particular direction you want to approach your target area?' the pilot asked Jason over the intercom.

'Dan, from the south, flying to the east of the Gunong up the river until the tributary comes into sight then follow it to its source up the mountain and then over the mountain at its highest point. At the top of a cliff. That way we might even see a tall, flowering tree.'

Some chance. 'Yes, we might. I'll do that,' and Dan Foster glanced down at the map spread out on his knees.

Pressing the intercom switch Jason told the Int Corporal to look out of his left-hand port hole.

The pilot and Jason recognised the main river at about the same time. They were about five miles south of the Gunong. The plane nosed its way north, Dan Foster peering equally carefully at his instruments and at the ground. By then a wind had sprung up, coming from the west. None of the passengers ever thought that that would make a difference to the noise of the plane being heard more or less loudly ... but it did.

To get the most out of the recce – *after all we're looking for a single tree!* – the pilot slowed his speed down to just above stalling speed and, following the smaller river to its source, saw how steep the mountainside was. Jason put his binoculars to his eyes, looking out of the window, the plane's vibration making it difficult to hold them steady. So intent in not stalling his plane was the pilot he came well below his 'nothing under five hundred feet' insistence. As they came over the top of the steep side Jason saw, just for a flash, something – or somebody? – move in a tall tree with red flowers.

'Dan, fly north for a few miles then come back higher. We've enough time, haven't we?'

The pilot, sweating at the effort he'd just put into a difficult manoeuvre, glanced at his watch. 'Yes.'

As they flew forward Jason asked his Int Corporal what, if anything, he had seen. 'Saheb, I thought I saw the top branches of a tall tree move but I'm not sure as we were above it for so short a time.'

As they flew south they approached the steep bluff and, to both front passengers' astonishment, noticed a horizontal black gash in the side of the feature. They flew over it, both men realising that such a 'hole' in the side of a hill would not be visible from any upright angle.

'Back we go, Dan,' said Jason into his mouthpiece. He had not taken his binoculars from his face – in the distance he saw an area of tapioca, distinguishable by the change in colour of the green and saw a few men at the edge looking up at the plane before darting back into the jungle. *Two lots of movement. One, the wind; the other some locals – but together? It must be the guerrillas trying to find the plane!*

Back at the airfield Jason thanked Dan as he got out of the plane. 'What did you make of it?' he asked the pilot.

'On the way back I was thinking that a sudden blast of wind could easily have tilted a plane, especially one where the pilot had lost control. Also, and I agree that this is a very long shot, pushed it between the sides of the gap in the feature and so it would have fallen to the bottom. Had it not been almost perpendicularly tilted its wings would surely have broken so have been able to be spotted, otherwise no plane, not even one as small as an Auster would have had any chance of falling down from up top.'

'I agree and if, another big if, those branches were moved by a climber trying to look down to see if anything was there ... ' his voice trailed off. 'And did you see movement by the side of the tapioca patch we flew over about five minutes after we left Gunong Rajah?'

'No, I was concentrating on my flying.'

Once back in Battalion HQ Jason and the Int Corporal went to the IO's office and had another good look at the air photo to see if they had indeed flown over the territory they had thought to be their true target. 'Even if what I thought I saw through the small window in the plane as we flashed over the top of the precipice was not a person, there was no doubt that there were people at the edge of the slash and burn cultivation,' said the Int Corporal, with his finger on the place on the photo.

'Yes,' agreed OC A Company. 'I had a clearer view than you did and whatever it was I saw, there was movement. The question is "man made or monkey made"?'

'Did you see any other scared monkeys?' inquired the IO.

'Now you mention it, no, I can't say that I did,' Jason answered.

'No, nor did I' added the Int Corporal.

'And the people you saw at the edge of the jungle,' continued the IO. 'Can you remember any colour of the clothes they wore?'

'Some dark colour,' said Jason. 'It was only when they moved that we noticed them. If they had been government loggers or villagers gone hunting, with spears as no one now has shotguns, their clothes would probably have been of a lighter colour and, if they did not have a guilty conscience, they would not have tried to hide.'

'Good point,' said the IO. 'The CO said to take you to his office once you had finished checking on your return.'

'Let it wait until tomorrow. It's a bit late now and I'd also like to slip over to Yasin's place and tell him just what we saw and see if he can confirm it fits in with what he feels it should. If you think the CO should be told that, well and good, otherwise let it be and book a time for me, the Int Corporal and you, through the Adjutant to meet him. By then I'll have written what I hope will be a succinct report.'

He was forestalled by the CO's stick orderly, the smartest

man on Guard Mounting that morning – saluting and saying the CO wanted to see Rance saheb so please go to his office.

Jason told the CO what he wanted to do before fully reporting on the morrow, 'Just to squeeze the lemon to its last drop, sir.'

'Yes, that suits me as I have quite a lot of office work I must get through.'

About the same time as Rance and the Int Corporal had left Battalion HQ for the airfield, Lin Soong's group had reached the slash-and-burn area, guided by the *t'o yan*. The *t'o yan* had pointed out the tall tree at the top of the steep hill to their front then left them.

'Little Sister, her escort and I will go and investigate, you others stay here,' said Lin Soong, and off the three of them went most cautiously, on the lookout for any Security Force traces as they did. They reached where the flat ground started climbing without seeing any enemy traces. 'We're safe now,' said Lin Soong. 'No Security Force soldier would waste time and effort to climb a steep hill just to have to come down again. Let's go on up.'

It was a steep climb and when they reached the top they were gasping for breath so had a short rest. 'Now we're here let's go and look for the tallest tree and see if you can climb it,' said Lin |Soong. They searched around and the one they thought was the tallest had no low branches or creepers to reach from the ground so Siu Tse climbed its nearest neighbour that had and halfway up, bravely, jumped from the one into the other, reaching the top without any more difficulty. She peered down into the dark depth and, was it her imagination or did she see something that gleamed? She stretched her back and all of a sudden an aeroplane swooped up from the other side, so close to her it almost knocked her over in her surprise. She felt dizzy and stayed where she was, the branches swinging from the air disturbed by the plane's propellers.

'Are you all right?' came up from below, Lin Soong worried about her and the plane.

'Yes, yes,' she shouted back. 'But it so surprised me I nearly fell over.'

'Wait till the plane has flown out of the area before coming down,' he shouted up at her. It was a sensible precaution because a few minutes later the plane did fly back towards them but higher this time so there was practically no danger of their being seen. It flew off – *in the direction of the others* Lin Soong cursed – and Siu Tse climbed down.

'While you were up there did you notice anything that would make you suspicious of an aeroplane at the bottom?' Lin Soong asked.

'I was just craning my neck to see if there was anything there and my efforts were making the branches move as the plane came over so suddenly. I wasn't sure if the smell of petrol so near came from the plane or from below. I did see a gleam of something but my eyes could have been playing me tricks.'

'That's hardly enough to say either way. I wonder if another look tomorrow is worthwhile.'

Siu Tse felt it was not up to her to answer so she shook the twigs off her clothes and sat down for a breather. Lin Soong wanted to smoke a cigarette so he did and having thrown the butt away, not bothering to bury it, they made their way back to their overnight camp as fast as they dared, packed up and moved to a new site. 'Because we think the pilot could have seen you it is too dangerous to stay here any longer,' Lin Soong said when the others told him that the plane had flown over them so unexpectedly – 'the wind was in the wrong direction to have had any warning' – it was too dangerous to stay there any longer. In fact, their standing orders dictated the move. That night as she lay thinking over the day's unusual events, Siu Tse would have never believed that her youthful heartthrob and her enemy, in one body, were in that aeroplane, which was just as well for her peace of mind.

Luckily for ex-purser Law Chu Hoi, he had managed to get some paperwork fixed for use in Singapore before leaving Hong Kong but even so he kept in the shadows as much as he could, not that he knew the phrase 'borrowed time' but he knew the feeling well enough. He was coming to the end of his tether, having waited for about six months in the employ of Chen Geng when a stranger visited 47 Pedder Street. It was Ah Ho, the courier, not that Law Chu Hoi recognised him until Chen Geng introduced him. Ah Ho had been responsible for contacting Chen Geng about Ah Fat's journey on the SS *Eastern Queen* early in the previous December but, as normal communist working went, he only knew the next link in the chain, Chen Geng in this case, not the one after, the purser.

Ah Ho came to Singapore to brief Chen Geng on another matter and they met when Law Chu Hoi was out on a job. After their current business Chen Geng brought the matter of Law Chu Hoi to Ah Ho's attention, telling him about Comrade Ah Fat and a *gwailo*, named as Captain Jason Rance, about whose provenance there was some doubt. Ah Ho knew that there was no 'case' against Ah Fat but this Rance person was out of his ken. 'Introduce me to this Law Chu Hoi man and I'll make up my mind,' he said.

Unluckily for Law Chu Hoi the six months' waiting had done his temper no good so when introductions were made he stupidly blamed Ah Ho for 'not bothering to come early to help me in my quest.' He had yet to appreciate that sitting in a purser's office and taking the odd person to meet one of the two Hakka agents in Tangra posed no dangers as opposed to being the Secretary General of the MCP's personal courier, which Ah Ho was, was one of the most dangerous jobs of all.

To Ah Ho's credit he showed no disquiet although he felt it deeply. The two men also took a personal dislike to each other, the courier still not showing it. At the end of a lengthy conversation when Law Chu Hoi became short-tempered Ah Ho said, 'Leave it with me for a bit longer. I can report it to the Central Committee and then bring their answer back, or get the answer to you else how.' He took the address of where Law Chu Hoi was staying – it was not 47 Pedder Street, as Chen Geng had to be protected.

'Well, make it quick,' the ex-purser snapped as Ah Ho left. Law Chu Hoi would never know what Ah Ho did: feeling that such an unexpected maverick was a danger who should never come anywhere near the Central Committee, he went to Kuala Lumpur where he met Chan Man Yee, the woman MCP 'mole' in Police HQ. She had a job as the clerk who looked after the secret archives of the Police Special Branch. She was irreplaceable therefore highly valued by the Politburo. Ah Ho was only allowed contact with her if his task was of the highest importance to the Party's safety. This was one of those occasions. Ah Ho contacted her and together they concocted an anonymous letter to be sent to the Head of Special Branch and signed 'by a secret friend'. Chan Man Yee knew exactly how to write the letter, the contents of which were about one Law Chu Hoi, a one-time purser of the SS *Eastern Queen*, who was living – address given – on false papers and known to be a dedicated communist, properly based in Hong Kong.

The name of Captain Jason Rance was also given to the female 'mole' for passing on to anyone who approached her from the Politburo who could take 'preventative action' were the occasion to arise. Ah Ho went back with other intelligence he had picked up, one item being the government and army reaction to the lost Auster, to deliver to the Politburo.

And it happened as both expected: the Head of Special Branch contacted his opposite number in Singapore and Law Chu Hoi was arrested for wrongly living on false papers. The captain of the SS *Eastern Queen* was unobtrusively contacted, confirmed that the man concerned had once been employed by him but had been dismissed, and for what reason. After considerable correspondence with the senior Special Branch representative in Hong Kong, the ex-purser was sent back to Hong Kong under arrest with a police escort for banishment to China. He never knew what had gone wrong for this to happen and, to his intense disgust, his wife was banished with him.

<h1 style="text-align:center">6</h1>

Captain Rance, happily oblivious of the fact that his name was now registered by the powerful 'mole' in KL for any future interest the Party might have – unsaid but fully understood by the Party hierarchy – that any undercover pseudo-communist activity would merit condign punishment if it were ever discovered – went to brief the CO as arranged and told him about their suspected findings resulting from their air recce. 'Sir, I grant you it was inconclusive but all three of us, the pilot, Corporal Mangalsing and I myself reckon it is "odds on" that the plane could be down that narrow cleft in the hillside. I thought I saw the top of the tree moving at our approach. None of the other tree tops were moving so there was no strong wind at that level. Is it just possible that the guerrillas were told by some of the locals that they had heard the crash and the only way of seeing if the plane was there was by climbing a tree? I know that that is an inspired guess. Overflying the feature we saw it was impossible for the plane to have gone down the cleft from the top but on a return flight along the flow of the river the hole in the side could, with a big gust of wind, have turned the plane on its side so slid it in.'

The CO stroked his chin and merely looked enquiringly at Jason as he asked him, 'Do you mean that had there not been such a gust of wind, the plane's wings would have been torn off on impact with the rocks so be visible outside that gash?'

'That, too, sir, we all considered would have been the case,' and continued, 'on a patch of slash and burn we saw a small group of whom we took to be guerrillas from the colour of their clothes turn round and run into the jungle. Malays don't slash and burn but the *orang asli* do. I ask myself if it is possible that the guerrilla group met some of those people whose knowledge of Malay is so poor that sign language was used. Could the tree recce group have gone to see if it were possible to recover any documents from the plane?'

He left off and the CO considered such a scenario. He picked up the pens on his desk and re-arranged them neatly. 'So, what are you proposing?'

'I'd like to take my reserve platoon in by chopper. Let me be winched down over the slash and burn site with an LMG Number 1, a radio operator and my batman while the rest of the platoon under the platoon commander, Gurkha Lieutenant Danbahadur Rai, is lifted into a position say a thousand or at most fifteen hundred yards north and try and lay an ambush on any northward guerrilla movement. Were I to establish that, indeed, there is something at the bottom of the cleft, the nearer of my other two platoons would stay out after being re-rationed and the farther off one brought back here to act as a reserve or even an escort for any engineer recovery group that might be needed to go and see what they can find.'

The CO thought that suggestion appropriate and nodded his assent. 'That would be expensive in flying hours but, seeing the rank of the dead man, it would be better for us to recover what is there rather than the guerrillas doing so,' he said as though talking to himself. He looked at the map on the wall as he considered all possible options. And as though it were the same sentence he continued, 'Though how they'd manage if the plane is so deeply down the cleft I don't really know. Is there anything else you'd like me to consider?'

Now it was Jason's turn to dwell on his answer. *Keep it easy. Don't muddle him.* 'If you agree to my plan, sir, I'll take a long rope from the QM, tie it round that tall tree, or any tree that will bear a man's weight, round my waist and abseil down as far as necessary to confirm that the plane really is there and not a figment of my imagination, bolstered by vain hope. Dropping some stones might, who knows, get a reverberation showing something that's not rock.'

The CO picked up a pencil and scratched one side of his nose, taking a moment or two to answer with 'Yes, I agree. Not much choice, is there? Anything else before you go and give your orders?'

'I'll take a powerful torch and, just in case we meet any locals who need a bit of cajoling, I'll take some fags, a lighter and some sweets for the children, sir.'

'Isn't that overdoing it somewhat?' The CO seemed a tad grumpy at the idea of cajoling locals.

'It has worked in the past so it may work again.'

'Have it your own way,' the CO said as Jason saluted and left the office. *A few extra bits and pieces for locals wouldn't do any harm really, would they?* He knew that under Jason Rance the soldiers had learnt the necessary talents of silence, patience, near invisibility, the skills of a hunter and the relentlessness of born trackers, as well as being as reliable as sunrise: *and Rance, having been born in this country knows how to get the best out of the locals.*

The IO requested Brigade for the helicopters and the reserve platoon was made ready, with orders for the nearer platoon to be re-rationed for another five days with the farther off platoon going to the nearest LP and getting ready to be flown back to Seremban. Jason detailed Corporal Jaslal Rai to be the LMG gunner to stay with him. 'Bring ten loaded magazines with you, every fifth round to be tracer.' He, a signaller and Kulbahadur Limbu, his batman-cum-bodyguard were designated the 'plane-search party'.

The purser of the SS *Princess of the Orient*, Liu Yew Kui, arrived in Calcutta and on the afternoon of the third day, business being slack enough, decided to go to the Hakka tanneries in Tangra to meet the next link in the chain to somewhere else, as he saw it, never having been indoctrinated into the mystery. The contact he met was Wong Kek Fui and he, and one other, either took notes or certain selected visitors to the MGB secret office, which they still thought was an over-cautious consulate.

After greetings and small talk that included the almost obligatory glass of brandy, Wong looked at Liu and said, 'Comrade, only now let me know what I can do for you.'

'The next time you go and meet Comrade Sergey Siderov tell him that the job I was given has been done.'

'Only that?'

'Yes. There is nothing else to say and anyway the less said is always wise and he will know all about it.' The purser looked at his watch. 'Time to go. Thank you for the brandy. Don't bother to go with me to the gate as I know my way around – should do after all these years.'

They shook hands; the purser went to his boat and the 'link' got into his car and drove to the Soviet consulate to deliver his message. He had to go himself as the phone number was never given him. He had not seen any need to tell the purser that Sergey Siderov had been recalled to Moscow, nor did he know why. He gave the message to the new man who dismissed it without any interest as his predecessor had not mentioned it when he had handed over the job. Through inefficiency the project to kill the purser of the SS *Eastern Queen* died a natural death much more easily than the originally planned deaths would have done.

In his group's new temporary base in the jungle, Lin Soong went over in his mind's eye the events at the top of the high ground. He had been worried about the unexpected and sudden appearance of a *gwailo* flying machine that whooshed out from the other side of the steep feature so very unexpectedly – any nearer and Little Sister might have been blown out of the tree so low did it seem. The branches at the top were not all that strong. He still wondered if it were more than a coincidence and his worries were increased more when it flew back over the feature at a higher level along the flow of the river. 'Come on down, quickly and safely,' he had called out. She had already started her descent.

On their arrival at their temporary base at the edge of the

slash and burn area the others told him that the aeroplane that had suddenly come from the east while they were out in the open was most likely the same one they had heard in the distance. Two such planes had never been seen together or near each other. They could not say if the pilot had seen them or not but 'standing orders' were definite, weren't they? If a plane flew to a side of any guerrilla camp, 'stand to'; if it circled it, 'evacuate'. This time it was a circling movement but overhead when the men below could, just, have been seen.

'We'll make a move tomorrow,' said Lin Soong. 'That diversion has already cost us some time and could be difficult to make good.'

By now most guerrillas moved in the early morning and late afternoon but not during the day because they thought that that routine made it less likely for them to meet any Security Forces who didn't seem to move during those times. And, in general, working that way did save casualties.

Such was the worry over the lost aeroplane in HQ Malaya Command, intensified by an almost hysterical wife's pleading for 'something, anything' to be done, that this new demand for helicopters was speedily met. The CO had given the slash and burn as the nearest place for Jason and his three men to deplane and the two choppers to fly on to an LP, the grid reference taken from the air photograph, drop their load, go back to Seremban, re-fuel and take the rest of the men to the northern LP before going on farther to fetch the other platoon to Seremban before returning to KL.

By ten o'clock next day two Whirlwind choppers had touched down on the football pitch alongside the battalion's lines without shutting down and the platoon, divided into two, was ready to emplane. All had taken the precaution of putting their hat in their trouser pocket as a hat flying off and caught by a rotor could break it, forcing the heli to close down and wait while a new three-blade rotor was flown in – expensive and time-consuming.

The IO climbed up to brief each pilot, orally, with the correct grid reference for deplaning. Sometimes pilots used a quarter-inch-to-the-mile maps which made finding the LP more difficult than were one-inch-to-the-mile maps used but these larger sheets were clumsy to use as they took up too much space on the pilot's lap.

The pilots put their headset back on after the IO's briefing and the IO signalled to Jason for the first lot of men to emplane. A Company's men were well trained and when he made a circular arm movement the soldiers moved in single file to their designated machine and stepped up into it, helped by the crewman because when wearing heavy big packs upward movement was not easy. Once seated each crewman tapped the pilot's leg and the two helis flew off.

After about thirty minutes flying time Jason's heli circled the LP, all inside hoping there were no guerrillas to shoot at them, and came down to within six feet of the ground. The crewman indicated 'jump' and, as quickly as possible, not easy with an LMG or a radio set and a loaded big pack, jump they did. Away the chopper flew and moved up to its mate to continue the journey northwards with the depleted platoon.

Lin Soong's group, halfway between the two LPs, was worried. *So the plane yesterday must have seen us* came into everyone's mind. 'They are not near so we will move on, taking all necessary precautions as we do,' ordered the leader. 'Everyone listen for the engines to make a different noise for if that happens it means it has landed to let troops get out. Then we must decide just in what direction that is and try to avoid them.'

Before they moved off towards the high ground Jason searched where he had seen men dart under the trees and had his suspicions confirmed. 'Daku were here,' he said, looking at the tracks. Jason's batman-cum-escort, Rifleman Kulbahadur Limbu, also looked around. 'Saheb, they only left this morning,' he called out. 'They can't be so very far away.' Kulbahadur was the best tracker in the battalion and had been of immense use when tracking turncoat Alan Hinlea. He could read the ground for signs like most people read books.

'Good man. It is too early to tell the others. Off we go. As the daku have moved off not in the direction we are going we can move non-tactically.' He had measured the angle of march from the LP to the top of the high feature and the four men set off on that compass bearing. On the way they met a group of men who were neither Malay nor Chinese. 'Sakai,'[12] said Jason. 'Stop. Put your weapons on the ground. I've been told that they are easily frightened.' The Gurkhas did so, smiled and waved at them. They remembered their OC having previously warned them about the

---

12   A general term formerly used in Malaya to describe various *orang asli* or indigenous groups.

Sakai, timorous, gentle and not used to living anywhere else.

Jason called out, smiling broadly, using easy Malay, 'Don't go. Stay.' He turned to Kulbahadur Limbu, 'Kulé, get those cigarettes out and give each person one.'

The men saw cigarettes and came to take one each, Jason using the lighter for all of them. Grins of appreciation were even broader when sweets were also given: '*Anak anak*' – for the children – made everyone smile.

Jason's boyhood Malay could easily cope with the unsophisticated men's language and he put his arms out like wings and made a 'brrr' noise with his lips. Yes, it was immediately understood – *they asked that yesterday* – and without further warning the senior man went to a tree trunk and embraced it. '*Tahu, tahu*' – know, know – and again everyone smiled.

'Saheb, I have an idea,' Rifleman Kulbahadur Limbu said softly to Jason. 'Can you ask if any daku have contacted these people recently?'

'Good thinking, *keta*,' and turned and saw that the oldest man had a small boy sitting next to him, happily sucking a sweet. *A grandson? If I can get him to smile maybe granddad will answer me.* He went over to them and, taking a sweet out of his pocket, held it out to the youngster and, as if by magic the sweet said, coaxingly in Malay, 'eat me, eat me.' It was a gamble as both of them might have been frightened and run away but no, it was a sign of power and so the sweet was accepted. Then, slowly, taking another gamble and, pointing north and west, asked which way the *orang Cheena*, the Chinese men, went yesterday.

It never occurred to the headman to doubt Jason's question

and pointed in both directions. So, *they split! How wise to have sent the rest of the platoon farther north.*

'On our way. This old man pointed out that the daku also went this way, towards the high ground.' Waving goodbye to the cigarette-puffing men, his small group moved off. When out of sight Jason told the others what the old man had indicated, 'So that means the daku are in two groups, just like we are. We did not pick up their tracks earlier so we're just that bit lucky in moving the way we did. Move carefully now although I rather doubt there are any of them around here now. It really does look as though the plane is where we suspected it might be,' said Jason.

The others nodded agreement and, with Kulé leading the way, they moved in the direction of the high ground. They reached the bottom of the steep ground without any incident and had a rest. They decided that the signaller and the gunner stay together at the base and Jason and Kulbahadur to go up the steep ground, with weapons and the rope but no packs. By then it was one o'clock. 'Let's have a hot brew first. Water from our bottles will do till we find a stream.'

Firewood was quickly collected, a fire lit and, while the tea was being brewed, Jason told Kulbahadur to collect as many stones that would fit into his pocket, explaining that the rope was not nearly long enough to get to the bottom of the cleft but stones thrown down might hit the damaged plane's fuselage and the different noise would be ample proof that the plane was at the bottom. As they sipped their hot drink Jason told them what his plans were: 'If we're lucky we can do what we need to in one day. The two men remaining down here will look around for a stream and we'll make camp by it. There's no point in trying to go any farther today. Sig-nel, you open at the next battalion opening time and, if I'm not back send a message telling battalion we are at the base of the hill where we think the plane crashed and the guerrillas were here yesterday but have now moved north. If they need a grid reference, I'll give you the correct GR when I've come back.'

Kulé soon found the tracks for two going up and coming down again the side of the feature and led the way up. Near the top, Kulbahadur looked around and pounced. 'Saheb,' he called out. 'More proof! Look at this,' as Jason joined him. A cigarette butt was lying on the ground. It had not rained the night before so it was dry. Jason bent down, picked it up and sniffed it. 'I am not a smoker so I can smell it easily. It is fresh enough to have been dropped yesterday and it doesn't smell like the ones you smoke.'

Kulbahadur again pointed to the ground. 'Saheb, tracks, and one looks like a woman's. Do you know anything about the daku who operate in this area?'

'No, Kulé, I don't but if you say it's a woman's, a woman's it'll be.'

They climbed to the top of the feature. At the very top there were more definite signs of a visit as they could both see where someone had climbed a tree. Jason remembered the *bomoh*'s description and asked his companion if he could see any red flowers. 'It may not be the time of year for flowering but can you have a look?'

The Gurkha climbed up the tree next to it as there were no holds near enough the ground to start up the target tree. He managed to jump across where the branches of both trees were nearest: he was an expert tree-climber as were so many Gurkhas, from an early age, having climbed trees in the hills of Nepal to cut foliage for their goats and cattle.

'There are one or two old red flowers, Saheb,' he called down to Jason's great relief and satisfaction. 'Come on down,' he called up and down Kulé came, jumping the last ten feet from the limbless base of the trunk and landing easily.

'Which is the best tree to tie the rope round?'

They searched and found one of few hardwood trees – in Malaya only one percent of the trees were such – and they tied the rope around it. 'You or me, Saheb? I am lighter than you so it should be me.'

Jason agreed and they tied the other end of the rope round the rifleman's waist. 'When you feel you're low enough shine the torch down as it will be too dark to see anything low down. Also don't forget to drop the stones in as many different places as you can. One of them might make a different noise if it does hit the fuselage.

Slowly Kulé let himself over the edge and Jason, as slowly, paid the rope out. It was almost its full length when the Gurkha's voice came up, faintly, 'I am shining the torch and there seems to be what looks like the tip of an upturned wing below but it's a long way down. I'll drop the stones and try and get another noise.' Jason could just hear the stones rattle as they hit the sides of the precipice.

'Chha, chha' came some little time later. Jason presumed that meant the noise from the stones had indicated a different surface from the sides of the precipice.

'Shall I pull you up?' Jason shouted.

'Wait. I'll tug when I'm ready,' came the faint answer.

When Jason felt a tug on the rope he started to pull the rope up. Down below, the Gurkha, using his feet where possible and trying to keep the rope from swinging, slowly ascended, sweating as he did, arms desperately tired. Just below the edge he shouted out, 'Saheb, help. Pull me.'

Jason lay on the ground and reaching down managed to catch hold of one of Kulé's wrists. He dug his toes into the ground and pulled his hardest. Those final five feet were a challenge and when the Gurkha's head came above the rim of the big drop, Jason stood and grasped him under the arms and hoisted him those last few feet to safety. Once out of the cleft, he lay on the ground recovering his breath. Jason gently untied the rope.

'*Keta*, you did wonderfully well. You really had me worried at the end. Just as well you went down not me as I'd have been harder to pull up,' and they smiled at each other.

'Saheb, the plane is there. That bit of upturned wing and the noise from the stones prove it. It was a long way down from me.'

'Well done, *keta*. That was typical Gurkha guts that got you down and up again.' The Gurkha nodded and smiled. 'There's no hurry. Rest for as long as you want to. All we have to do is to go back downhill.'

As Kulbahadur rested, getting his breath back, Jason coiled the rope and, slipping it around his shoulders, waited for the Gurkha to get to his feet of his own accord.

They made their way back downhill and found that the

other two had indeed made a rudimentary camp near a spring of delicious cold water. They had collected a lot of dried bamboo leaves and laid them around their camp about ten to twelve paces away from where they would sleep: anyone treading on them would make enough noise to wake them up thus negating the need to have a sentry all night.

Kulbahadur took his bottle of rum out of his pack – all, or nearly all, Gurkhas carried their bottle – and, having drunk his first tot, told the others what he'd found out. 'Yes, the aeroplane is there.'

'Kulé, I meant to ask you,' said Jason. 'Did you smell any rotting flesh when you were down there?'

'Saheb, now you make mention of it, yes, there was a faint smell of something different but it did not strike me then as rotting flesh. It could well have been human rather than animal.'

'Was the journey up and down difficult?' the signaller asked.

'Going down, no, but coming up I nearly ran out of strength. There was no fresh air down there and that must have weakened me. I expect my arms will be stiff in the morning.'

Jason made out a sitrep and as he was far enough from any suspected guerrillas not to have to use key but voice he could give as many relevant details as he considered necessary to convince Battalion HQ that the wreck was indeed where he had intuited. He knew that the CO would need sufficient relevant details to convince higher formation that his report was accurate. It would be easiest for him to report personally so once contact made been made he told his signaller to ensure that control had contacted call sign 1 then to say: 'Fetch Acorn.'

'Roger. Wait out,' came back instantly as reception was good. Jason's call sign was '1 Able', '1' being the rest of his platoon.[13]

'1 Able, Acorn on set. Send over.'

'Sunray 1 Able. I can confirm that an aeroplane is wing-up in the cleft at … ' and gave the grid reference. 'Presume it is the one we were searching for. Do not know how far from bottom it is. Roger so far, over.'

'Roger. Wait out.' A pause then 'Sunray on set' and the CO's voice came across. '1 Able, are you positive in your identification? Over.'

Jason made a moue, thinking *would I be so idiotic to say so if it was not so?* but answered '1 Able, one hundred percent. Intend moving north tomorrow to join the rest of my call sign. Over.'

'1 Able. Excellent. Congratulations. Now what do you recommend at your end? Over.'

'1 Able. Doubt very much any effort to recover aircraft worth the effort but expect an attempt to salvage bodies will be ordered. My batman who went down by rope smelled a smell that could have been rotting flesh but was unsure if human or animal. Propose joining up with my platoon before returning to base. Expect it will take time to arrange recovery of bodies and presume a guide from my small group will be needed. Roger so far, over.'

The CO acknowledged what had been said and waited for Jason to continue. '1 Able, I have also established that the Charlie Tare' – codeword for CTs or Communist Terrorists – 'were in

13   Able, Baker, Charlie, Dog, etc. changed to Alpha, Bravo, Charlie, Delta, etc. in 1956.

two groups. One was in my present location, presumably also searching for the plane, probably yesterday and the other moved north towards my other code sign. Over.'

The result was that the CO told Jason to move north and meet up with the rest of his call sign and try to contact the 'Charlie Tare'.

Battalion then contacted all the other sub units and told them to stop patrolling and an exfiltration plan would be passed on the first call next morning. Jason managed to speak to his platoon commander and told him in Nepali, rather than in English, about the guerrilla group going his way. 'Fix an ambush position on any likely approach. I'll be coming your way tomorrow. I'll let you know when I am in your immediate area.'

They closed down after that was acknowledged and, in both cases, prepared for the night. In Jason's group that meant checking their dried bamboo leaves after their meal. Before settling down to sleep Jason told his men that there had been another plane crash like this one earlier on in the Emergency that had been lost. It was rumoured that it went down a crevice that was so deep it could not be reached. 'No, I never heard if it was found or it the corpses were recovered.'[14]

---

14 A plane carrying a Brigadier MD Erskine, DSO, was lost on 27 October 1949, having taken off from Seremban. Despite extensive ground and air searches, nothing was found for five years. Among parts of the wrecked plane and scattered bones an old medal ribbon with the DSO ribbon was found. The brigadier was wearing medal ribbons when he went on the ill-fated journey so the bones were taken as his. (*History of 656 Squadron, Army Air Corps*.) Your author heard strong rumours of searchers being directed by a medium, an elderly English woman living in England.

During the night there was an unexpected thunderstorm and an explosion like an artillery piece that was being fired. 'What was that?' asked Jason,

'A thunderbolt, Saheb,' answered Kulbahadur. 'Centipedes attract them.'[15]

Lin Soong was worried, though as a good leader he tried not to show it. The helicopters flying both to his north and later back south so soon after the Auster's flight over the steep hill and their position near the cultivation of the *t'o yan* had confused him. Although he knew the exact area where he was to hand over the girl he was escorting to the next group – an old tree struck by lightning at a stream junction – he had no idea where the troops that the helis had brought were. Even if they had heard the noise of the helis settling on the ground it would have been too far away to pinpoint. The only clue of the possible landing area was the time they'd heard both machines fly back. That was less than twenty minutes ago, he surmised, though he foolishly had not checked exactly how long on his watch. He certainly did know that one of the helis had landed to his south soon after he had left the slash and burn cultivation – he did not know enough about the engine noise to divine that the machine had not landed but only hovered, not that it really mattered which it was – but the speed of its onward flight was such that some troops must have quickly left it for another task. *And that can only be the downed aircraft* he realised.

---

15 Your author has asked for an explanation of this many times but has not received a convincing answer.

He had only been to the RV three times before and had always used the same approach, walking along a small stream. He had been able to find out if there were any Security Forces from the *t'o yan* – the area had been clear so far – but the route he used was easy to ambush and he was unwilling to use it now without a decent recce. He was due to reach it next day but with a detailed recce it could be the day after. *Well, it would not hurt the other group to wait an extra day or so, would it? It often happened like that between courier zones so let it happen again – and stay alive.*

The countryside was flat and, in places, swampy. At a midday rest he told his group that they would make camp on the early side and, having sent out a patrol to see if there were any signs of movement from the other heli lot, they would go on cautiously for their RV, 'but it will only be before eight in the morning or after five in the evening as that is our safe time.'

The others knew what he meant although Siu Tse was, by now, so tired, that it meant nothing to her. *I wonder if my Alan was ever as tired as I am?* she asked herself.

The rest of Jason's platoon had been taken to an area about four hours' walk from the target mountain as the Platoon Commander thought of where the downed plane might be found. The pilot had seen that the area he had been sent to was marshy so he told his crewman to warn the men that they'd have to jump out. He also told the other pilot, some little way behind him, of his decision. At the hover, men gingerly jumped out of the machine, weighed down by their packs, and not wanting to jump on the man who had just jumped out but knowing that helis didn't like hovering over much. Deplaning was slow and the pilot was glad to be able to fly away.

The platoon moved onto drier land on the jungle fringe and Gurkha Lieutenant Danbahadur Rai decided to recce the area for any signs of guerrilla movement. He would make camp and ask his OC for orders the next time they had to open their radio so it was only then that he learnt about his OC's success. At his 'O' Group that evening he once more asked his section NCOs how many good ambush positions they had come across during their recces. He decided to make his base a hundred yards or so from a site he felt was one easily recognised by guerrillas: an old tree struck by lightning at a stream junction. His own base was in a position to its east on the edge of the swamp so that when he put some two-men positions around it to ambush the guerrillas moving up from the south, their footprints would not warn any daku advancing from the south. He also warned them that the OC's four-man group would probably steer clear of his ambush positions by approaching from the east.

Jason's depleted platoon commander had passed his proposed ambush position's grid reference to control in Seremban and to the OC. One thing OC A Company had always stressed was that crossing platoon or company boundaries was always a dangerous time. He and his group had moved from the steep ground early and had stopped for a brew shortly after midday. 'We are not so very far from the rest of our men. What I propose is not to go straight there as it might well spoil their ambush. We'll move to a flank and make camp then when we open our sets this evening or even tomorrow morning I'll contact them.'

Everybody in A Company knew that their OC never did anything without a good reason and what he told them now made good sense. After their brew he changed the bearing of their move about five degrees to the east and shortly before sunset came to some swampy ground and, after looking round, chose a position in a sheltered area a few yards from the edge of the swampy ground. 'Sig-nel,' he said in a low voice, 'key this evening as we have not been able to clear the area. Here is our position,' and handed it over on a piece of paper. 'Ask control to pass this to call sign 1 but if there's too much interference, only tomorrow morning.'

The signaller nodded and looked around for some trees on which to hang his aerial. The others looked for any recent marks then, slowly and silently, carried out normal routine, arranging night sleeping places, fetching water and fire wood, cooking then eating before sleeping.

Lin Soong's position was also carefully sited and he, too, was concerned whether the group for the next stage had managed to arrive – hanging around under present conditions was not wise. He had not gone straight to the RV but veered to the east. He found that it was too late to try and see if the other group had arrived as well as make camp so, not completely satisfied – *is one ever?* – decided to make a simple night stop on the edge of the swampy ground. If either he or Jason had shouted as loudly as they could the other would have heard it faintly and the platoon ambushers would have heard both voices somewhat louder.

Early next morning with a light mist yet to evaporate, the leaders of all three groups left the edge of the surrounding jungle where they had spent the night: the daku to find the other squad, the depleted platoon to their ambush positions and the four-man group to assess the situation. So quiet and almost animal-like in the way they could move Lin Soong's group and Piggy's group – yes, his men also used that soubriquet – had only been about one hundred and fifty yards apart, Piggy's group to the north. The two groups saw and, recognising each other, cautiously waved. They moved towards each other and, although Lin did not like being touched, endured an embrace, repelled by the other's bad breath.

'Are you ready for us to take your passenger?' – a strange word to use – asked Piggy.

'Yes, I'll go and fetch her, the quicker we can both be on our way the better. There are too many enemy soldiers in the area for safety and for comfort.'

Piggy nodded. 'Yes, you go and fetch him.'

'It's not a him, it's a her,' said Lin. As he turned to go he did not see the smirk on the other's face.

Searching the area through his binoculars, Jason saw movement. He softly called out, 'Jaslal guru-ji, load and cock your weapon and bring it here now. Kulé bring me my big pack.'

Both men came in an instant. Jason quickly put his pack on. 'Jaslal, you can't see the target by lying on the ground. I'll bend forward and you put your LMG on my big pack and aim at the daku from a standing position. I can't direct any fire. Choose any obvious target yourself and Kulé will help you as and how he can.' He bent down and Corporal Jaslal put his gun on the OC's big pack, squirmed around as he tried to get a firm position.

'Saheb, better if you stand up until we see a target.'

Jason stood up.

Lin Soong came back with Siu Tse and approached Piggy's group. Piggy himself was not in the front so she did not see him. Lin said farewell and rejoined his men prior to moving away. Siu Tse's escort took her to the new lot and quickly disappeared. The new group waited on the track by the side of the swamp until Piggy came back to join them. At the same time Piggy and Siu Tse saw one another – he did not recognise the woman but she recognised him in one look. She screamed shrilly and tried to run away, heedless of the direction. She blundered into the swamp. *Where's my saviour now when I need him?* she thought, as she wormed her way towards a pile of stones she could see through the thick swamp vegetation.

As she ran away, Piggy suddenly remembered who she was and without a second thought plunged into the swamp after her.

To Jason's amazement he saw the top half of a man and just the head of someone in front of him moving as quickly as conditions allowed in the swamp, finding it difficult to keep their balance. He bent over as he said. 'Jaslal, put your gun on my back and shoot those two running, and any others you can see.'

By then the two half-submerged people were about fifty yards into the swamp so Jaslal, placing his gun on his OC's back, said 'ready Saheb' and aiming at the taller man, fired a short burst, catching him in the head. He sank down out of sight. *Has to be dead*, the corporal said to himself. Aiming now at the shorter of the two he saw the head disappear. Without a target he did not fire.

Siu Tse, completely flummoxed by the unexpected noise – she had never heard LMG rapid fire before – tripped and fell headlong inside the swamp. She lay there breathless.

'I've got one, and one's disappeared, Saheb,' Jaslal shouted down to Jason.

'Good. Spray the area once more,' shouted Jason and this Jaslal did. He came to the end of his magazine and took the LMG off Jason's back. Jason stood up and stretched, his ears 'ringing' with the noise of the firing. 'Did you see which way any others guerrillas went?'

With no more noise of firing of the *ngau gok*[16] Siu Tse came to her senses, picked herself up and crept deeper into the swamp, desperate to hide. Jaslal answered his OC's question. 'Saheb, if there were any more daku they'll surely have turned back into the jungle. I know I shot and killed one of the two. The mist did not let me see all that clearly.'

The four men stood there, searching for any more movement, as Jason wondered what best to do next as various courses of

16   *Ngau gok*, cattle horn. The Chinese CTs used this term for the Bren LMG because of the shape of the magazine. But the transliteration of the word 'Bren' was also often used with the characters bo leng. The word for 'light' was often omitted, so the weapon was termed '*bo leng gei gwaan cheung*'.

action went through his mind. *What do I know? My men are somewhere to the west. The enemy group moving north that I was following – either those were they or ... or, if not, could it be another group coming from the north?*

'Lads, we are too few to go and search for the dead man and the one in front of him. The group that Jaslal saw must have gone into the jungle to get away from our fire. They won't know the rest of our platoon were following them. We will wait a few minutes and if we hear nothing we'll move over to our men and call out it's us coming. Only then will we check for dead and any wounded.'

Safety, especially crossing sub-unit boundaries, was a constant concern. Better the odd guerrilla get away than one his soldiers be killed by 'own fire'.

7

Gurkha Lieutenant Danbahadur Rai was briefing the men going on ambush when firing broke out. 'That gun means it's the OC Saheb's group,' he said, looking in the direction of the noise, 'very near and just to our east – the swamp area.' They all listened expectantly and were surprised not to hear any more firing. *Is he in danger? Shall we go and help him? No!* 'Without any delay, go to your ambush positions. The daku could be trying to escape our way. Move!'

Away they went, knowing exactly where to go. With camouflage fronds already in their jungle hats they were virtually invisible as they took up their positions. They didn't have long to wait. All of Piggy's group, not knowing about any troops there because the helicopters were miles out of sound when the Gurkhas were deployed and who had not made any sort of recce before their night's halt, ran straight into the ambush which opened fire immediately on seeing them. Four were killed, three others wounded and captured.

Lin Soong's group immediately moved some hundred yards to the west, into thicker jungle, and took up positions facing east. 'If the other group needs help we must be able to give it,' he said quietly. 'We must ensure that Little Sister has got away.'

His men nodded agreement. It would have been a dereliction of duty not to ensure her safety.

Jason and his men looked across the swamp. No movement. Then they heard firing to their half left. 'The daku have been ambushed by the other part of our platoon. Pack up. Sig-nel, no time for a sitrep now. Get your aerial down and we'll go over to the rest of our men.'

In no time they moved off towards where they had heard the noise of the firing. At the top of his voice Jason yelled 'O ho. We are coming to join you. No firing. We won't be long.' Even though he knew it was a risk to give his position away to any guerrilla by shouting it was less risky to do so in a situation like they now found themselves in with their own men in the offing.

'Saheb, it's all right. We are ready for you,' came the comforting answer.

They met up some five minutes later and Jason was delighted to see the success of the platoon's ambush. He saw that four corpses had been stacked together and the three wounded guerrillas were having medical dressings put on their wounds, disarmed, bound and placed under a sentry.

'Excellent work, Saheb. Congratulations. No casualties ourselves?'

'No, Saheb.'

'That's good news. Did any daku get away?'

'I don't think so but we'll have another search for any wounded if you like.'

'Yes, do that but only locally. Don't bother about the swamp.

Meanwhile I'll write a sitrep for Battalion HQ and give it to the signaller to send next opening time. We'll tell them the news and ask for a heli lift for us, the wounded and the corpses. Keep sentries out, Saheb, and when it's time, cook a meal.'

The Gurkha lieutenant gave the necessary orders and said, 'Saheb, we were alerted by your firing. What happened?'

Jason gave a rueful smile, remembering he still had to go and search for the corpse of the man his gunner had felled, told those around him what had happened.

'That was lucky, Saheb. Good shooting in all that undergrowth.'

'No, Saheb, I told the gunner, Corporal Jaslal Rai, to shoot his LMG off my bent back otherwise he would not have been able to aim properly. I wore a big pack to save being burnt by the empty cases and braced my knees with my hands. Saheb, give me three men as escort and hunters, yes – this is "Operation Hunter" isn't it? – for the corpse, and I will take them with the gunner guiding us to look for him. In fact there were two people who were running into the swamp.'

'Without trying to conceal themselves? In the open?'

'Yes, just that.'

'Curious,' said Gurkha Lieutenant Danbahadur Rai. 'Not like them at all. What did you see, Saheb?'

'Nothing. I had my head between my legs, trying to keep steady for Jasé's aiming.'

The Platoon Commander looked with astonishment at his OC. *There's nothing he won't do, is there!*

Jaslal, listening in, said, 'Lieutenant saheb, it was as though the person in front was trying to escape, panicked, fled and the man behind was trying to catch them.'

The three wounded men had been given as much first aid as was available and were now tied to a tree, zealously guarded by a rifleman. They were in pain but managed to conceal it as stoically as they could. After a while, the senior softly said, 'We'll be severely interrogated. It is incumbent on us to say as little as possible. Let's get our story ready. We will only say that we were on a routine patrol from the north moving down to our southern border. We must not mention we came with firm orders to take Little Sister back or that a party from the south was to meet us here to hand her over to us. We must protect the others by not talking about them. Got it?'

The others nodded their agreement but before they could say any more the sentry told them, in fractured Malay, to keep quiet.

After discussing such a curious incident a bit longer Jason said, 'Bring two poles and a poncho to carry the body back on.'

'Saheb, before you go, would you like to talk to the prisoners?'

'Yes, there might be something to add to the sitrep.' He was led to where the three men were and the sentry gave him a butt salute. The three prisoners saw a *gwailo* and felt afraid. *Don't such people torture prisoners?* The leader was glad he had given instructions but all three were utterly taken aback when they were greeted in fluent Chinese. 'Do your wounds hurt? We don't have all that much medical equipment with us but I have asked for some *chek seng gei*' – navigate-leave-a-space machine, a helicopter – 'to come and pick us up tomorrow. You will be taken to a hospital, kindly treated and not tortured as your propaganda chiefs like to lie about. Only when you are fit will you be interrogated.'

He let that sink in. 'Now, tell me where you have come from, where you were hoping to reach and why.'

One man answered as though he had rehearsed the answer already. 'A routine patrol to our southern border to see if there was anything new to report.'

To Jason that was not a complete answer at all. He bent forward and said *'paan chue sek lo foo'* – feigning to be a pig you are trying to vanquish tigers. Once more complete surprise was registered in each face and smiles appeared, albeit briefly.

'What did you say, Saheb?' the Platoon Commander asked and Jason told him that their reply 'going on a routine border patrol' was probably a lie but 'let's leave it to the police to do the interrogation.' A few minutes later Corporal Jaslal Rai, now armed with only a rifle, and an escort of three men joined their OC and they moved off towards the swamp.

It was only during the second burst of gunfire that Little Sister bravely plucked up enough courage to worm her way back to where she had been when the first lot of firing had broken out. Water got in her eyes. She took her lucky handkerchief, her keepsake, out of her pocket to wipe her face. She heard a rustle, looked down and saw a snake coming towards her. Without thinking she screwed up her handkerchief and threw it at the snake. It hit the snake in the eyes, which then veered off. Siu Tse jinked her way back and as she had heard nothing suspicious since then and the activity was away to a flank, she was at odds what to do. *I can't stay here forever. I must try to meet up with my men. If I can get on firm ground I have a much better chance of being rescued.* She reached where she heard flies buzzing and, yes, there was a very dead Piggy, leeches and ants already crawling over the corpse. A faint smell of bad breath nauseated her and brought those years of long ago nearer still. Seeing him dead gave her heart and, keeping her head below the level of the long grasses – *oh, what moving with a bent back means* – she reached the edge of the swamp. Cautiously, oh how cautiously, she looked around. No one in sight. Holding her breath, up she got and slipped into the undergrowth, shivering with fright, and wet through. In front of her was a tree with hanging vines she could easily climb. She stepped close to it then something made her go round to the other side of it, the side facing the jungle and, without a second thought, nimbly climbed up into it. In a small bole next to two forked and sturdy branches she found a place where she could not be seen from the ground. After moving about to get comfortable and getting her breath back she opened her pack, took out some dry clothes, wriggled out of her wet ones – *my knickers will have to dry on me* – and squirmed into her dry ones before taking out a canteen of water and some tapioca. She wolfed it all down then curled up and, so shattered was she, bodily and mentally, she closed her eyes and dropped off to sleep.

The search group soon found tracks of the guerrillas from the north and easily saw where at least two people had gone into the swamp. Buzzing flies revealed the corpse for them. They neared it and saw it was covered in leeches, busily sucking away, and ants devouring the still warm flesh. Leeches that live in water are long and can suck up to a pint of blood. Jason knew of a case when a woman had tripped into an area of such creatures and four of them had sucked her dead.

Jason looked at the dead man's face for longer than his men thought he would. *Can it be the same?* his thoughts going back how many years was it now? *Fifteen. Must be the same one. Can't be two such men.* 'Get him bound and carry him out,' he said, his men noticing his voice unusually shaky. *And the girl I rescued?* He shook his head. *Stop dreaming.*

Just as the carrying party left Jason called his gunner over. '*Keta*, think back to when you opened fire.' A nod. ''How much did you see of the person in front?'

'Only the head, Saheb.'

'Did you notice anything about it?'

The LMG gunner thought for a moment. 'It was small, Saheb.'

Jason took a gamble. 'Do you think it could have been a woman?' he asked casually. 'Woman, Saheb?' surprise in his voice. 'No, that never struck me.'

'Not at all?'

The saheb is strange today! 'No, Saheb. Not at all.'

Later he asked himself if it was only idle curiosity that made him go a few yards farther along where bent reeds and rushes revealed tracks where a person had moved both ways. They then jinked off to the left. He followed them. A little way off he saw something white hanging on a bent stem of long grass. He made his way over to it. *A handkerchief?* He bent down and picked it up. *Yes, that's what it is.* Something familiar immediately caught his eye: its blue edging. Childhood days swum back into his mind: his mother not liking to share handkerchiefs so having separate colours for mother, father and son. He examined it closely, wondering if it was pure coincidence. *But it this one is old and frayed no, can't be ... but it is ... that stain of blood is the same as when I wiped her cheek.* His mind churned. *Can't still be hers, can it? Not after all these years. A coincidence, surely? But there's dead Piggy so does that mean Siu Tse is somewhere here? Was it she who climbed the tree and was surprised by our Auster? If so, one chance in how many million?* His mind spinning, he started back to the dry land ... memories of years in the past with his first kiss coming back. Intuitively he touched his lips tenderly.

Faithful and observant Kulé followed him unobtrusively. *My Saheb is in deep thought: why?* Jason reached the jungle edge almost oblivious of the group with Piggy's corpse. He stared into the jungle, mind a-whirl. *What was it that surprised me that time?* He thought hard. Yes, some remark about climbing trees. He saw a small print at the base of the tree he was standing under, but there were no marks of anyone having tried to climb up. His unconscious mind broke loose as he remembered the lullaby Ah Fat had taught him so many years ago and which he had sung when he was comforting her. He sang the first six lines to himself:

> *The sun shines its bright light on the hill,*
> *Bright Virtue, be good and go back home to bed,*
> *For tomorrow morning mummy has to rush to plant seedlings,*
> *And grandpa has to go up the hills to tend cattle.*

Bright Virtue, will you grow up quickly,
To help grandpa tend cattle and sheep?
but, unthinkingly, sang the last two lines:
The sun shines its bright light on the hill,
Bright Virtue, be good and go back home.

Out loud ... loud enough for the girl up the tree to wake and hear them. As he sang the words he took the handkerchief out of his pocket, looked at it, and put it back again, quiet once more. The words gently drifted around the otherwise voiceless jungle, adding its cadences to the normal voices of an early morning under the trees. The Gurkhas following Jason momentarily wondered if a message was being sent *but surely that's impossible.* Kulé was even more perplexed when he saw Jason taking an old white handkerchief he had never seen before out of his pocket, looking at it before putting it back.

He turned on hearing footsteps behind him. Two riflemen were approaching. One called out 'Saheb, you are wanted. Sunray on set.'

On hearing voices Jason came out of his reverie with a start, annoyed with himself for being so absorbed in those years of so long ago. *But the coincidences had to be thought out.*

'Kulé what are they saying?' he asked. Kulbahadur told him.

'Coming,' Jason called back. 'Go on back and tell the operator to say I'm on my way.'

The operator, looking miffed, handed the spare headset over. 'Saheb, I was asked why you were not here.' He felt that Sunray thought it was his fault that Captain Rance saheb was not there when Sunray had said 'Fetch Sunray'. His face did not have his normal smile.

Jason put on the headset and, talking into the microphone, told Sunray he was 'on set'.

'Hello 1,' came the CO's voice. 'I dislike you not being near your set at times like these. I have had your sitrep and spoken to your Sunray minor. I understand you have five killed and three wounded and captured Charlie Tares. Congratulations. No casualties own troops, correct or not, over.'

Jason confirmed that Sunray was correct, wondering why his affirmation was needed. The CO asked if Sunray1 had found any more clues in the swamp 'where Sunray minor told me you were.'

'I. From traces I found it is possible that one other Charlie Tare had been in the swamp. Tracks were inconclusive.'

The next question from Battalion HQ was had Captain Rance got the mandatory box camera and fingerprint outfit. Jason confirmed he had.

'In that case, photo and fingerprint the dead now and bury them in your location. Prepare an LP as near as you can to your present position. I am sending in a platoon of call sign 2 to relieve you. ETA 1100 hours tomorrow. The three wounded Charlie Tares will be ferried out in the first flight. You will stay behind and brief Sunray 2 and come out in the last flight. Roger so far, over.'

Yes, that was clear enough.

'Your immediate task on your return is to escort a group of rescue technicians and medical men to the scene of big Sunray's plane crash as only you and your small escort know the way. Out.'

Jason called his 'O' Group after the transmission had finished. 'Tomorrow a platoon of B Company is flying in to relieve us. We have to send the prisoners out in the first lift so, Saheb,' he told the Platoon Commander, 'I think you had better go with them. I have been told to brief the new Sunray so will fly out on the last lift.' He looked around those sitting in front of him. 'How far away is the LP you landed on when you were brought here?'

'Saheb, it took us a slow two hours to reach this location. We did not know if the noise of the helis could be heard by any daku so we moved slowly.'

'Did you notice any possible LP nearer? Between the one you were dropped into and here?'

'Yes, there is an old Sakai cultivation place about twenty minutes' walk from here.'

'Good. That'll do. Saheb, send as many spare men as possible to prepare it as best they can after their meal. They can spend the night there to save them coming back and the remainder of us will move after an earlyish meal tomorrow. Any questions?'

There were none. Before he dismissed them Jason told them that he and Kulbahadur would be returning almost as soon with a rescue party at the site of the plane crash.

Lin Soong was a determined man, who had a sixth sense of jungle craft, as indeed had many other guerrillas who spent their life almost as animals in their sensitivity to danger. Even before the second round of shooting, his group had reacted according to their standing procedures: scatter and wait, either until more firing presaged another move or it was safe to gather at the appointed

RV. Guerrillas seldom if ever made any move without selecting an RV, bound by bound. It soon came second nature to them. There was so much noise of talk in *Loi Pai Yi Wa* – such troops were normally so silent – that he could now tell where soldiers probably were not. However, he was worried that a couple of them might still be searching in the swamp. And that did worry him, not only because he had seen the leader of the group that was to take Little Sister on the next stage killed there but also because, for whatever reason, the girl had tried to escape as soon as she saw him. As for that man who ran after her, it was either fear of losing her or, hadn't there been a curious expression in his eyes when he told him there was a woman to escort back? Yes, could there have been a more personal cause?

His men slowly collected in the chosen RV and Lin Soong quietly collected a canteen of water and some of the emergency rations they carried. 'Just in case Little Sister has dropped her pack we must help her if she is still alive, as we all hope she is. If we find her she will be thirsty and hungry.' The others agreed. 'She ran into the swamp. She'll be wet through. She may still be hiding there. We just don't know but we must find out. Let us take some of our spare, dry kit just in case … ' and he left his sentence unfinished. Individually each guerrilla thought that she was probably dead if not badly wounded.

With the extra stuff in one of their packs Lin Soong with one gunman moved north, away from the noise of the Gurkhas for a couple of hundred yards. He saw no enemy tracks. The two men then moved northeast and then back southeast. As they went they 'croaked' from time to time. When the swamp came into view

Lin Soong softly said, 'If we get no answer now that'll mean her corpse is in the swamp.'

They 'croaked' together twice and, having heard nothing, were about to move away, bitterly disappointed, when a soft croak came from a branch high in the tree they were standing beside. 'Little Sister, we have come to collect you but first we will climb up and join you,' Lin Soong quietly called up to her.

Siu Tse pinched herself, thinking it just had to be a dream but, no, it was true, true, true. Hope flooded back into her and she smiled for the first time in ages. *I wonder who the singer was. Just can't have been ... what did he say when I asked him his name?* It came back in a flash, *Shandong P'aau.* She knew it could not have been that wicked man who had killed her Alan because she was sure he'd have told her if that Rance man could speak Chinese – *in any case most unlikely. Such people just wouldn't bother, would they?* Then another idea struck her: *as I know my girlhood rescuer is dead, do you think I only dreamed I heard that song?* Her head spun in bewilderment.

Lin Soong and his escort climbed the tree and were delighted to see Little Sister was safe and surprised to see her clothes were dry. They sat near her, opened a pack and offered her some food. She was still hungry as she had not had much in hers. She also welcomed more water. While she ate and drank the two guerrillas listened attentively for any Gurkhas who might come their way. Having finished eating she looked for her lucky handkerchief – *didn't it save me from that snake?* – but to her dismay she couldn't find it. *Oh dear! Lost!*

She put a brave face on it and asked, 'Have our comrades

suffered much? I know that the man running after me was killed.'

'Do you know why he chased you?'

Why hide the truth? She told them all that had happened so many years earlier, even how she had been rescued. 'But I never heard of my saviour again. As soon as I saw who would take me on I just had to get away. I suppose I thought the swamp the safest place to hide.'

'Yes, that makes sense but the firing of the *ngau gok cheung* certainly took us by surprise,' Lin told her. 'It probably meant that there was a splinter group of soldiers we had no idea about.' He smiled at her. 'Yes, you were lucky. If you had been any taller you'd have made a better target.'

'Were any others killed?'

'Not from our group. The people from the north were a rough lot who seemed to lack basic training. They were all either killed or wounded and captured. None of us was.'

'Where are they?'

'The *Goo K'a bing* have captured them, at least we think so because of the noise they made as they gathered the five corpses and the three wounded comrades.'

'What happens now?' she asked, realising how lucky she had been.

'Without an escort there's no chance in your trying to go north now. We'll get you back. It won't be easy but we'll manage, especially if this lot of *Goo K'a bing* fly back, as I am sure they will with our wounded comrades. That is always what they do, so it seems.'

She shuddered. 'And torture them I suppose.'

'Yes, if we believe what we are told by the Politburo but I somehow doubt it. Now we can't sit around all day,' and he told his escort to go back as silently as he possibly could, get the others to the tree and they'd endeavour to move off in a northwest direction. 'Not so far away there is a *t'o yan* settlement. I am sure they can look after us till this present excitement is over.'

A thought came to Siu Tse: *if I don't have to go all that way north, maybe there'll be a chance somehow or other to see my baby boy again when we get back.*

That evening after the wireless had closed down, sleeping platforms built, sentries detailed and food utensils had been cleaned to keep rats and cockroaches away, the soldiers had their tot of rum and a mouthful of *ikan bilis*, dried prawns, a great morale booster after a heavy day. Kulbahadur brewed his Saheb some tea and brought it over to him as he sat by the side of where he was to sleep. The Gurkha saw him looking at the handkerchief he had taken out of his pocket earlier on – it was not one he recognised as he knew all the Saheb's kit. Jason looked up as Kulé gave him his tea and said, 'Kulé, bring your tot of rum over and we'll drink together.'

They sat together, saying nothing for a while, then, in an indirect way, the Gurkha tried to establish why his Saheb's behaviour had been so different from normal. He looked at his OC's eyes, normally keen, kindly and shrewd but now with a hint of haziness in them. *Why does a brave, cool and resourceful officer such as he behave so unlike his normal self?* The question chased through his mind as it searched for a rational answer.

Almost unintentionally Kulbahadur said, 'Saheb, you

surprised us when you asked if the person you went after was a woman. What gave you such an idea? You have never asked such a question before, or if you have, not in my hearing.'

Jason felt he had to talk about his problem and he and Kulé knew each other as well as almost anyone else did. He took the handkerchief out of his pocket. 'How old do you think this is?' was a question that was probably the least of all that the Gurkha expected to be asked.

Kulbahadur looked at it and examined it. 'It definitely isn't new, Saheb.'

'It is at least fifteen years old,' Jason answered flatly. 'You are correct. It is not new. It was mine until fifteen years ago … ' and his eyes took on a look of deep thought.

He pulled himself together. 'Kulé, I had no idea about who the dead man was before I saw him but on looking at his unusual features I knew I'd seen him before … ' and out the story came – of how the dead man had killed two men who were molesting a young Chinese girl all those many years ago. He described how he had frightened the now-dead man away, helped and revived the girl, taken his handkerchief out of his pocket to dab to blood off her cheek. 'I knew she was frightened so I had sung her a song to comfort her. It was a song mothers sang to their babies to get them to sleep.'

That answered part of the Gurkha's doubts but he said nothing. Gurkhas are good listeners.

'It would be too much of a coincidence if it was the same man chasing this same girl. I had to find out and, although I never saw her, I found this handkerchief in the long rushes off that trace of a track in the swamp.'

Kulbahadur shook his head in wonder as Jason continued, 'And as my memory replayed those times I also remembered her saying that had she known about the attack she'd have climbed a tree to escape. I had seen no return tracks. You know how difficult it is to track people in such places so, as I walked near the trees, that song came to my lips unbidden.'

'Saheb, if you had found her, what would you have done?'

Indeed, what would I have done? 'Kulé, if she was wearing guerrilla uniform and was armed there'd be no option but to treat her as an enemy soldier and she would have been tried by a judge and most probably hanged. If, on the other hand, she could prove she had been kidnapped and was not a guerrilla and had thrown away, say a pistol in the swamp, I expect she'd be allowed to go free.'

Kulbahadur thought that over and, saying nothing, got up and took the used drinking containers away to clean them. *Fate plays strange tricks to others than us Gurkhas!*

Lin Soong's men, using supreme fieldcraft, had gathered near the tree by five o'clock. It was always safer to move after the Security Forces had bedded down for the night. 'It will take quite a time to reach the *t'o yan* settlement. This is how I intend to get there,' Lin Soong quietly told his men. 'I will go in front, using a shaded torch until we reach that bamboo grove we know of. There we will make some firebrands. We will try not to make a noise by using bits of dry bamboo that are already on the ground, if there are any. We will shred the ends then light them. We have a lighter and then, when lit, we will walk openly, singing a song. We have all heard the type of song the *t'o yan* sing when they have their communal dancing. Not that we know the words but the *Goo K'a yan* will never credit it is guerrillas singing so not bother. In any case, they won't come and investigate.'

His men silently clapped their hands in appreciation of such a daring and clever plan.

The sentry in the platoon camp heard some singing. It was in the distance and too far away to see any flame from the burning bamboos. Just in case, he went to wake his section commander. 'Guru-ji, can you hear any noise?'

The corporal listened carefully. 'Yes, it'll be those Sakai going round and round till some of them fall to the ground in a trance. There's no need to worry about it. The daku would never dare to imitate them.'

As usual the members of the Politburo of the MCP, hiding in their deep jungle lair, listened in to the Chinese-language news, the Red channel, on Radio Malaya. They learnt to their horror that they had suffered a further loss of five men killed and three wounded and captured by 1/12 GR down in the south, in the Gunong Rajah area, Bentong, Pahang. The name of the senior guerrilla leader was given. It was not a name normally used as the man was generally known as Piggy. 'We'll have to discuss that at our meeting later on in the day,' muttered the Secretary General, Chin Peng. 'It may be more serious than an ordinary contact,' though he could not immediately think why that thought assailed him.

The non-voting member, Ah Fat, had immediately pricked up his ears at hearing the name of the unit involved in the contact. *I wonder if my friend Jason Rance,* Shandung P'aau, *was involved.* He often thought back to the time he had convinced the Soviet 'Rezident' in Calcutta that his boyhood friend was a deep-cover agent working against the British as an officer of Gurkhas. Back again in the mind-deadening atmosphere of the Politburo he had had to spin a convincing yarn about that incident when he gave his report. He hoped that no investigation would be instituted by the propaganda people, suspicious of every unusual feature, to Jason's detriment.

This latest report was indeed discussed in their regular meeting later that day. One of the Politburo said, 'It is not usual to have military activity in that Gunong Rajah area.'

Heads nodded. Another said, 'It could be to do with that crashed plane. Wasn't that the area Radio Malaya said it was probably lost in?'

'Yes, it was but not to start with, one later and the report first said that nobody had any real idea where it had crashed so a large search party had been deployed to try and find it,' came another comment.

Lee An Tung put up his hand, a habit he had learnt somewhere when he wanted to make a point. 'I know our people are much thinner on the ground than the *gwailo* but any in that general area will also be keeping an eye open for the wreck in case it contains important documents.' Yes, that was well known but it never did any harm to be reminded of it.

Lee's deputy broke in. 'There's another point about that area, isn't there? I can't put my finger on it. Can any comrade help me?'

Ah Fat thought it was wise for him to take part in the conversation although he seldom did. 'I think I know what you're thinking about, Comrade. Isn't that one the boundary RVs we use when we want to escort someone from down there to us here?'

'Yes, of course,' the deputy said with a short, self-conscious laugh. 'So, who will it be if the *Goo K'a bing* have met such a group and it is nothing to do with the crashed plane?'

Chin Peng cleared his throat. 'It can only be Lin Soong's group bringing that woman friend of the captain who was killed on his way to join us.'

'In that case we've lost her and anything she could tell us about the *gwailo*,' said Lee An Tung.

'There may be a chance she is not one of the dead or captured,' said the General Secretary. 'So, just in case that is correct, next time we send any message down to the Seremban district we'll tell her to continue her good work there. Let us vote on that.'

Comrade Lee An Tung had another idea: 'Comrades, before we do, I have another suggestion. Ever since we had that report from Comrade Ah Fat of a British officer being on our side, is it possible, do you think, that, presuming Comrade Little Sister does get back to Seremban, she can be targeted towards him?'

Muted gasps of pleasure greeted that idea. Ah Fat was asked for details and, pretending to dig them out of his memory, gave them.

The vote was passed unanimously even if it were an unlikely 'starter' and arrangements were made to find out as quickly as possible what had happened to Comrade Siu Tse.

Next day as scheduled, two helicopters flew to collect the platoon and the captives, the stiffs having been photographed, fingerprinted and buried the previous day. Jason was able to brief the new platoon commander, a sergeant, in depth as well as show him the swamp where the body had been found.

'Do you advise anything special?' the sergeant asked.

Jason remembered the noise of the night before. He did not have any experience of working with Sakai but, even so, suddenly to hear such a noise was, indeed, worth looking into. 'Yes, Guru-ji, once you have satisfied there no daku hiding around here or in the swamp, go to the nearest Sakai community,' and he showed him on the map about where he thought it was, 'and see if they can tell you anything.' He looked at his watch. 'Time to go to the LP.'

Back in base Jason prepared himself for another short visit to the area with the Engineer recce team, a couple of senior members of the Army Air Corps who had flown out from England and a padre – obviously there was no need to take any medical staff. Once there the problem of the plane's recovery was seen to be more than the Engineers could deal with. The padre stood on the edge of the cliff and said a short burial service for the three dead men.

Lin Soong's jungle navigation ability was good enough to take his team back to their base in the jungle near Seremban but, of course, he had no control over the weather. One most uncomfortable night of heavy rain and thunder had interrupted the guerrillas' sleep early on with cascading water flooding their bashas. In an unusual lapse of jungle lore, they had not taken notice of the trees nearby. The heavy rain had made some of the older trees so waterlogged that the extra weight of that night's rain made them too heavy to stand upright. Around midnight, huddling under what protection they had managed to re-arrange for themselves, they were scared stiff by the heavy creaking that heralds a tree fall. Everyone's nerves tingled, knowing that a large tree was about to crash down, each one of them knowing that there was no chance of running away to safety. Siu Tse tensed her body as, with a rending, tearing sound, a tree fell with a sickening thud as it hit the ground. Silence was broken by some of the smaller branches whipping down around them. 'Comrades, are you all right? Is anyone hurt?' called Lin Soong, not that he could have done much to help if anyone was. Luckily no one had been hit. But later on for Siu Tse it was even worse. She was by then so tired that she had gone to sleep once more with her right arm flung out. Towards dawn the rain stopped. She woke up and her right arm seemed numb. She rubbed it with his other hand and only felt rough skin. Not her own, which was itching. She was at a loss to know what to make of it and put it down to having slept on it. She tried to move but was unable to. She moaned and whimpered until the sentry came over to see what the trouble was. There was just enough light to see the unblinking eyes of a large python glared at the girl from just below her shoulder. She fainted in fear.

The sentry saw that the snake was stuck. It could not go back nor could it move forward. He quickly called Lin Soong. 'Comrade, come and help kill a python that has swallowed Siu Tse's arm.' He came over with a parang and cut the snake in two, making sure that the girl's arm was safe. The python squirmed with all its might and lashed its tail, but in vain. By the third stroke the body was severed. The next job was to slit the piece that was still round the girl's arm.

She had regained consciousness and, in a daze, was helped to the stream by which they had camped, and she washed her arm. Meanwhile the guerrillas sliced up the python to cook it for their morning meal. It was too much for the girl who, although hungry, declined any. She was never to know that her Alan's arm had similarly been eaten by a python.

They were all thoroughly relieved to get back to their main camp. The Chinese girl had much to think about; all her unexpected adventures, the camaraderie of her 'fellow comrades' as she thought of them, the drama of meeting her smelly lecher, running into the swamp and, strangest of all what she thought she must have heard in her dream when hiding in that tree. She had never heard the lullaby ever since that time so long ago. She often shook her head in bewilderment, unable to come to any hard conclusion as to what had actually happened.

The Political Commissar decided to send a message by the next courier from the MCP HQ asking what to do with Little Sister. He was saved this as the next courier brought instructions for her to return to plain-clothes duty in Seremban where her task was to try and join up with a Captain Jason Rance, who was thought to be an officer in 1/12 GR and known to be a secret comrade under deep cover. Any news she could get about operations would be told to the Political Commissioner and the Military Commander of the Regional Committee.

On hearing the name of the man who had killed her Alan, Siu Tse's initial inner reaction was that she could never get herself to work that way – even on Party orders. However, on mature consideration, it would make her task of killing him so much easier, wouldn't it? She thought it over before she went to sleep that night and decided that she had had enough of this rough life and that if she said that she was ready to carry out the Party's idea – she had yet to realise that an 'idea' like that was really an order – she would once more be able to live with and look after her son. Surely anything else she had to do was worth the effort. Her last comforting thought was *the longer I don't get my enemy dead, the longer I can live at peace with my baby boy. Better, much, than the loss of my lucky charm – at least it did save me from one snake: now I know enough to kill another snake ...*

Back in Seremban Jason Rance was unsure whether to keep his secret boyhood flashbacks caused by that handkerchief and the dead Chinese in the swamp to himself but who would listen to such, what? Too many coincidences to be completely ignored but, even if true, did it matter? Yes, he had been shaken by it but at least he had unburdened himself to Kulbahadur Limbu who had not dismissed it as impossibility.

After deep thought he decided to talk privately with the Head of Special Branch, Ismail Mobarak, known as Moby, and his deputy, an ebullient Teochew, Tay Wang Teik.

At a private meeting in Moby's house he apologised for what he was about to say, 'possibly so irrelevant it may well be'. The other two nodded, sensing Jason's inner difficulty. 'As background you are fully aware of all who and what went into our Operation Janus. There is one person in the drama I'd like to draw your attention to one who might, just might, be of significance. Please don't be surprised if I start my story as far back as 1938 ... '

Tay Wang Teik and Moby returned to the sitting room after they had said farewell to their mutual friend Jason at the front door. Moby called for a fresh pot of tea and, once they had refilled their cups, said, 'Well, what do you make of that? A most unusual story by all counts. Haven't heard the like of it ever, have you?'

'No, can't say I have. On their own, each episode, the one when he rescued the girl and the incident in the swamp are seriously interesting.' He took a sip of tea and Moby nodded his agreement. 'Yet, without the first one, the second would lose much significance.'

'I ask for answers to two questions,' Moby said. 'One, why did the woman keep that handkerchief for so long, presuming it is the same one, of course. The second is what were a one-time taxi-girl and the mother of a British turncoat's illegitimate son doing in that area, again presuming she is the same person.'

'That gets me to ask a third question, Moby. Do we try to answer your questions?'

Moby smiled. 'On the face of it I think a "yes" is in order if it only means asking the captives if there was a women in their group and, if so, were there any reasons for such an unlikely person to be with them?'

'So far they have said they know nothing, even under a certain amount of pressure.'

'That means that there probably is a reason they've yet to tell us,' was Moby's rejoinder. 'Have you got a copy of the photos Jason took of the corpses before burying them?'

'Not on me but, yes, in my office.'

'Be a good chap, Tay, and run and fetch them.'

His deputy disappeared and soon returned with copies of all three. 'Here you are, Moby. Fine looking bunch aren't they, especially that one with up-and-down eyebrows. You sent a copy of these to your opposite number in Bentong, didn't you?'

'Most certainly, yes. And, here I apologise for not telling you, in yesterday's mail I got an answer. They recognised two of them as low-level members of the MRLA but could not place the one that has a porcine face and uneven eyebrows.'

'The phantom Siu Tse's potential rapist.' Tay Wang Teik looked excited. 'That, to me, means that he was being escorted and, both of us knowing the way these people work, that can only mean he was based with the MCP up north.'

'Yes, I was coming to the same conclusion myself. That means my next move is to send yet another copy up to KL to our mutual friend CC Too to get one of his men to look through their rogues' gallery and tell us who he is.' He was referring to Too Chee Chew, known to all as 'CC Too', a brilliant propaganda expert who worked in HQ Malayan Police. 'And when we get his answer back we'll have another session with the captives.'

'Yes, that's sensible. Also, by then they'll be fit enough to answer our questions in a better frame of mind – especially after rehearsing their answers!'

Moby said, 'I have another idea, Tay. Jason Rance was

obviously most impressed by witnessing the murder of those two men and his inordinately successful method of getting the other, third, man to leave the scene as fast as he could. If, and it is still a big if, if the owner of the handkerchief Jason found in the swamp and showed us is the same girl, what memories of the whole business does she still carry? And her feelings towards Jason must still be more than grateful.'

Tay Wang Teik said, 'She certainly cannot have forgotten it. Do we know if she similarly suffered under the Japs?'

Moby shook his head. 'No idea.'

'Doesn't matter now anyway. Can't matter. What I'd like to do is to go and see the manager of the Yam Yam, Yap Cheng Wu, and try and get him to talk about her. He knows we take an interest in him but there won't be any politics in this, at least as far as he is concerned, and so that may let him tell us more than if we were making it a personal checking.'

Yap Cheng Wu showed no outward surprise when he was visited by Tay Wang Teik. At eleven o'clock in the morning the staff were cleaning the place up and there was no pressing reason for the manager to refuse to meet his visitor. He did wonder if it was anything to do with that missing *gwailo* they knew as *Sik Long*. Yap had been wholly instrumental in arranging for the *gwailo* to leave Seremban, nothing more. In fact he did not expect to hear about him until he had reached the Central Committee when a gloating announcement would have been made to try and embarrass the colonial government. Certainly nothing had ever been announced by the Security Forces of any such man having defected, being captured while trying to defect or even being killed while trying to do so. What had he heard the English say? *No news is good news*. But then those rumours had started and the gwailo's pregnant girlfriend, Siu Tse, was worried. She fully knew about and approved of what her hoped-for future husband was intending to do and that it would be a long time before any news could filter back that he was well and happy working with the Central Committee of the MCP, which she merely thought about as 'them'.

The manager knew that before any definite news of her Alan's arrival with his escort had been received, Siu Tse had begun to hear niggling rumours that Hinlea was dead – *didn't we all hear them?* It could have been nothing more than just careless talk or mere speculation that Hinlea's so-called friend Captain Rance – never any proof, mind you – had killed him. He had told Siu Tse all that class were just the same, none could be trusted. Certainly, there was evidence that Captain Rance had not been in the camp after her man had left her. Good enough!

Deputy Tay was shown into the manager's office and offered a chair. 'Yap *Sinsaang*, I won't take up your time by any customary small talk as you are a busy man, but I would like to ask you a question that is worrying us.'

There was no need at all to explain who 'us' were.

'Yes?'

'We have heard that the *Sik Long*'s girlfriend, whom we believe gave birth to a son, has not been seen about the place for some time. We know that she is not at her home and that her mother is looking after the baby. My question is how did she react when she heard the rumours of her man's death? If you have any knowledge you are ready to tell us, or if not us, me, are you willing to pass it on?'

The manager grinned slyly as he cleared his throat, thinking about the difference between 'us' and 'me'. 'Us' could mean endless questions possibly resulting in difficulties one way or another. 'Me' would have no reaction. It could also, at sometime in the future, reap a reward.

'Yes, to a "me" and not an "us".'

It was Tay Wang Teik's turn to grin as he offered the manager a cigarette. The manager opened a drawer, took out a bottle of brandy and 'buzzed' a bell on his desk.

'With water at this time of day?' as a youth came at the noise of the buzzer.

'Yes, a little water will make the drink last longer.'

The manager ordered the youth to bring water and, glasses filled, 'yam seng', drink to victory, was said aloud. Empty glasses were put on the table.

'Another before I answer?'

'After your answer if it is as satisfactory as I think it'll be.'

'No comebacks?'

'I can't see any.'

'The girl came to me, worried at the rumour that a Captain Rance had killed her man. No, she had never seen him and never heard his name other than from *Sik Long* ... Hinlea. By then she was heavily pregnant and vowed that her baby would be a son – it was – who would make amends. I told her I could in no way help her. It was beyond anything I could do.'

'Can you tell me about when that was?'

The manager thought for a while. 'To the best of my memory sometime in early December 1952.'

The Deputy Special Branch nodded. It had never been announced or even hinted at that renegade Hinlea had been killed on 28 August of that same year.

'Thank you, most helpful,' said Tay as he got up to go. 'Nothing else, then?'

'Yes, now I've cast my mind back so far: I can remember her saying she would go and ask her uncle for advice. That's all I know.'

'Who is he, please? My last "me" question.'

'Only if ever I want a "me" question.'

'Done.' *It may never happen and I can bluff my way out of it.*

'He is Deng Bing Yi who works in a garage here in Seremban. I am not sure of the address but it is the last garage on the left as you leave the town on the KL road.'

Tay Want Teik shut his eyes as he tried to place it. *Got it!* 'Thank you for your trouble. I'll now leave you alone,' he said as he got to his feet.

The manager also stood up. They shook hands and Tay Wang Teik left. What the manager had kept secret was that, long after the events *he* had been asked about, he personally had taken the Chinese girl to see an old schoolmaster at Mantin for advice on her wanting to get revenge herself, so becoming a guerrilla herself. He hadn't evaded the question as that was not specifically asked, was it?

Back in the office, Tay Wang Teik and Moby once more discussed what had been learnt. 'That man Deng Bing Yi is a shady character,' said Tay. 'He is clever at his job. During the war he managed to sabotage a number of Japanese vehicles before having to into hiding. I learnt that his niece went to him to see if he could help her eliminate Captain Rance. Have we any idea of his answer? Can we guess it?'

'Can't imagine, other than sabotage his car,' said Moby, half in jest.

'Well, if he did, he was not successful, was he?'

'I have a man who has a distant relative in Deng's garage. I'll get him to ask some questions. If a blank, that'll be that!'

'Fully understood.'

The contact in the garage was the friend of a distant relation who lived in Mantin. It meant Tay Wong Teik taking a bus ride the next Saturday which, luckily, happened to be his relation's wife's birthday. There was quite a gathering and brandy flowed. Among the guests was the elderly wispy-bearded schoolmaster, Ngai Hiu Ching, who, for whatever reason, liked his tipple more than most. He did not recognise Tay who, when introduced by his distant relation, was announced as 'one of us', meaning the family, not the political persuasion of the one-time schoolmaster. It was a lucky break, and one most unexpected.

Each man, Tay and Ngai, holding a full glass of brandy in one hand, retired to the back of the room where there were some comfortable chairs. 'Let us sit down, Ngai *Sinsaang*, the joints of our bodies don't get any stronger even if the brandy makes us think so.'

Conversation turned to mutual friends, some of whom went back to pre-war years. Tay Wang Teik's head was stronger than was Ngai Hiu Ching's and Tay now remembered what he had read about the man when he took over the job of deputy to Moby: be had been an agent for wartime guerrillas against the Japanese, be they comrades or not. So he had more than a suspicion of what part the old schoolmaster played in affairs. 'One person I had hoped to meet here,' said Tay after a break in their conversation to refill their glasses, 'but can't see is Comrade Deng Bing Yi. I was going to ask him about his niece, Fong Chui Wan. I heard she had a son born to her but there was no news of the father. I hear she is no longer at home. As a *tung chi*, equal thinker, I am worried.'

'Equal thinker' is a term that almost invariably defines a 'comrade', nearly always a communist one.

The old schoolmaster sighed deeply. As far as he was concerned her case was the one he was most proud of. 'Such an example of a girl with a big heart and such spirit ... Yap Cheng Wu brought her to me ... ' He looked around suspiciously before continuing 'when I heard her story about the father of her son trying to join the Central Committee, I saw her as Central Committee material herself.'

He stopped and Tay poured more brandy into the old man's glass which was empty and proposed a toast to Fong Chui Wan. They drank and as the brandy warmed the old man's stomach he leant forward whispered 'I told the Politburo about her. They sent for her ... '

'Did she go there and then?'

'No, I sent her to Jemima Estate near Lukut village.' A pause, then ' ... and the Central Committee asking for her to go them instead of ... I told her to tell nobody ... '

Tay saw he was getting muddled as his voice trailed away in a drunken stupor. He recovered enough to take another gulp of brandy and then said, 'Her one and only ambition was then and still is ... ' he slurred his words so Tay had to put his ear closer to catch what was being said, 'kill her man,' gulp, with spittle drooling, 'so entrance.' The old man's 'kill Rance' had sounded like 'entrance' and the meaning was, somewhat naturally, lost on Tay. The old man passed out and Tay, seeing the glass in his hand about to drop, took it, put it on a table and edged his way back to the main party. He had certainly learnt a lot, especially that the Yam Yam manager had not been as straight with him as he had originally thought, *but yes it had been just a shade too easy – but 'entrance'?*

Talking it over with Moby on the Monday they decided that what must have happened was that Siu Tse was so incensed by the rumour of Jason Rance killing Alan Hinlea – almost correct but he had not fired the fatal shot – that initially she had tried to get her uncle to arrange matters. Here was a blank: the only way would have been to sabotage his car ... 'Moby, can you remember that burnt-out car someone found on the road leading south from Seremban and reported to the police? Now when would that have been ... before the turn of the year surely?'

'Yes, I do. I'll call for the file.' Tay continued with his account of the birthday party until the file came. Moby looked at it. 'Yes, as far as anyone could make out it was not an ordinary accident so we called the forensic people in. It had been tampered with. And,' he looked once more at the file, 'it happened on the night that Goh Ah Hok, the fresh ration contractor for 1/12 Gurkha Rifles, gave his Christmas party.'

'Got it!' almost squealed Moby's deputy. 'I had heard a rumour about it so I went snooping to see who had been invited. Always useful to have a look-see when possible. I was on the opposite side of the road from the house, standing behind some trees. Yes, it's all coming back. I saw Captain Rance with one other, the adjutant was it? I've known the captain since 1948 so I wasn't mistaken. The adjutant parked his car outside Goh Ah Hok's main door and Rance got out. The adjutant then drove his car a little distance off. By then I thought that most of the guests had arrived so I was just about to move off when another car drove up and parked outside the front door, where the adjutant had first parked his. A Chinese gentleman got out and went inside. I waited until he was under the light in the main room to see if I could recognise him and as I strained my eyes I saw someone go up to the car. He looked around, opened the front door, put his hand inside and unlocked the bonnet. I saw it was Deng Bing Yi. He then crawled under the car and I couldn't see what he was doing. I thought maybe the driver had phoned him to come and correct a fault.'

Moby was listening intently. 'And then what happened?'

'What happened?' Tay echoed. 'Nothing happened. He got up, closed the bonnet and walked away to another car, presumably his own as he got in and drove away.'

Moby whistled. 'Just suppose, just for one moment suppose,

he thought it was the adjutant's car he had come to sabotage and did not notice it had been moved so sabotaged the wrong car … '

' … and some other unfortunate fellow died instead,' Tay finished the sentence for his boss.[17]

'Exactly that,' breathed Moby. 'I can't remember any Missing Person notices around that time so whoever the other man was it could be that he was one of those who live just below the level of truth in the level of deception. Even so let his soul rest in peace,' said Moby, as a practising Moslem he knew all life was sacred.

The upshot was that, apart from adding this latest item to Siu Tse's file, she was not thought to be enough of a menace to warrant any extra watching. There were more than enough more important and dangerous people to keep tabs on already and resources were always tight, weren't they?

---

17 See *Operation Red Tidings, Operation Blowpipe* and *Operation Tipping Point.*

PART TWO

8

It was not until three years later, in early 1956, that a strange twist
of fate linked the now Major Rance with Siu Tse, happily reunited
with and mothering her small son, neither of them knowing
anything about it. And even if, however remotely unlikely, either
did, both would have dismissed it as having nothing to do with
them. In fact, had a lowly member of the Chinese Communist
Party in far-off Peking not been sent down to the HQ of the MCP,
now in the Betong salient in south Thailand, with a message and
to repair the Politburo's radio set that had been broken for the
past six months, the lives of both English officer and Chinese girl
would probably never have impinged on each other. But come
from Peking this man had and so impinge the other two did.

In the intervening three years, Major Rance and his A
Company had taken part in a number of operations, some more
difficult and dangerous than others but all successful enough to
add laurels to his military crown as far as his Gurkha troops were
concerned but, sadly, not so in the eyes of some senior officers.
His tactical skill, his relations with the Gurkhas, his Chinese and
Malay linguistic ability set him as being different from the normal
run of British officers – 'hardly Sahib-like' being heard more
than once. Jason's reaction was to ignore all such comments. His

current Commanding Officer had a grudge against him because he reminded him of a dead younger brother. Rance could never understand why the two of them never quite seemed able to 'hit it off'.

The crunch unexpectedly came from a completely unexpected source, not even in Malaya but neighbouring Thailand. The comrades in Peking were worried at the radio of the rump of the MCP, now hiding in the Betong salient in the very south of Thailand, not receiving their messages for so long that something had to be done to remedy affairs, so frustrating had it become to both ends of the link. At a meeting of senior cadres in Peking it was decided they simply had to issue a most important and secret message to the MCP so a courier had to be sent, by an emissary, there being no electronic method. So secret was it, it was never trusted to paper. The emissary had to be a good radio repairer as well as being able to commit the long message to memory.[18] The man chosen was middle-aged, not particularly fit as his job was a sedentary one. He was of medium height, with high cheek bones and a slightly protruding chin. His steady eyes that seldom blinked were calm and reflective. It took him many months to reach Betong, being escorted from 'bound to bound' from north China, across North Vietnam, Laos and Thailand by dedicated comrades. At his age it was a great physical challenge and he was dead beat on his eventual arrival, hardly able to walk.

Even though he was physically exhausted on arrival he gave as much of his important message as he could remember before

---

18   See *My Side of History*, Chin Peng, Chapter 22.

repairing the radio. In fact he never did remember the most important points so it was slightly ironic that his name was Meng, the same as the surname of Mencius, the Confucian philosopher, and Ru, a scholar or learned man. Even with the repaired radio set allowing communications with Peking, the missing part of the message was not allowed to be sent over the airwaves. So impressed were members of the Politburo at Meng Ru's dedication that, after his briefing to them, he was allowed to stay with them in their camp for as long as he wanted to: he was known by all and sundry as 'Emissary'.

As a dedicated communist 'cadre', he was entirely devoted to the cause, if only because he had never known any other. He was like millions of similar featureless functionaries throughout the 'workers' paradise', doomed to the treadmill-like monotony of constantly coping with trivia without ever having properly to exercise brain or talent, despite the grandiose eloquence of superiority such a system aired because he knew of no other nor could he imagine anything different.

However, during his slow journey through western Laos, Meng Ru gradually noticed a change in people's demeanour. He had no idea what people were talking about but they smiled, laughed and joked without looking over their shoulder to see if Big Brother was listening in so being reprimanded by heavy-handed authority. It was so different from the non-smiling, furtive glances when passing strangers he had grown up with, and so become used to. There seemed to be no worry as to the 'is he an enemy?', 'can I trust him?', 'will it count against me if I talk to him?' frame of mind installed into every citizen of a communist, nay authoritarian, country.

In Thailand it was more obvious than it was in western Laos. On one leg of his journey his main companion worked with the Americans and, rather spitefully, quoted what the American military were saying about the Thais: 'the nicest people money can buy who play at their work and work at their play.' True or not he didn't know but mulling over the difference, and trying it out himself with each lot of comrades who helped him on his way, he felt something deep inside him telling him that this was the way to live, not the way he had known till then. It only later struck him: *rather than trying to keep the people in line through fear I like the feel of how happy people seem when not bullied by the Party.*

One of the people he had grown friendly with in the MCP camp was the Politburo's non-voting member, one Comrade Ah Fat. There was just that 'something' about him that made the man from China keen to know him better by talking to him, however stilted it had to be to start with. What really intrigued him was when he overheard the Secretary General telling the comrade to go to Malaya, to the capital that he knew as Ka Lum Po, and carry out some job. Before he went, greatly daring, Meng Ru asked Ah Fat to go for a walk with him. 'Comrade, the birds and trees are different here from where I come from. Please teach me their names.' Totally innocuous if overheard!

'Yes, I'd like that,' said Ah Fat, sensing clever tradecraft as they walked away towards the wooded part of the camp. When no longer in earshot, the Emissary said, 'I overheard you being told to go to Ka Lum Po. What is it like there? I was told about it by my grandfather who was born there but, quite why I never discovered, he moved to Peking and never went back. That is why I was born in China.'

'Oh, how interesting,' Ah Fat answered in a neutral tone of voice, only showing peripheral interest and purposely not using the almost obligatory use of 'Comrade' when addressing him.

'I expect in your job when you go to the capital city of Malaya you have lots of sensitive contacts, one way and another … ' and the Emissary wistfully let his voice trail off.

Ah Fat noticed that the initial 'Comrade' also had not been uttered following his own non-use of the word, thereby deliberately ignoring a required courtesy. *Tradecraft still sharp!* he thought happily. After a judicious silence he said 'Well, yes, in my job I am bound to, "one way or another" to have contacts,' letting the emphasis sink in.

By this time Meng Ru had a burning ambition 'to change sides' but it seemed an almost impossible thing to do. It would have to be thought out oh so very carefully, indeed it was most unlikely it could ever happen. Once started only one false step would lead to perdition. Both men understood what, mentally at least, was as yet unsaid, only implied and both fully realised how necessary it was for both of them to take one cautious step at a time. For about five minutes they walked on without talking. Ah Fat waited for the Emissary to break the silence, wondering how not to let his own double life ever be thought to exist. His companion stopped, turned and faced Ah Fat, looking at him eyeball to eyeball. 'Is there anyone among those who you meet who knows how to get me back to my grandfather's Malayan standing and be ready to advise me how to set about it? Would it be possible for me to go to Ka Lum Po also as my grandfather was born there and I'd like to see the place.' *And leave no traces here* Ah Fat thought.

'You won't see it until you can pronounce it correctly' said Ah Fat judiciously, 'as well as learning some Cantonese, if only to understand it when spoken to in it so you can give a simple answer.'

'You mean my northern dialect, my *kwok yi*, not being understood by you southerners who speak *Hak Ka Wa* or *Kwang Tung Wa*?'

The Emissary grinned with eyes button bright. 'That is clever of you: yes. I can quickly get used to a southern pronunciation.'

'In Cantonese you'll be known as Mang Yu not as Meng Ru. Will you be ready to recognise your name then or will your ignorance give you away?'

The grin left the Emissary's face and he looked a bit disappointed. 'I do have a lot to learn, don't I?' he acknowledged, with a trace of sadness in his voice.

Ah Fat decided it was time to return to the main part of the camp so it was only a few days later, in fact the day before he himself left for KL, that there was a further opportunity for another talk. His companions were so suspicious of any degree of fraternity turning into friendship so keeping relations cool – deliberately.

'Tomorrow I go to KL. I will try and broach the subject. If, for planning purposes, the answer to your request is "yes, but only provided he can come here without any official help and without any family members" that will put a different and difficult complexion on it.' Ah Fat scratched at a tickle on his nose. 'Now the Federal government is no longer under the English but the Malayans and all matters of protocol are not as easy as they were for the type of problem you are raising.'

'Do you really mean "no"?' asked the Emissary, glumly.

Ah Fat hid his impatience. 'I said "for planning purposes, yes". Have you thought how you will get down there, unknown by your present hosts and without any paperwork?'

Meng Ru looked even more glum. 'Is there an answer?'

'Off the top of my head I'd say your only safe way of hoodwinking your hosts here is to pretend you are going back to China and I will arrange to take you to the Malay-Thai border and then you walk. But those are only first thoughts. Have you any immediate reply to being told the only way you'll be allowed to come is by walking, without any official documents?'

Needing an answer quicker than it seemed to come naturally, Ah Fat coughed and looked at his watch. That jolted Meng Ru into saying 'I would only come down if I can come with an English escort. Why?' He answered his own question. 'Only such a person can be a substitute for an official piece of paper in once-colonial Asia.'

The upshot was that when Ah Fat reached KL he went to visit his only pro-Government contact and old friend, CC Too, in HQ Malayan Police. One point he had for him was about Meng Ru. He explained the Communist Party emissary's background, his potential use if he came, that he wanted to come south 'but he would have to be escorted through the jungle in Betong to the border and then on south. Now there's a problem that not even you on your own can answer.'

CC Too agreed and said 'I can talk to the Commanding General who is still a British officer. The Malayan authorities are not yet, militarily, ready to take over the top job. This is something we just cannot waste.' He searched for a phone number and rang it, holding the phone away from his ear so that Ah Fat would hear what was said. The phone rang and an answer came, 'ADC to GOC.'

'Good afternoon,' answered CC Too. 'I am Mr Too speaking from Police HQ. Please be good enough to put me through to the General. Tell him it's too important to use the phone and I have a visitor who will be of the greatest interest to him. One he already knows but no more details till we meet up.'

The General himself spoke. 'Mr Too, as you only ever contact me with a cast-iron reason, come round as soon as you can. Give me your car number and I'll get my MA to warn the gate.'

'Thank you sir, I'll be with you in a jiffy' – he was proud of his English – and waited to tell the MA his vehicle's registration number.

Within half an hour there were four people in the GOC's office other than the General: CC Too, Ah Fat, the Director of Intelligence, Colonel James Mason, and the MA. Ah Fat was asked to give 'chapter and verse' about the possible communist defector, which he did in an exemplary fashion and Meng Ru's potential value was assessed as well as a probable Malaysian reaction. Colonel Mason asked questions gained from secret 'signals intelligence' and the answers Ah Fat gave confirmed both the Emissary's potential use and the veracity of the secret sources.

The upshot was that it most certainly did seem worth trying the get the Emissary to Malaya and that, as it could not be done without a Chinese speaking Briton, the choice of escort was a narrow one. After considerable discussion, Major Jason Rance was the best, nay only, man for the job.

The longer Meng Ru was in camp the more and more was he pumped by the Politburo to tell them about life in Peking, Party matters, discipline and what was done to traitors? This led to a talk on deep-cover double agents. That in turn led on to how the MCP was nearly destroyed during Japanese times and, in answer to a question by the Emissary, 'do you have any hidden agents working for the Government? I know I shouldn't really ask you this but if I am asked when I get back I can tell them one way or the other.'

Such subject matter was normally sacrosanct in being kept secret but under the pertaining circumstances, some details being told senior men in Peking in no way seemed heinous, so the question was answered openly by the Secretary General when he and Meng Ru were together. The Secretary General had warmed to his guest and hoping that, on the man's return to Peking, a good report about his activities would be of value for his own imminent move there, was unusually forthright. 'Yes, we have a British officer of Gurkhas. We don't know his real name so there is no harm in telling you he is known as Captain Jason Rance.'

'That is good news,' the Emissary said, neutrally.

'I'll let you into a secret,' said Chin Peng confidentially. 'It is a curious case indeed. A Chinese woman's British officer husband was to have joined us but never arrived although we know that he started on his long journey. One of our trusted men, you have met him, Comrade Ah Fat, was involved and indeed was lucky to escape some battle with his life. This woman thinks her man was killed by the man who calls himself Rance, so now she wants to kill him. Wants personally to kill him in revenge. She was going to join us but she, too, never arrived because her escorting group was ambushed on the way up to us. She returned to her base near Seremban ...'

'Excuse me, Comrade, where? These names mean nothing to me.'

'Oh, sorry, of course they don't. I'll say it again more slowly, Se-rem-ban.'

Meng Ru nodded. 'Sorry for the interruption,' he said, having made a mental note of the name.

'Yes, as far as we know she is in or near this Seremban place biding her time to kill him and get her revenge.'

'Comrade Secretary General, I thank you for telling me, with such openness, about this most strange case.' The Emissary shook his head then stifled a sneeze. 'Once I get back I won't mention it if you don't want me to. I do know that were such to happen to us neither person would be allowed to carry on as they are doing for much longer. I am glad I won't ever meet either of them.'

Down in KL the meeting that CC Too had arranged hung in the balance. On the one hand the GOC felt that missing such a rare opportunity to tap a root of knowledge would be negligence amounting to irresponsibility; yet if matters were to turn sour the political ramifications would cause such embarrassment that no one would profit.

'I met Major Rance and thoroughly approved of him,' the GOC said, 'the last time you, Mr Ah Fat, and he so skilfully managed to extract sensitive documents before the Baling peace talks of December 1955.'

'Yes, sir. It was a close-run affair and had Major Rance not taken Mr Too's small case with its secret bottom with him to give me, I'd not be here today.'

'As close-run as that, eh?'

Ah Fat nodded but added no more details.

The GOC well remembered how he had to ask for Rance by personally ringing his CO and, using veiled speech, spell out how urgently Jason's especial talents were needed. He never knew how bitterly the CO had taken the request so when yet another request was made in this case his CO left Rance with no doubt in his mind of his inner objection to going on yet another 'one-man cowboy show' he privately called it while telling the GOC 'of course I have no objection, sir.' He was never told any details except that it was of the greatest importance.

The operation to extract the emissary was eventually approved subject to it being undertaken by Major Rance – 'and a small party of Gurkhas' was unsaid but understood – moving secretly up to the Malay-Thai border. When the CO sent for Major Rance he almost blamed him for getting detailed although he knew that was obviously untrue: however, to show his wrath at the whole affair, he forbade Rance to take any Gurkhas with him. 'The GOC only asked for you, so you are the only person I am sending,'

His OC A Company said nothing but remained facing his front, looking over the CO's head.

'It'll be good not to have you around for a while. I have two large bones to pick with you so pin your ears back and listen. The first is that I was going to punish you for, when Duty Officer, not knowing the Guard Mounting drill properly. After you had ordered "withdraw khukris" from their scabbards and had inspected them you forgot the correct drill to put them back. Didn't you?'

'Yes, sir, I had an unfortunate lapse of memory.'

'I heard you had to ask the Guard Commander and only gave the correct order after he told you. I won't allow any Gurkhas to go with you as only you personally were asked for. I had planned for a month's extra Duty Officer for you. I'll keep it until you come back from leave. The second thing is that when you were at the Divisional Commander's cocktail party I gather he said to you "Rance, your only hope of promotion is another war" and you turned to him as said "that makes two of us." Can you deny that?'

Jason remembered the occasion: when that remark had been made to him he jokingly indicated his friend and said, "that makes two of us". He had not realised that the General had taken the remark as being address to him! Now he felt it better to say nothing.

'I have apologised on your behalf so apologise to me, *twice* over, and dismiss,' he spat out.

Jason said, 'Sorry, sir, sorry,' saluted and left the office, inwardly fuming. *I am expected to go on some operation about which I have no idea with no soldiers ...* A lesser man might well have said 'no' but Major Rance was not a 'lesser man'. The only way Jason could manage was to 'borrow' some of surrendered guerrillas with whom he had already worked, now under Moby's control. He went to Moby's house to arrange for them, unofficially, and it was during their meeting that Moby told him what Tay Wang Teik had found out about Fong Chui Wan's intention to kill him. As Jason had no idea who she was or what she looked like he shrugged it off. *Now had it been Siu Tse whom I rescued all those years ago it would have been a different story, wouldn't it? Nor would it have been about killing me, only killing time with me* and he chuckled softly.

Ah Fat returned to Betong and reported to the Secretary General on how he had managed to check that his special 'mole' in the KL Police HQ had not been affected by recent political events before contacting Meng Ru. Preparations for Meng Ru's move southwards were most carefully worked out in the greatest secrecy and to a strict timetable. This was to ensure that his move down to the international border coincided with Jason Rance's reaching it.

Jason went to HQ Malaya Command with his team and reported to Colonel James Mason for orders. The Colonel nearly didn't allow him to go with only surrendered guerrillas and no radio but, having quizzed Jason why he had no Gurkhas and expostulated angrily at Jason's evasive answers, eventually allowed him to go in a 'blood-be-on-your-own-head' tone of voice. Jason met up with the emissary on the Malay-Thai border and once safely on Malayan soil and happy to talk Chinese with an Englishman, whose name he then didn't know, one evening he told him what he'd learnt about a Captain Jason Rance being a deep-cover agents and a Chinese girl, named Fong Chui Wan, wanting to kill him.

Safely back in Seremban Jason handed his company over to another OC and departed for England on his six months' leave that came along every three years. He was badly in need of a rest as this last journey up to the Thai border without his Gurkhas and only with the surrendered guerrillas, had been an immense strain. Had he met active guerrillas on the way up he'd have to be ready to pretend he was a turncoat deserting to the MCP HQ in Thailand or, on his way down, a Russian spy. Meet the most senior Communist Terrorists still in Malaya he did and his superb knowledge of Chinese got them talking freely.

When he returned from leave there was a new CO, Lieutenant Colonel Adrian Forbes, the last one having been posted out at short notice. The new CO had been his platoon commander when he was a Gentleman Cadet at the Indian Military Academy in 1940. They fully understood one another so Major Rance was once more as he had always been: ready for anything and at peace with the person he had to live nearest for longest, himself.

9

Major Jason Rance was delighted to find himself posted back to his beloved A Company as indeed were the men of his company to have him back with them. 'He understands us better than the others do' was admitted in a number of small ways as Gurkhas seldom make outright comments about their superiors. He was overjoyed to see that his one-time batman-cum-gunman, Kulbahadur Limbu, was now a lance corporal who had been 'mentioned-in-despatches' in the Honours and Awards that had been announced while Jason was on leave – *that means a party to congratulate him*. His new man was Hemlal Rai, as sturdy as anyone, whom Jason had known since he was a recruit.

The CO's temporary absence meant it was a week after Jason's return before he was called to meet him. Jason knew him well: a round-faced, tall man, tough who wore tortoiseshell-framed glasses and walked with a forward, slightly stooping gait. Giving him a cracking salute he said, 'Colonel, I am delighted to see you and serve under you, having first met you when I was a Gentleman Cadet at the Indian Military Academy all those years ago.'

Colonel Adrian Forbes stood up and extended his hand. 'Glad to see you, Jason. I have been told everything "about it and about" before you went on leave and all I need to say is consider yourself back in Square One as though nothing untoward ever happened.' *And no mention of a month's extra Duty Officer!*

'Sir,' grinned Jason back at him, 'you have lightened my spirit. Thank you.'

He was told to sit down, and the CO took a piece of paper from the safe that was behind his desk. 'Here is a letter from the Director of Intelligence, Colonel James Mason, about what he picked up from your four SEP, Surrendered Enemy Personnel, our old friend Moby and one I have not met, CC Too, about your amazing journey to the Malay-Thai border and back again with the man from China when you met the chief daku, Ah Soo Chye and his two lieutenants, Tek Miu and Lo See.' The CO looked up at Jason. 'How did it feel?'

'Sir, it certainly was a new situation and one I had never dreamt would come my way but one thing I have learnt is that when taking on a new persona, you cannot act it; you have to be it. Had I shown any other facet at that encounter we would not be having this conversation today. As a matter of interest, two of the SEP, one-time ardent communists were, by then, sincerely normal citizens.' He did not add that the four called him *Fut Sum Pao*, the Buddha-hearted Leopard.[19]

The CO nodded his appreciation of what Jason had said. 'I totally agree.' He looked at the piece of paper in his hand. 'Meng Ru, the man you were escorting, spoke highly of you and related something you said to a,' he looked at the paper studiously,

---

19 See *Operation Red Tidings*.

'Temiar named Senagit who showed you a dead pig he had killed with his blowpipe dart. Apparently you took it from him and made it grunt but when you tried to give it back he jumped away. Correct?'

Jason nodded. 'I could have spoken to him, and the three guerrillas come to that, in Malay but being a Russian from China I wouldn't have known it and so would have given myself away. Doing that to Senagit's jungle pig was the only way that occurred to me of showing I was completely unconcerned about being in their company.'

Once more the Colonel nodded. 'That makes good sense,' he said. Then, after a short silence, 'how much else do you remember of your conversation with those men? You were there long enough to have had a good chance to pick up quite a lot the Int boys never hear about. Colonel James Mason up in HQ in KL would like you to scratch your head as much as it takes to record as much as you can remember what went on between you.'

'I have not forgotten it at all, sir, but if I give it a lot more thought I might find some nugget that I have temporarily mislaid were I to give chapter and verse as of now.'

'He feels that with your report there might be a chance of using you as a small squad, or a company, or the whole battalion on a follow-up operation, depending on what you can tell him.'

Another jungle operation when everything seems to have quietened down! The CO broke into his thoughts by saying, 'Suppose one of the guerrillas mentioned the east of the main Divide, over in Kelantan, not where there is an "open", shall I call it, population of Malays but where there are many aborigines,

Temiar is the name I see on the page here.'

Jason screwed up his face in concentration. 'Yes, I have heard that Temiar are not good explainers or general conversationalists, living such a remote life in such a restricted community. They are short, dark people with naturally curled, peppercorn hair, who frighten easily and often they will allude to something they take for granted which means nothing to a listener not used to their jargon. Hint and inference play a big part in their conversation. Also, at the time, what I call my "snail's eyes" were fully out, probing how to react, ready to withdraw at the first sign of giving myself away by an incautious reply, or even a stupid question.'

'Yes, I can quite see you had to keep all your wits about you. Almost like a tight-rope walker trying to smile when concentrating on not falling off.'

Jason laughed outright at that. 'I like it, I like it. I wish I had thought of it myself. I'll have to give a lot of thought. If I'd had my own men, great observers as they are, I could have gone over matters again. One of the conditions of getting my own guerrillas – they were my own from an operation I had captured them in and handed them over to Moby who went too far with them ... '

'Too far?'

'Yes, sir. After I had captured four of them and handed them over to the police he pretended he was going to shoot them dead if they didn't help him and roped me in to "save" them. He had them in a row, each bound to a stake and a police squad aiming their rifles at them when I arrived. I remonstrated, asking for mercy, in Malay so they could understand me. They never knew it was fake and were so thankful to my intervention that they became mine, so to speak.'

'Helped by your Chinese, of course.'

'Yes, one of the conditions of their helping me instead of Gurkhas was to be able to become complete civilians again, doing their own thing with no more obligations to anybody official. That means I can't check anything with them were I ever to want to.' He broke off with a tilt of his head. 'Of course, I could always ask to see Meng Ru to get confirmation of any point I needed. There just might be something, either seen on our way down as well as hinted at by my new-found friends.'

'Yes, I am sure the Director of Intelligence could arrange that somehow. I expect it would mean a journey to KL. No sweat there.'

Jason stood up, there being nothing else to talk about. 'I'll bring it in to you as soon as I have finished it.' He saluted and went back to his company lines where he asked the office runner, as a special favour, to get a large mug of tea for him.

During his leave, Jason had not told anyone about his unusual adventure, feeling it unwise on his part and unsafe as far as Meng Ru was concerned. He never forgot the warnings during the late war against 'careless talk' that were plastered everywhere in England. But that in no way prevented him from going over it in his mind's eye as he looked back on the whole business, even if he hadn't wanted to. There was something that he skimped over on the way down because he was worried about his escort not being physically up to the job and remembered saying to himself he'd think about it later but it had sipped his mind. He sipped his warm tea as he thought back. No, it wouldn't come.

Hemlal appeared in the open door bearing a plate with some fruit on it. He brought it over to Jason's table and put it down in front of him, smiling. 'Saheb, the Quartermaster guruji says you will like this fruit. I have peeled it for you. It may be a bit bitter but your sweet tea will put the taste in your mouth back sweet again.'

Jason thanked him, rather wishing he had not been disturbed, and Hemlal saluted and marched out. Jason looked at the fruit. A lime. Lime. Lime? Lime! *Got it!* he almost yelled. *Yes, that's it, limes!* On the way down Meng Ru had seen three limes lying under a tree and had stopped to pick them up. He had called out for Jason to slow down and Jason had looked around to find out why and seen his charge holding three limes in his hand. 'I like them and I can suck them when I get thirsty,' he had said. It had not occurred to Jason that sucking a lime to refresh one was much good, oranges, yes, but limes ... Jason had glanced at the tree under which the limes had lain before being picked up and now – *YES* – it was not a lime tree they were lying under. Another flash as he remembered seeing three old, rotting limes not far from where he had taken charge of Meng Ru but had taken no notice of them. Jason knew his trees and nowhere around the route they had used were there any limes so they had to have been placed there. *Why?* he asked himself. There was only one answer: a code to show when couriers had passed the place. Those old limes, what, four months old by the look of them as far as he could remember and those new ones? At least a week as there were no fresh tracks and there had been rain more than once. *Didn't I tell*

*those guerrillas there were no tracks and their answer was in that
case we'll go on up and the Temiar with us can hunt game which
will be a pleasant change from what we've been used to.*

If the courier with the latest lot of limes had been known
to Ah Soo Chye, surely he would have mentioned it when they
were talking about movement? Jason had flown up the river on
a recce the day before moving up on foot and Ah Soo Chye had
been worried about it being something to do with Security Force
movement in that area but with Jason's assurance of there being
no military traces, the guerrilla leader's worries vanished. He
had looked relieved. The odds, then, were that the couriers were
nothing to do with the guerrillas working in the west of the main
mountain range known as the Divide, running down the central
part of Malaya, but to the east, over in Kelantan. Jason had not
operated as far north as this before so could not tell if there were
any lime trees in that part of the jungle, but, even if there were,
it was unlikely they would be used for signalling purposes. No,
there had to be a grove of them somewhere near any courier
movement axis. Near to where the main settlement was, surely?
Ah Soo Chye had mentioned *t'o yan*, earth people, the aborigines,
during their talk and, to Jason's mind, that pointed to indigenous
groups over in the east of Malaya.

He now knew what to write in his report which he quickly
finished and gave it to his clerk to type out for him, three copies,
one for the file, one for the CO and one for Colonel James Mason.
He looked at his watch. 1600 hours. Time for basketball. He
went away to change. Tomorrow was soon enough for the report.
What was one day after a lapse of nearly seven months?

The Director of Intelligence found the report of more interest than he had thought he would. *How many mostly town-bred British soldiers would ever have even remotely thought of any fruit lying on the ground not having fallen from the tree above it?* He called for the relevant files about the aborigines, chiefly the Temiar people, but they were not much use as there was almost nothing about any group of them to the east of the Divide. *Blast it!* Those people were the personal bailiwick of the Department of Aborigines, a bunch of prickly, inward-looking anthropologists. He had come across the rather below-par Director, Norman Helbit, whose one aim in life seemed to be unpleasant to everyone not in his department, less, so it was rumoured, the Chinese contractor who 'ran' him. *No, no direct approach there.*

James Mason had a fruit farm in England that he proposed to develop when he was pensioned off from the army and the mention of limes interested him. *Is England too cold for them?* He had a pal in the Department of Agriculture and, on the spur of the moment, decided to ask him. He looked up the number and dialled it.

'Hullo, yes, who is that?' No name given.

'Peter, hold your breath, it's James here, James Mason.'

'What can I do for you, James? Make it short; I'm just off to a meeting.'

'Can you tell me, without too much difficulty, where there are lime groves in the north of the country?'

'James, it so happens that I can answer your query in one: where the Sungei Puian and the Sungei Blaur meet in Kelantan, near a ladang, the headman of which is one named Bongsu

Helwood. Must fly,' and the phone went dead.

So nothing he knows about in the area Rance visited. He again reached for his phone list of numbers and dialled Police HQ and asked to be put through to Mr CC Too.

He was just about to put his phone back in its cradle when an ebullient voice came over the line. 'Sorry to keep you waiting but here I am now. Can I help you, whoever you are?'

The Colonel smiled as he answered. 'Mr Too, I have never heard you when you don't seem to be in a happy mood. It is Colonel James Mason this end and I have a question for you I hope you can answer.'

'Tuan Colonel, all I can guarantee is to listen. If you are asking it over the phone on a clear line it can't be all that sensitive, can it? Let's hear it.'

'What can you tell me about the Temiar aborigines over in the east of the country without going into too much detail?'

'The salient point in a nut shell?'

'In or out of a nut shell but the salient point, please.'

'The chief headman of all the other headmen was appointed by the guerrillas now ensconced in Thailand and the government accepted him as being the senior Temiar headman in Kelantan. He is a dangerous and tricky man, named Bongsu Helwood, whose ladang is at the river junction of on the Sungei Puian and the Sungei Blaur, and he is a known friend of the few guerrillas who visit his ladang every three months. Pause for breath, Colonel.'

'Thank you. Couldn't be more succinct or more useful. I'll reward you somehow or other some other time.'

'Tuan Colonel, my pleasure,' and the conversation ended.

Colonel James Mason stared out of the window, lost in thought. *Two for the price of one. Does this need looking into? And if so, how?* He called for as large-scale map of the area as was in his stores and, after it had been given it, studied it carefully. He had it on good authority – sources never divulged – that the MCP still had hopes, however residual they might be – of making one last push on the capital in a vain hope of at long last gaining superiority over the elected government. *Stupid, forlorn, unachievable but that uncommon virtue of common sense is never a factor of Communist planning, is it?*

If Meng Ru was to be believed, he had picked up some surreptitious talk as he passed through North Vietnam of their aiding the MCP, outlandish though the thought was at first blush. There had even been a rumour that guerrillas had been seen wearing khaki-coloured uniform over in the Sungei Puian area.[20] Could it just be possible that arms were being secretly being brought down the coast from Vietnam and infiltrated across country in dribs and drabs to the Bongsu Helwood person for any onward transmission? Security Force's eyes over in Kelantan were not, he knew, as sharp as elsewhere over to the west of the Divide. Was there even a one percent chance that secret efforts were being made to reinforce the communist terrorists this way? Even half a percent possibility had to be looked into. He knew that a Federal Brigade was planning an operation to try and

---

20 Your author may have been responsible for this rumour because when operating in that area his Temiar contacts told him that the 'bad men Cheena' were wearing different coloured, khaki, uniform and carrying weapons they had not seen before.

convince the aboriginal population that the Government was on its side – 'hollow laugh! as there had never been any meeting of minds between the two peoples – but that was for the aboriginal population in the west of the country.

Colonel James Mason knew he had to get into a huddle with the GOC.

'Well, James, what have you now to disturb the unruffled surface of my innocent life?' The General was obviously in a good mood. The time of his departure was drawing to a close and he found working in an ever-increasingly xenophobic atmosphere dispiriting in the extreme.

'Sir, I am sure you will remember all too well and probably none too happily, the time when you asked the late CO 1/12 GR for Major Rance to help him we knew as the Emissary escape from Thailand … '

'James, don't,' the General interrupted. 'I remember it all too well. It caused more grey hairs in more heads than it was worth. Why bring the subject up now, over half a year after it is over and done with?'

Tread carefully the director told himself. 'Sir, we never got Major Rance's own report on the operation as he went on leave almost as soon as he had washed the twigs out of his ears. He has now come back and I took the liberty of asking the new CO to ask for a report. I have it and can give it to you to read. It is not long but has one interesting facet I'd like to bring your attention to.' So saying, he gave it to the General.

'Sit down, James, while I read it.'

A couple of minutes later the GOC put the file down and,

looking at his Director of Intelligence straight into his eyes, 'James, this is interesting as far as it goes. If it didn't go any farther you wouldn't have brought it to me. Out with it.'

The Colonel told the General all his thoughts, the more obvious and the more far-fetched. 'So, it is a question of squeezing not the lemon but the lime dry and if so, how and by whom?'

Silence ensued while the General thought that one out. 'The chance of your thoughts being correct is one of the most unlikely I've ever heard. I used the word "chance" so however improbable, there is still a chance and until we have disproved it there remains a tiny, tiny risk of there being something.' He sighed heavily, exuding a long breath as he shook his head. He looked at his watch. 'Not too late,' he said, almost to himself and called in his MA. 'Richard, pop round to my deputy's office and ask him if he'd mind coming in just for a moment to discuss something unusual.'

His deputy was a Malay Brigadier who was destined to take over the post of Director of Operations and be promoted to Major General when the present British Army man left.

A knock of the door and after a 'come in', in came the Malay officer. 'Tuan, I am sorry to have given you no notice of asking you over but this is something up your street and without your say-so, I don't want to give an opinion one way or the other.' He handed over the file, 'Please sit down and read this while I order a cup of tea for us all.'

The Brigadier read it and a frown creased his brow as he did. One way or another he was clearly unsettled by it. He gave the file back and said, 'That's something we could have done without.

Those fellows don't like us however well we try and treat them but don't let us dwell on history.' He was referring to the time when, so it was still rumoured, minor Malay royalty riding elephants, would go 'Sakai shooting'. 'I think it is worth our while to have a look at the place but it can't be a, what, full-scale military operation. Logistics for one reason probably could only support it at the expense of more important operations which need to be maintained at the level they are now.' He took a sip of his tea and put the cup down again. 'And yet ... and yet ... as the detective novels have it,' and he smiled as he showed off his knowledge. 'I'd like it looked at. I don't think it is a job for any British troops, even the special forces, as it is so sudden for them and not of a high enough priority to distract them from their already planned work. So Gurkhas are the answer and the man to lead them is this Major Rance who seems an unusual linguist. So yes, go ahead with minimum resources is my recommendation,'

'Thank you for your thoughts,' said the GOC. 'That means I'll give the operation a green light and see if Rance can hunt out any skulduggery. James, if we have not used the code word "Operation Hunter" already, use it. Oh yes, I think we must let Major Rance have some money from your secret fund.'

The Brigadier got up. 'Thank you for bringing me into this. I appreciate it. But one thing, General. It won't be easy to get as many one-dollar notes as will be needed and the bulk, let alone the weight, rather puts the kibosh on that. I suggest five-dollar notes.'

'Good point, Brigadier, thank you. So be it.'

The Malay officer politely asked permission to depart, was

given it, saluted and left the office.

By themselves once more, the General said, 'Okay, James, now nuts and bolts. I am unwilling to even mention this to the Department of Aborigines as their man, what's his name? Norman Helbit, yes, doesn't seem to like anything the military puts its hand to and would only make objections. It'll have to be Rance once more. By the way, do you know his full name?'

The Director of Intelligence shook his head. 'Never bothered to find out. Why do you ask?'

'I happen to know it, Jason Percival Vere Rance and it you shorten one of the names and make a pun out of the last three you get "Percy Vere Rance. Perseverance". Neat!'

James Mason gulped his amazement. 'I wonder if he knows that himself?'

'That's something you can ask him when you next meet him, if you don't forget. Now, back to logistics,' said the General. 'Say maximum one platoon or maybe a strong section only; go with enough rations to last, what, ten days? If possible I don't want any airdrops. Let's look at the wall map.' They went over to it and found out where the Sungeis Blaur and Puian met at Helwood's ladang. 'Their approach march has to be from the east via Gemala and the nearest railway station is Gua Musang. There is a road to Gemala and they might be able to hire local transport and, once there, make their way across country to Bongsu Helwood's ladang. There are two wide rivers to cross to reach the ladang: the Sungei Nenggiri and the Sungei Blaur, both flowing from the high mountain chain and there are no bridges. Both will take some effort to cross. There may be some native rafts or even flimsy boats otherwise swimming will be the only answer. Once the strongest swimmer has crossed with a rope and tied it to a tree that others will find crossing the rivers easier by clinging to the rope as they pull themselves across. I see the need for a porter party from the battalion rather than local porters, but if the former they can walk back to the railway station after they have dumped their loads.'

'One point. Does Major Perseverance have any Temiar language ability? If not, can we get a phrase book or word list from somewhere? Give him a couple of weeks for background knowledge and he can be fluent in a couple of days working in it, if what I know of him is correct.'

'Good idea, sir. Leave that to me. I am sure I can rustle some material up somehow.'

'Right. To finish off, let the start time be up to 1/12 GR, obviously telling us well before they set off. Send a secret order by mail to the battalion as soon as you can get the language material to send with it.'

The Director of Intelligence said, 'A good session, sir, and from your briefing I could see yourself looking at a much younger infantry officer.'

The General smiled and almost looked guilty.

The Director continued, 'I can't see any insurmountable drawbacks – I hope, although it won't be all that easy.' He saluted and went back to his office where once again he phoned CC Too.

'Can you call round to my office, Mr Too?'

'I'd rather not: these days people are getting touchy if they see me in your HQ. Tell me where you live and I'll pop round in my car after dark and take a drink off you.'

'Excellent. Before you come, can you get hold of any Temiar language notes and bring them with you?'

CC Too chuckled. 'Are you a mind reader, Colonel? It so happens I got my hands on one earlier on today. Tell me where you live and I'll bring it with me.'

And in the privacy of the Colonel's study, after a meal that satisfied them both when the Colonel's wife's presence prevented any 'shop' and over a glass of brandy, all that needed to be said about Operation Hunter was told Mr Too and such crumbs of knowledge he had were handed over with the Temiar language notes.

Five days later the CO of 1/12 GR sent his runner to bring Major Rance to his office. 'Jason, it seems that you have "cast your bread upon the military water", or should I have said "cast your limes" rather than bread to good effect' said the CO with the ghost of a grin, holding up a type-written, A4-sized paperback book, a quarter-inch-to-the-mile map and some sheaves of paper stapled together, with the security caveat of 'secret' stamped on each sheet.

Jason's eyes brightened but he said nothing as the CO continued, 'the Director of Intelligence has read more into your limes not under a lime tree than a mere courier marker.'

Jason nodded, leaning forward eagerly, wondering what else could be read into them.

'The Colonel says he has spoken to two departments, one of aborigines and the other of agriculture. It seems that the only place where limes are in profusion is over in the east of the country – pity I don't have a larger scale map of the area than the one I've been sent but before the morning's out I'll tell the IO to get a set of larger scale ones – in the ladang of one Bongsu Helwood. He is, I gather, an interesting character, fully favoured by the Communist hierarchy who made him head man over, not only in his own intimate area, but over the heads of other adjacent head men with their own areas. Not popular it would seem but all that the government could do was to agree with what was by then an accomplished fact.' The CO could see that Major Rance was almost bursting to ask questions, so he put up his hand and said, 'Wait, there's more to come.'

The CO turned to another page and said, 'Colonel Mason has gone as far as thinking that, so quiet is that area in comparison with the west that it might just be possible for junks coming from North Vietnam carrying dribs and drabs of military goodies the MRLA, albeit now a rump, could use in any push south to threaten KL. What do you think of that?'

Jason shook his head in disbelief. 'Such a travesty of military planning had never entered my head, sir. I can't see that happening, but it could just extend their hold over the territory of northern Malaya to the government's detriment and embarrassment.'

'As I see it, what you say is but a one percent possibility but even that pinprick were better not there. Neither of us have the intelligence background that those privileged to think such things have. Anyway, they want it looked at, by you. They think a ten-man squad will be the best-sized unit to take with you.'

Jason looked more puzzled than happy. 'Of course, sir, it is a great challenge to be detailed for such a job but what will be my actual task? Go around with metal detectors to see if such stuff is buried?'

'No, that has not been suggested.' The CO took the A4 paperwork and gave it to Jason. 'This is rudimentary Temiar those aborigines speak. The GOC has given you two weeks to learn enough before going over to the ladang and, using your Malay to start with, to try and pick up anything the aborigines say to one another in Temiar which they think you won't be able to understand. Oh yes, I am to let you have S$500 in S$5 bills to take with you to use how and when you need them.'

Before saying anything Jason riffled through it, looking at some of the words and mouthing them to himself. 'That's asking a lot, sir. Even if I were to learn every word here before I started on this operation I would not be sure of the correct pronunciation until I hear it spoken and even then ... ' He left his sentence hang in the air then continued ' ... of course I'll try my best but it's asking a lot of me so if I fail I hope Higher Authority will not be too disappointed.'

'Of course not, Jason. That will be the least of your worries as I see it. The soldiers are good at picking up languages, even if they mangle them. You can learn the Temiar with the men you detail and have communal classes. Something or other is bound to show itself even if it is completely negative, so that will be one less worry for our lords and masters. Now, to the way I see you going about this. HQ Malaya Command want to keep this quiet so to start with you'll only be deployed on the ladang for a maximum of two weeks. You will have to take a porter party with you so as not to need any airdrops. You will carry five days' rations so be self-contained in the approach march that will be from the southeast. You will go by train to Gua Musang station, which is nearest to the village of Gemala, which is the last village before hilly jungle takes over, and get there by bus. Then it's walking. Luckily there is a long ridgeline running from east to west for you to follow. There are what look like two difficult rivers to cross, the Sungei Nenggiri and the Sungei Blaur. The nearest bridge over the first one you meet will be miles from your line of approach so you will have to choose from being taken over by aboriginal raft – if there is one – or by swimming. Take a rope that a strong swimmer can go over with and tie it to a tree and then the weaker and non-swimmers can clutch hold of it and pull themselves over. You have practised river crossings before, that I know, wrapping up your kit in poncho capes et cetera.'

'Yes, provided the river is not too ferocious, that will be the answer, sir.'

'And if it is too ferocious?'

Jason grinned back his answer, 'We can't cross our bridges, or our rivers, till we reach them, so we're told. I can see me asking for an Auster air recce to tell us how far away a bridge is or ask for a heli lift over the river nearer to or into the ladang, wait until the water level drops or, sadly, abort.'

'Yes, I don't want any of my soldiers, you included Jason,' said with a wicked grin, 'drowned when the odds are against finding anything with lethal capabilities other than the aborigines' blowpipes' poisonous darts.'

Jason stood up. 'It rather reminds me of the definition of these new-fangled hovercrafts, sir, "a solution looking for a problem". If that is all, sir, I'll go away to my company lines and think about what you have told me. It will be a pity to spoil what might be enjoyable as well as useful by not thinking of every aspect of it. One thing, sir, will be of enormous help is asking for an aerial photo of the rivers taken from a direct line from Gemala to the ladang. It may be a lifesaver.' He saluted and left.

The CO looked at his retreating figure and thought *so far nothing has been beyond that man's capabilities, why should this be?* and turned to his office work, which included asking for an aerial photograph of the area Jason had asked for.

Bongsu Helwood's ladang comprised an area of about two acres. It was on the only flat ground within a great distance. Huts were made almost entirely of bamboo and built on stilts. Previously the only time limit of living in their rural settlement was to remain there until a death by illness, especially an unexpected one, rather than by, say, a person being killed by a tiger. That meant burning every shack and moving where the shaman, a most powerful person, had dreamt was the best place to move to. Then the jungle would be cut down but until that happened miserable temporary shelters were made. Cutting the jungle was done on a hillside with the lower trees being half cut on their upper sides until the top trees were reached then the whole line of trees would be fully cut. They fell onto the half-cut ones which were knocked over like a house of cards, with a tremendous noise, echoing many miles and shaking the ground. Having cleared the land vegetables, hill rice and tapioca were planted.

The Department of Aborigines tried to prevent, or at least limit, this slash-and-burn method of cultivation. Helwood's ladang was the prime one in the area and lesser ladangs had been 'closed down' and their dwellers moved to Helwood's. This was unpopular for the minor head men who resented being under one they had never had to be under hitherto. Each individual's area, known as a 'saka', was jealously kept as 'mine' and if 'foreigners' tried to hunt or fish in them, friction arose.

There was also a medical post where basic first aid, for cuts and burns as well as for basic skin diseases, could be given on the resident medical practitioner's recommendation. The three guerrilla leaders, Ah Soo Chye, Lo see and Tek Miu, used it when they visited, which was roughly once every three months, and always at the annual harvest time, *iwoh*. The medical practitioner was expressly forbidden to issue any medication without seeing the patient but Helwood would tell him the stuff was for his wife's private parts so she felt too embarrassed to show herself so he, as the husband, would take the medicines for her. 'Fine, but they always went to the guerrillas.'

Likewise, even when unexpected deaths occurred, Bongsu Helwood had been strictly forbidden to move so there was a graveyard at one end of the area. The Sungei Puian was on the west of the ladang and steps were dug into the twenty-foot bank for water to be fetched. The Sungei Blaur on the other side of the ladang was a bigger river, faster and fiercer. The two rivers met just south of the ladang.

All went barefooted. Most women went about bare-buff though some were covered. Men wore a loincloth but not much else. All of them carried a blowpipe, a long cylindrical pole with a mouth piece to shoot darts that were poisoned by the sap of the *ipoh* tree. There were no shotguns, much though all the men wanted to carry one.

Cattle were not kept so the only milk babies knew was their mother's and the only wheels they had ever seen was those of visiting helicopters that mainly brought medical stores when needed. Each time one came it was the centre of interest. No foreign troops had ever been stationed there, only a lacklustre group of quasi-military men, known by their Temiar name, *Senoi Praaq*, Fighting Men. Of course, military units were known about as the inhabitants would cross over the Divide into Perak and see soldiers, chiefly Gurkhas, on ladangs there or meet them patrolling.

But soldiers on my ladang? The thought horrified Bongsu Helwood. No. He thought of the visitors they liked, the *senoi cheena* or Chinese guerrillas, who themselves liked the Temiar women although only the guerrilla leaders were allowed to take a wife, none of the others being so accommodated. They were much more popular than were the Malays. The Chinese guerrillas also seemed to like their limes because they always took some away with them, never eating them. *I wonder why.*

Back in his company lines, Jason called all his Gurkha officers, the CSM, CQMS and senior NCOs, together. 'We have a different type of operation given to us. It is the GOC saheb's personal order that I must be in charge. Apparently he has heard about my Chinese and Malay language ability,' and he smiled disarmingly, not really wanting to have to say it – after all, everyone in the battalion knew that already – but the reason why 1/12 GR was chosen was needed to be given. 'The background is that before I went on leave I had to go to the Malay-Thai border, not with any of you as the then Commanding saheb refused any Gurkhas to go with me but with four daku who had surrendered and knew me.'

Yes, they all knew about that, but no one wanted to talk about it.

'On my way down with a man who had come from China, yes all the way with a message for the daku HQ because their radio was useless,' he laughed as he shook his head at the very idea and the men looked bewildered at such a rudimentary organisation. 'On the way down he saw three limes lying on the ground and picked them up to suck. Nothing unusual in that but they were not under a lime tree. Someone had put them there as a code the daku use to show when a courier came that way. A little later we met the three senior daku themselves. I got away with it by pretending to be a Russian coming from China to be a spy in Malaya and while we were chatting the daku told me about themselves.'

He could see intense interest in every face. 'Luckily I hoodwinked them sufficiently well not to be taken for a British officer. After I came back I was immediately sent on leave, as you all know. Only on my return has HQ Malaya Command asked for a report on what happened. I wrote it out, you probably saw me writing away as you passed my office,' – yes they had and had wondered what it was all about – 'and that report went to the General saheb. There he ordered some research about the limes and who was putting them down as a marker when the daku I spoke to didn't know anything about them.

'It has been thought that the place where the limes are, over in the east of the country, with the "bare ones"' – the way the Gurkhas described such people – 'could be the place where weapons are being brought in by small sea-going junks from, would you believe it, as far away as Vietnam? Our job is to go and see if that is true or not.'

He let that sink in before going on. 'We won't be moving for at least two weeks as I have been told to learn their language so I can talk to them in it or, using Malay, understand what they are saying in their language without them knowing I can understand it.'

The men shook their heads almost in unison at the thought of learning enough language from a book in that time to be any good.

'I have been told to take only ten men with me and once we have decided who they are, I intend to take some classes so that they can recognise some words. But you all have enough Malay to be able to talk to them, or rather to those who know a little. I have a map here and I'll show you where we are going.'

He opened out the map he had taken from the CO. 'This is too small to see enough details but roughly we will go by rail to Gua Musang,' he pointed it out, 'then on to Gemala by bus then walk to here, crossing two large rivers that flow down from the mountain.' He showed them where he thought Helwood's ladang was, on the river junction of the Puian and Blaur. 'I have been told to take a porter party made up of the strongest men in the company, with ten days' rations who will return, either to Gemala and buy more rations or go come back here if an airdrop is allowed. Now I can't say which.

'We should all be back well within the month but, as we all know so well, life is full of surprises,' and he laughed delightfully, and the others joined in. 'Captain saheb,' he addressed his Company Second-in-Command, 'please make up a team of ten men who are the best Malay speakers and can swim. This is because we must cross two rivers to reach our objective and there are no bridges so we will have to swim across. The best swimmer will take a rope over first, tie it to a tree and we others will use the rope for safety. I'll get a strong rope from the QM, like when my then batman Kulbahadur had to go down the crevice to see if the crashed plane was there.'

He looked around and asked if there were any questions. One was what they were expected to do once they had reached where the bare ones lived?

'I asked the Commanding saheb that same question and he had no answer except to try and find out if the head man, Bongsu Helwood, who is a friend of the daku who are reported to visit him four times a year, is involved in any arms for the daku. But quite how we do it I really have no idea. Maybe once we are the ladang one of my men will find out. This is one of the most unusual operations we have been sent on and it looks as though we'll be learning on the job. If they have a secret we must try and find out what it is.'

It was only much later that Jason learnt that the Temiar language has no word for 'secret'.

10

At the end of two weeks trying to learn Temiar, Jason's head was in a whirl with new words, the pronunciation of which he had to guess – that there were some sounds found in neither English nor Malay would only be found out later. The language had nothing in common with Malay or Chinese so there was nothing to 'hang' a word on. After the first two lessons it became clear that his Gurkhas would not benefit by any further instruction. He managed to get them all some swimming practice, first in swimming trunks only, then fully clothed and lastly with their equipment and weapon wrapped up in a waterproof 'poncho' cape. It was found that the normal one poncho each man carried was not big enough so each man had an extra one issued him. The signallers – both the one to go with Jason's group and the one with the porter party – had to buy some large sheets of polythene in the local bazaar to ensure their sets were kept dry. They also fired their rifles, no automatics, on the range. Each man took fifty rounds and the signallers twelve rounds of pistol .38 ammo.

Jason minutely studied the aerial photo that had been delivered within ten days of asking for it. His gaze was chiefly concentrated on the two rivers he had to cross to get to the ladang area. The nearer was far wider than the second one but both looked fast-flowing from the amount of white froth visible as the water rushed over rocks that stood proud of the surface. Based on the scale of the photo he worked out the length of the rope needed to cross the river to be asked for from the QM. The river nearer the ladang area was only as half as wide as the first one but its source was higher up so, even without the impetus of any rain, the current could be as fierce as the broader one.

The amount of rations to be taken was a problem; in the end it was decided that both teams would carry five days' worth for themselves and the porter party of seven men an extra five days' worth for Jason's men. One unknown was whether there would be any extra five days' rations on the ladang and another unknown could such a heavy load be swum over the two rivers, even using a rope?

Jason also arranged for the men to draw a month's pay as he had permission for money to be spent where necessary provided a receipt was produced for later claiming the amount spent.

The IO rang Gemas station to book thirty seats, Jason plus his ten, the seven porters and space for their large loads. The office provided return rail warrants that the station master at both ends of their journey would submit for repayment. The group went in one of the battalion's lorries, seen off by the CO and GM.

The journey to Gua Musang went without a hitch but once they had unloaded their kit onto the station platform then taken it outside, transport became a problem. No local bus had room for all of them and their loads at once, and Jason did not want to split his party. He went back into the station to see the elderly Tamil station master – he had never found either a Malay or Chinese in that job.

'Tuan Station Master,' he said in English, 'I have a problem. I need to take my soldiers to Gemala but we are too many to fit into a bus because of the other passengers. How do you advise me to get there? I don't want to walk – it is too far and too hot!'

'In no way is that possible,' said the Tamil, with a wry smile. 'I have a friend who has a lorry. I'll ring him up and if he is not busy he will take you there. As he is my friend and you have asked me so kindly, all you will need to pay is the cost of the diesel, full tank to full tank.'

'That is most generous. Thank you, indeed.'

The Station Master lifted his phone and talked away in Tamil, which Jason did not understand. The phone was put down and: 'You are in luck's way, Tuan. It is empty and the driver will come over here in the next twenty minutes or so.'

Jason got up to go but the Station Master stopped him. 'I have not talked to such a polite Englishman for so long, let's have a cup of tea together.'

Jason blithely thanked the Tamil man and, once it had been brought in, they had a lively chat about nothing in particular until the lorry driver came to report to the Station Master. Jason was introduced and, saying farewell to the Station Master – 'perhaps we'll meet on our way back' – he and the driver went outside. The lorry was parked in the forecourt and the men were ordered to load up and get in the back. 'I have a full tank,' the driver said. 'I will fill up in Gemala and you will pay.'

The journey to Gemala was not long and once there the driver filled up at the only place there was and Jason paid for it. Kit was unloaded in the centre of the village. 'May I have your phone number just in case I need you again?' Jason asked the driver and made a note of it before the lorry went back to Gua Musang.

Such a military gathering in Gemala was obviously unheard of and their presence caused much excitement.

'Gather round. We are all a bit hot and sticky. What I think is the best idea is to stay here the night in a hotel, pay the money from your own pockets, get a receipt and put in a claim when we get back. It will also save one meal of our rations. We can also have a refreshing wash and start off early tomorrow morning.'

Yes, that seemed a sensible idea. 'Guruji,' Jason said, 'Come with me to what looks like a hotel and we'll try and fix us up.'

In fact it was the only hotel in the village, run by an elderly Chinese man with his wife. The manager had a limp but Jason refrained from commenting on it. His use of Chinese so pleased them that, despite there not being enough rooms or beds, arrangements were made for them to sleep on what beds there were and the others to sleep on the floor – at half price! Jason ordered a rice meal for them all before sending the NCO back for the soldiers. It was all a bit squashed but no camp had to be made and someone else cooked the food so life was easy enough. Weapons were stacked and a toggle rope was bound around them. They were put in the corner of one room and one man's sleeping space was on the floor athwart them with another rope tied loosely around the pile and his wrist so not needing a sentry all night.

One of the signallers asked Jason if a sitrep was to be sent.

Jason did not like the idea of rigging up the radio in the middle of the village so shook his head. 'If this hotel has a phone I'll send a message saying "In Gemala, NTR" which should be enough. There was no telephone in the hotel, which rather vexed Jason. His thoughts were interrupted by the local Malay policeman who approached him. 'Tabek, Tuan' and continuing in Malay asked him who the soldiers were and could he help?

'Encik, we are Gurkhas and have been told to visit the *orang asli* in the high mountains and need to spend the night before we start our long walk. If you like I'll come to the Police Station and explain it to the Tuan Inspector.'

The policeman smiled. 'Tuan, a man speaking our Malay language so fluently can only be a good man. There's no need for you to bother. I'll report it myself.'

Jason smiled back. 'Encik, may I come back to the Police Station with you and use your phone? I come from far-off Seremban and need to tell them I've arrived safely. This hotel has no phone.'

He saw a frown cross the young policeman's face. 'I'll pay for the call, so there's no worry.'

The policeman's face looked happier. 'Let's go there together,' said Jason and off they went. The Inspector said that there was always a delay on that line but if Jason gave him the phone number, the message to be delivered, and five dollars for the call, he'd look after it.

'Yes, that is most kind, Encik. Thank you.' Once again Jason blessed his ability to speak Malay like a native. He bowed his head in thanks and went back to the hotel to have a cool shower before his meal.

Next morning it was raining heavily when they woke up. 'I don't think it's sensible to move off in the wet,' Jason told them. 'We all know how rain mightily increases the weight of packs. What are your thoughts of staying here for our morning meal and then moving off? If it is still raining then we'll just have to cover our loads with our poncho capes.'

The men discussed the proposal among themselves but before they had come to a conclusion Jason said, 'No, I have just had an idea. Hemé and I will go on a recce to find out the best path to take so not waste time looking for it when fully loaded.'

That made good sense to them all. 'Before Hemlal and I go out I'll tell the manager what time we want our meal. I'll say ready for half past eight and ask him if he knows the best way out of the town and if there are any tracks towards the first river we have to cross.'

Jason sought out the hotel manager to ask him about tracks. Luckily it turned out that before running the hotel he was a logger so knew the countryside all the way up to the Sungei Nenggiri. 'It's quite a way but there is a logging track that takes you up to the ridge line that leads to the first big river. I'll give you someone to lead you out and show you. I'd go with you but I badly hurt my leg when I did not get out of the way of a falling tree so had to leave logging and try to make a living by running this hotel. Not the same,' he said ruefully.

Jason commiserated then asked him about the country both sides of the Sungei Nenggiri. 'I am going to the junction of the

Sungei Blaur and the Sungei Puian to visit the ladang there.'

The manager shut his eyes to picture the best track to take. 'You have chosen a difficult place to try to get to. Nobody I know has gone there. The ridgeline is easy to follow and the track you'll be shown will take you to where the high ground starts. On the other side there are steep hills but we never logged there so I can't tell you about them.'

'Are there any bridges?' Jason asked hopefully.

'No, none on the way you are going. The nearest bridge is so far to the south that it would add at least two days to your journey.'

'And the river? Wide? Fast? Any fords?'

'Wide and fast and no fords,' a flat answer, given with conviction.

'How would you cross it if you had to?'

The elderly man looked at his questioner with steady eyes. 'I couldn't have.'

'I had planned for one man to swim across with a rope round his waist and once on the far bank tie the end round a tree on the bank and we others use the rope to help us across. We will have securely wrapped our kit, our belongings, up to keep them dry.'

That made the manager think for some moments as he tried to visualise what he had been told about. 'Such a method had not occurred to me,' was his only comment.

'I have another question: what sort of people are the *t'o yan* and can they be of any use to me?'

'They are a race apart who try to keep away from everyone else. Once they see your weapons they will disappear into the jungle and can keep away from you for as long as you are in their area.'

Having no more questions to ask Jason went back to join the others to tell them of what he had learnt.

After their meal, the rain having eased off, Jason went to collect their guide and they moved off shortly after ten o'clock.

The journey through the jungle was slow, muddy and leech-ridden. They stopped every hour to rest, inspect their loads and take leeches off various parts of their body. By four o'clock they were all tired and they were still some way from the river. 'When we reach a suitable place for a camp we'll stop for the night,' Jason called out. There was a collective sigh of relief.

Luckily one was close by, and loads were taken off till the morrow, with some men looking after the cooking and others construction overnight shelters. Men slept side by side the length of a stretched poncho cape and, less than Jason's singleton, four were got ready. While work was being done, Jason wrote out a sitrep to send to Battalion HQ and, detailing his one-time batman, Lance Corporal Kulbahadur Limbu as escort, said they would go forward to see if they could find the river. 'If Sunray wants to speak to me, let the senior man answer if I'm not back. Also, once the meal is ready, eat it even if we're not back by then. Food is better eaten fresh and hot,' he said with the familiar twinkle in his eye.

The two men set off, Jason's eye on the compass and Kulé's on the track. After a quick walk of about twenty minutes they came to the Sungei Nenggiri – and stared at it in dismay. The earlier rain, heavier upriver than in Gemala, had swollen the waters into an ugly brown torrent about twenty yards wide. Anyone stepping into it would immediately be swept downriver and, with the noise of a waterfall just out of sight round a bend, probably drowned.

'What do you think of that, Kulé? Doesn't look at all safe, does it?'

'No, Saheb, as it is I think we will have to stay on the near bank until that heavy rain has flowed away. If it doesn't rain tonight it may be possible to cross it tomorrow.'

'Let's hope so. Let's do this. I'll walk upriver for,' looking at his watch, 'fifteen minutes and you downriver for the same time and back here. Have you a watch?'

He hadn't but 'I am a good judge of time, don't worry' and off they set.

On their return neither had found anywhere easier to cross than where they were but Kulé's sharp eyes had spotted what looked like a raft under some tall trees on the opposite bank. 'See there, Sabeb, surely that is a bamboo raft that these people use?'

He pointed it out with his chin and Jason, screwing up his eyes, dimly made out what indeed could be a raft. 'What that tells us is that the Temiar cross the river here so that here is the safest and easiest crossing place. Whether they know how to swim we don't know but for us, once the rope man has managed to cross and tie the rope to a tree we can use the raft for ferrying the stores over as well as making it easier for the weaker swimmers.'

The two men got back to their temporary camp at last light to find a meal ready for them, the others having already eaten. By the light of the cooking fire, not easily lit because of the paucity of dry kindling, Jason told the men what they had discovered and gave orders for the next day, move off after a brew, get to the river and depending on whether it had rained towards the source of the river during the night, either wait until it was crossable or cross it straightaway. The raft should be of great help.

The senior man of the porter party asked Jason if his group was to stay this side of the river for five days then give the remainder of the rations when Jason's group came back to fetch them.

'A good point to raise, Guruji. So much depends on the unknown as ever, doesn't it? I mean if, after five days, the river is higher than it is now, we'll go hungry on the far bank yet if there is no rain between now and then, ferrying the loads over the river will be easier then than now. We'll wait until we get to the river tomorrow morning, already loaded.'

Sentries detailed they passed the night with no trouble.

Next morning at the river's edge Jason saw that the water level had indeed dropped significantly, with the main surge by now well downriver. 'Good, it is safe for all of us to cross over.' The best swimmer by far was Sergeant Chijbahadur Tamang, the battalion champion, as well as being in charge of the porter party. 'Rance saheb, I'll strip to vest and underpants, tie the rope round my waist and swim over. I will try and reach the other side as near as I can to a strong tree by that raft.' He looked at the current. 'I will have to start at least fifty yards upriver as the current will be too strong to cross straight over. Once I have reached the far bank and knotted the rope you must bring this end back here for a straight crossing.'

Jason ordered the rope to be taken out of the load it had been packed in and, with three men, all armed, went with Sergeant Chijbahadur along the bank to where he felt was the best place to start his journey. They found a flat space on the edge of the river and two men, rifle slung over their shoulder, found a suitable tree and tied it, knotting it as had been practised in Seremban. The Sergeant had brought all his kit with him and he took out the poncho from his big pack, into which he put the clothes he had just taken off before making a watertight bundle. 'Once I am over I may have to come back for it or it may be possible to put it on the raft.'

'Guruji, from here over to where you think you'll end up, is the rope long enough?'

'I'll try it as I think so. If not, help me back and we will have to join toggle ropes to it to make it the correct length.' He left unsaid any other alternative.

Taking off his clothes, socks and jungle boots, he tied the rope round his body, went to the water's edge, put his hands in the water, stood up, joined his hands together and put them on his forehead before plunging into the water. Everyone watched as he made his way almost straight to start with then, once he was in mid-river, was suddenly taken almost straight down with the current. With a supreme effort he broke free and reached the far bank, almost level with the raft. Spontaneous clapping broke out, which the Sergeant heard and he waved back. He disappeared into the trees and, unseen from the near bank, found a suitable one, undid himself and tied the rope around it, making sure the knot was close-fist tight.

The rope on the near bank was untied and carried back to opposite the raft and re-tied to another tree. 'What now?' called out Jason.

'I'll come back over with the raft and collect my kit,' the Sergeant shouted back. It was a skilful task coming back with the raft as Chijbahadur had to pull the rope with both hands and control the raft with his feet. 'Saheb, we need to fix a toggle rope onto the raft and hold it as we cross over so that it won't slip away downriver.'

The raft was made of hollow bamboos with space for up to four men each load. However, before the first load was taken across Jason made three men sit on it in the shallows and a fourth, holding the toggle rope, see how easy it was to pull the raft over. Everyone watched with much attention and saw that the raft was at least one foot under water with so many men in it so the drag on the puller with the toggle rope would be too much.

Everybody looked at Jason for an answer. 'The best solution is this. Before the ladang group strip and go over the river one by one holding on to the rope, they will ensure they have six days' rations. Heavy, I know, but that should give us six days' rations on the ladang and that, I hope, will be enough to find out what is needed for HQ. The porter party will come over later in their own time, with one or two men, whichever Sergeant Chijbahadur decides. He can take his time over that for even if my group needs ropes for the second river, from the air photo I have seen, our toggle ropes will cross it if we find a narrow place or if we can't swim. The quicker we can get on our way the better for all concerned.'

Taking matters slowly it was nearly one o'clock by the time the last of Jason's team was across, having stocked up before crossing, and got ready to move off.

He called over Sergeant Chijbahadur and said, 'You may be able to supplement your rations by firing on animals, yes, you have my permission for that, but anything you get that way will not replace a day's rations. I can't tell if I will be back, sometime within the week I hope. Only then will I be able to give you any firmer orders.'

'Hunchha, Saheb, leave this end entirely to me. You have enough worries of your own without bothering about me.'

With an extra day's rations Jason's group was too heavily loaded for anything but plod, plod, plod through thickening jungle, slowed by constantly having to untangle themselves from creepers. There were no tracks to follow but Jason could see from his map that the best way to the next big river to cross, the Sungei Blaur, was along the east-west high ground that acted as a watershed for streams flowing north and south. That and Jason's compass bearing of 153 degrees, a difficult angle with no thick lines to look at as he moved forward, were their aids to their destination. They moved so quietly they came across wild animals, chiefly monkeys but also deer and porcupines. They saw tracks of tiger twice and a family of boars. There were no traces of any human movement.

They left the high ground and, once they were much lower,

heard the noise of a river. 'That must be the Sungei Blaur,' said Jason. 'I know it's late and we're tired, but I think it's worth our reaching it today and so save time tomorrow.'

Yes, that seemed sensible, and in less than a quarter of an hour were on the banks of a fast-flowing river, significantly narrower than the Nenggiri but fast enough to pose its own problem for crossing. A stream of pure water was nearby, which was a boon, saving them from having to boil possibly polluted river water. That night each member of the group, Jason included, did an hour's 'stag', just in case of inquisitive wild animals. Jason remembered how earlier on in the year he had taken his A Company to Kelantan and the only Communist activity had been much farther to the south of Kelantan than they were now, near the Perak state border.[21]

There were no animal interruptions during the night, much to everyone's relief, inquisitive elephants being the main menace. In the daylight they could easily see another river gushing out from the far bank and the map confirmed Jason's suspicion that it was the Sungei Puian. Jason wrote out a sitrep for the signaller to send out when he had rigged up his aerial and said, 'Homé and Kulé, while the others are preparing our morning meal let's first go upriver to see what it's like and try and choose our crossing place.' Twenty minutes later when they were about to turn back they saw movement on the far bank, about a hundred yards farther on. The three men stopped and stayed still. A party of about twenty Temiar, men armed with blowpipes, women with

---

21 See *Operation Tipping Point*.

back baskets, some with infants in them, young children and dogs came to the river's edge. With the children on their father's back and, holding on to one another, they crossed over the river, the water only coming up to their knees although the current tugged them strongly.

'How lucky we came just at this moment otherwise we might not have realised that here is a ford, possibly the only one,' breathed Jason although there was no need for such furtiveness as the Temiar were, by then, moving along the near bank away from them. 'Back we go,' Jason said happily, now much less worried than he had been. Jason's next problem was whether to move up to the ladang with everybody, fully kitted, or to take half his small group, weaponless and not wearing any equipment for a recce to see what reaction there was from their unexpected and surprise presence. After their meal he told his ten men the alternatives. 'I feel it more propitious to make haste slowly, and the less frightening we first appear the less likely are the "bare ones" to run away.

'Saheb,' Kulbahadur looked around him at the others. 'We don't know if they will understand our attempts to speak Temiar and even if they do if might be the wrong word. We must appear peaceful and happy, in no way a danger. I have an idea how to do that. May I mention it, please?'

'But of course, you must tell us. Let's have it,' Jason said and the others joined in with 'yes, yes'.

'Leave our rifles behind us. Sing a song as we slowly move towards the first group of people we see, you in the middle and all holding hands.'

Everyone roared with laughter at such an idea. 'If we are holding hands we can't be in any danger of hurting them,' continued the Gurkha, resolutely sticking to his idea.

'Kulé, that makes good sense. Well done. What song does anyone suggest?'

'Saheb, you seem to know more songs than we do so what is your choice?'

'How about this one. There are three verses but we may not need them all. Shall I sing them for you?'

'Yes, yes,' his men chorused so Jason obliged by singing, in Nepali:

'I was due back from leave on the twenty-first

It is now the twenty-fourth

And because of you my darling

The Colonel will be wrath.'

The next verse had to be sung as by a woman, so Jason changed his voice to a shrill falsetto with:

'Take me if you're going to

When you go tomorrow

If you don't I'll kill myself

To everybody's sorrow.'

Then back to a man's voice for the last verse:

'My darling says she'll go with me

Whatever else I urge.

But I have not brought a family pass

They're bound to start a purge.'

The effect was almost electric in the men's appreciation, one man laughing until he had tears in his eyes. 'Saheb, we'll sing that and then once we are in touch with the "bare ones" we'll leave off and you have your say.'

By mid-morning Jason and his five men were over the ford and in the jungle below the ladang. Up they went, Kulbahadur leading, following the traces of those who had been seen crossing the river earlier on. Jason thought back to the Temiar notes he had studied and tried to remember typical Temiar names, Pedik, Mudak, Alang, Duwin, Kalusa came to mind, but at the bottom of that page of notes it said that names, as such, were seldom used, nicknames or relationships being the norm. *Much too soon for anything like that.*

At the top they found themselves on a plateau of ground bereft of trees except round the edges for about two acres. They were, in fact, standing on the communal graveyard although there were no signs to show that's what it was. About a hundred yards in front of them they could see some shacks. There were some children playing around them, some men sitting and talking together, and women hovering nearby.

'Now, from here, hold hands and start singing,' said Jason. They linked up and walking slowly, broke into song. They whole group in their front stopped talking and stood up, with even the women looking at them, the youngsters clutching their knees.

Twenty yards from the shacks Jason stopped singing and told the others to. They let go of each other's hands and watched as their OC moved a couple of paces ahead. '*Meed, hup.*' Happy heart. '*Tata.*' Old man, a term of deep respect. *Tongoq?*' Headman?

'Pedik, Mudak, Alang, Duwin, Kalusa.' Their faces showed they understood so the pronunciation must have been good enough.

It had the desired effect. Nobody ran away – they were too intrigued to be frightened. No European who had visited them had spoken basic Temiar.

Jason put both his hands on his head, covering his mouth as he did, and made his head squeak. His men smiled, each correctly guessing what was their OC's next trick. Jason took his hands, fists closed, off his head, put the right one out in front of him and made it say what he had already said. The Temiars looking on jumped back in horror. He then did the same with his left hand and said what had been said in Malay. The Gurkhas couldn't help laughing so Jason laughed with them and the Temiar men returned where they had been.

Jason then asked, again in easy Temiar, 'Where is Bongsu Helwood?'

'Gone hunting. Back later. Not now.' That was almost too much for Jason to fully understand so he repeated his question. The look on the men's faces showed that he was not with them.

Jason thanked them and said to his men, 'Let's walk around the ladang before we go back. These people will have to discuss us before we can return here.'

A Malay voice sounded at his elbow, 'Tabek, Tuan, who are you?'

Jason, looking around to see who was so unexpectedly speaking Malay to him, told him, rank, name and unit. 'And, Encik, who are you, please?'

'I am the medical practitioner and look after our little surgery, which is over there,' indicating where with an outstretched arm. 'Please come and see it.'

The Gurkhas followed him to his small dispensary and were invited to sit down on what chairs there were or on a bench,

'Why are you here, Tuan? This is most unexpected. Is anything wrong?' he asked in Malay.

Answering likewise, Jason said 'No, Encik, nothing is wrong. I was told to come here with a few of my Gurkha soldiers and see what Headman Bongsu Helwood was doing as some of the government do not believe in the reports they get from Mr Norman Helbit about various matters, timber concessions, hunting and I don't know what else.'

A look of loathing masked the medical practitioner's face and he said nothing for a few moments. 'Mr Helbit is my boss. I can say nothing about him but only about Bongsu Helwood.'

'Tell me about him.'

'He is his own man, Tuan. From what I believe he tells Mr Helbit, it is highly coloured and probably wrong. He also is on very friendly terms with the Chinese men.'

'Encik, wait a moment please while I translate that to my soldiers,' which he quickly did. He then took a gamble, knowing that a polite Malay, any Malay come to that, would never initiate a conversation about their superior. 'In your view and only between you and me, never to be repeated anywhere, would Mr Helbit be involved in illicit gun-running from the communists in Vietnam into this ladang and communist couriers take the arms over the Divide to the west of the country to be used against the Malayan government?'

The Malay's eyes were open wide in horror and disbelief. 'Tuan, I know much about the Director, how it is said he is involved with Chinese contractors to his own benefit but none of us talk about him and his dealings that are, are ... ' and his voice trailed off as he tried to think what best not to say but still say what most of his underlings suspected.

I'll knock the nail out of sight Jason thought. 'So, there is no chance, Encik, of Headman Bongsu Helwood playing a lone hand in a dirty game of arms brought by junks from Vietnam?'

'No, no, no. Never, never, never. And if you were not an *orang puteh*, a white Englishman, I'd think you had been drinking and lost your mind.'

'Encik, thank you for the compliment. As a long-service soldier I know when I see sincerity and I thank you for your kind words. So there's no worry *at all* about what I say?'

The Malay put his right hand on his heart then shook Jason's hand. 'I swear on the holy *Qur'an* there is no worry – nor can there ever be,' he added as an afterthought. 'All I do know for a fact is when the Chinese guerrillas come he gives them the limes they ask for, why I have no idea, but arms, weapons ... No, Tuan, no.'

'I have three days before I need return. Do you think it wise if I bring my whole team, eleven with me, up here for that time? Camp in a space at the edge over there,' and he pointed it out, 'where there are a few trees?'

'Yes, straight down from there is the Sungei Puian. It is good water to drink.'

Jason thanked him again sincerely and said, 'After I have told my Gurkhas what you have told me, and they won't talk about it.'

Back at the bottom of the hill the camp Jason gathered his men around him and told them just what he had found out. 'Now we are here, let's relax for a couple of days up in the ladang and our loads will be nice and light for our return journey. The Malay doctor has pointed out a suitable place for us. While you are packing up I'll send a message to Battalion HQ and if you're ready before me, Lance Corporal Kulbahadur will take you up and show you where to make another night stop.' He told the signaller to contact base and ask for Sunray or Acorn 'on set'. In no time at all Jason was called to the set.

It was the CO who asked for news, 'Send sitrep, over.'

'1. Sunray on set. I have had a long talk on the ladang with a Malay Starlight and in veiled speech approached the subject. Roger so far, over.'

'1. Heavy interference, say again, over.'

'1. Wilco,' and very slowly he described what had happened. He finished off: 'I am convinced that there is Nan Tare Roger in the original report. Temiar Sunray is away hunting. I plan to stay here another three days before starting back and try to confirm negative info. Over.'

'1. Read you strength 4. I read back … '

To which Jason replied, 'Correct over.'

'1, Roger. Out.'

Still on the set, Jason asked the rear link in Seremban to send that message to his other group at the next opening schedule then the signaller packed up and the two men moved up to the ladang to join their comrades. Kulbahadur Limbu had gone down a steep bank to see if the Sungei Puian was a good place to bathe. It was, there was a shallow crossing place to the far bank and about twenty paces downstream a steep waterfall. He returned as Jason and the signaller reached them and told Jason about it being a good place for a wash.

At about half past two Jason said, 'Let's go down to the small river for a wash and launder our clothes. The best will be in three groups of three men each: me, Kulé, Hemé and the signaller in the first batch, then three and three in turn. Just in case of any daku we'll take our loaded rifles.'[stet[to stand on it his mess tin 'cup' as a water sluicer, his fresh clothes on the bank WHERE his rifle was. He lay down in the water, soaked himself then mounted the stone to soap himself. Suddenly there was a manic cackle at which everybody turned to see where it had come from, and Jason found himself pushed hard so he overbalanced into the water. Taken by surprise, he managed to get out of the water about four paces before the waterfall would have taken him down.

'What was that?' he called out.

'As there was nobody seen and no shots it was not the daku but the "bare ones" showing their displeasure,' shouted one man back. 'Nothing to worry about.'

Jason had not finished washing properly so, soap in hand, climbed onto the flat stone once more. He was halfway through his ablutions when the manic cackle was repeated and once more Jason was pushed into the water. This time he only just managed to struggle out before being washed over the rim of the waterfall. He came back to where he had been washing, dried and, saying nothing, went back up to their camp. The others quickly joined him, unable to explain the affair but putting it down to Temiar hostility.[22]

That evening after their meal Jason gathered his men around him and said that, as he had always felt 'in the heart of my heart' there was nothing to find out because the premise of there being anything from overseas was wrong to start with. 'So, we have seen part of the world we had not seen before.' He shrugged and grinned. The men shook their heads at what he said. *The Sarkar is sometimes hard to understand. Who are we to argue with it?* 'We'll dry our washed clothes and wander around the ladang and see if the "bare ones" are really against us. If they are we'll go back, if not we'll stay our full time as, who knows, we may make it easier for any other Gurkhas who come this way.'

Next morning, Jason and Hemlal, leaving their weapons with a sentry, moved over to the Temiars' dwellings, rough bamboo hovels, basic and dirty with recalcitrant and fearful adults but, as everywhere else, inquisitive children. On Jason's and Hemé's approach those outside the hovels looked at them. Jason saw a stick on the ground in front of him and, bringing it up to his mouth, blew into it like a flute, making a whistling yodel as he did. He took his hand away and, looking at the children, wobbled his eyebrows, grinning foolishly as he did. Cautiously the little

---

22 When your author visited Helwood's ladang in 1963 with nine Gurkhas, he went to the Sungei Puian to wash after returning, with one Temiar, from visiting a platoon of his downriver. He thought the first round of manic laughter could not be a guerrilla because of no shooting. After another attempt at being drowned in the waterfall he returned to his own men and accused them of 'having fun'. Never. He was told by the Temiar, with whom he was fluent, that by making a camp anywhere near the graveyard, what else could he expect?

ones came up to him and he handed his stick to the tallest of them. 'Like this,' he said in Temiar and 'played' it again before giving it to the kid.

Greatly daring he puffed but made no noise except laughing at his efforts.

More 'funny faces' and more children's laughter, with the adults coming closer. A wild idea came to him and he sang 'Suzanna's a funny old man' with different farmyard animal noises in each verse. That was the key to acceptance and Jason was nearly hoarse by the time he was allowed to go back to his own place.

Next morning the medical practitioner visited him and said that the parents of the children had asked him to ask Jason to live with them because the children liked him so much. Jason looked embarrassed and said he did not normally make such a fool of himself but if that had made the Temiar friendlily disposed to Gurkhas, 'What else matters, Encik?'

They left as planned and, more lightly loaded, reached their other group easily in the day, having first warned them on the radio that they were coming.

Just as Jason's group reached the Sungei Nenggiri, ably guided by the irreplaceable Kulé, they heard shots from the area of the other group's camp. They seemed to be aimed away from them and for a moment Jason's men wondered if a group of daku, not knowing about the Gurkhas on the far side of the river, had wandered into them but there was no 'crack and thump' of any fire being returned. 'Not enemy,' said one of the soldiers.

'If not, why open fire?' asked another.

'That was no accidental discharge,' said a third.

'They'll be too busy to help us cross so let's wait until matters calm down,' said Jason.

Almost impatiently they waited, having taken all-round positions, the signaller with his set in the middle. Then they heard shouting and the man with the sharpest ears said, 'They are asking in what direction it went.'

'What went?' each man asked himself, eager to find out what the firing was about.

Jason stood up. 'All of you stand round me and shout "ayo"' he ordered. They shouted 'ayo', come, shorthand for 'we have come back to join you, answer us but don't shoot.'

Soon they saw someone on the far bank, looking their way. He disappeared and almost immediately came back with Sergeant Chijbahadur.

'Can we come over safely?' called out Jason, 'Now that the firing has stopped.'

'Yes, we had to fire to frighten a tigress with her cub. She was about to jump on a man who had his back to her so we fired to frighten her off. She has gone but left her little cub behind. What shall we do with her?'

'Bind it and keep a close watch so that the mother doesn't come back and attack you again. Now, please give us a man to help us over on the raft which I see is tied up your side.'

Once all were over and back as one group Jason went over to see the tiger cub. He loved animals and lifted her up tenderly, making little grunting noises at her. She nuzzled his hand and tried to suck a finger. 'She wants milk. Guruji, get some and feed her. Let's take her back to the battalion and have her as a mascot. A Company will be the most famous company of all.'

They decided to stay the night where they were and move early on the morrow. That evening Jason's sitrep was 'Mission accomplished. Nan Tare Roger suggested threat. Leaving Nenggiri tomorrow for Gemala. ETA Gua Musang day figures 1 6, I say again figures 1 6 of this month. Request you book seats for return rail journey. Out.'

He decided not to mention the new mascot which he carried himself in one of his pouches and put two spare jungle boot laces round her neck when being exercised.

They got to Gemas without any difficulty and were met by battalion transport for the last part of their journey back to Seremban. In A Company lines the office runner was made 'tiger master' and the CQMS made a small cage and fenced area for his charge.

The CO called for Jason the day after his return. 'Jason, before you write your report, just tell me everything. By everything I mean everything, no matter how insignificant it might seem to you. I must ensure that what we send in your report would make it seem likely that the rumours were true: essential no ruffled feathers' and he chuckled softly.

As Jason had rehearsed it all several times it came quite easily and the CO, a good listener, only asked a few questions at the end. He summed up by saying, 'Operation Wild Goose Chase would have been a suitable name, I think.'

'Yes, sir, but all was not lost. The Temiar are happy with Gurkhas even though I "broke them in" using antics with their children that any of my superior officers would have condemned me for,' and he gave an embarrassed giggle. 'But, sir, on the serious side, it does seem that a new Director of Aborigines would be a good idea.'

'Leave that to me. From what you say that is overdue. And, by the way, what name have you given the wee thing?'

'Dharké, the striped one.'[23]

---

23 A tiger cub captured by B Company of the author's battalion, 1/7 GR, was named Nepti, the flat-nosed one. She was looked after by a soldier who, after the cub was sent to London Zoo, cut his name from the army 'because serving in the army without a tiger to look after is no fun.'

11

By this time, Fong Heng Lit, the son of Fong Chui Wan, was a strong ten-year old. He hated his nickname, Yeh Gwai Tsai, wild little devil, that had been given him by neighbouring children when he reacted pugnaciously as they laughed and jeered at him for his mixed-race features. At first he was too young to understand it. 'Mother, mother,' he would cry, 'why do they call me that? Why do they tease me?'

His mother was unsure of how to reply. She told him not to worry and if he did not react it would stop. But it did not stop and as he grew older the bullying became worse. Being the only one so treated made him realise that he was, somehow, different from other boys. One day coming back from school a gang of them jumped on him and beat him up, severely bruising him but, luckily, breaking no bones. His mother was shocked when he came home, eyes swollen, bleeding and dusty.

'I hate them, I hate them,' he shrilled, on the verge of tears. 'You are the only one who treats me well. You are the only person I love. I hate all the others, every one of them.'

'Who did it?' his mother asked.

Various names were blurted out. Gulping resentment, he grasped her arms and, gritting his teeth, said, 'I have my own knife. I'll stab anyone who won't leave me alone.'

His mother looked at him in surprise. 'You will not stab anyone, my son.'

But could commit such an act? Siu Tse had never forgotten her grudge against the man she wanted to kill, even though she had been told to help him as he was a deep-cover agent who might want help. *That makes no difference at all. Even though I have not heard about him for a few years, somehow I feel in my bones my time will come …* and malevolence came over her features.

Her own mother came in from outside at that moment, interrupting Siu Tse's thoughts of the future, bringing her back to the present, abruptly. The old lady was crabbed and had a bad heart, so, ever since her husband's death, had insisted that her daughter live with her in her old place, not far from Sepang village at the jungle edge. That was soon after her daughter had returned from somewhere she never knew and she had had to look after the baby all by herself. Fong Chui Wan, as the mother preferred her to be known, had again helped Dow Gai Ngaan Yeh Yeh, Boss-eyed Grandfather, until she had made enough money to send her son to the local school when he was old enough to start lessons. That was when the bullying started.

'What are you two up to sitting down doing nothing, my grandson in tatters and you looking glum? You're no use to me are you? Disappearing somewhere you won't tell me about, leaving me with the brat, wasting my strength on something I was too old for. If only your father were alive he'd have beaten some sense into your brainless body, you, you … ' and, spittle oozing from her mouth, no more words were spoken as she keeled over, unconscious.

Her daughter and grandson stared at the prostrate body that twitched a couple of times before, with a rattle that signified her last breath, she died.

Siu Tse, eyes glazed with horror, stared at the corpse that lay on the mud floor. 'Quick, run for a sheet to cover your Por Por,' she said and, as her son obeyed her, she went next door where she knew there were two strong men to help her.

Luckily she knew where the nearest telephone was and she also knew the phone number of her uncle, Deng Bing Yi, who still worked in his garage in Seremban. As Fong Heng Lit was too young to do anything other than be guided by an elder relative, one as close as possible, she called him, told him what had happened. 'As you are the nearest male relative, please come and help.'

Within the appropriate time all necessary obsequies had been observed, the body taken to the nearest burial place and the police notified. Strangely Siu Tse felt liberated now she no longer had any duties for her mother to carry out: now it was time to leave the area, move into Seremban and start a new life both for her and her son. But exactly what?

When Jason was sent to escort the emissary from the Malay-Thai border he had taken four SEPs with him. They were so impressed with the way he could look fierce and also be kind they had given him the nickname *Fut Sum Pao*, the Buddha-hearted Leopard. Having successfully carried out their task, all four were allowed to slip out of sight and become normal citizens of Malaya. Two of them, Goh Ah Wah and Kwek Leng Ming, had decided to stay together and, after trying their hands at one job or another, finally settled on opening a new restaurant in the north-western edge of Seremban, on the Nilai road. They named it New Hope Restaurant and it had cubicles that could be shut off by curtains as well as having an open area with tables and chairs. Siu Tse knew nothing about it.

After her mother's obsequies, her uncle had asked his niece what she intended to do. 'I have not properly thought anything out, Uncle,' she said, 'but one thing is certain sure, I will not stay anywhere near Sepang ever again. If you can put me and my son up for a short time ... '

'How long?' her uncle interpolated.

' ... until I find a job in the cooking line, either in a restaurant or somebody's private house. I'd like a restaurant as my son has been taking lessons in carving meat with a butcher so he also could work there when he's older if I can't earn enough money to send him to school. It will take a little time to get to know my bearings, the only area I know is around the Yam Yam and that has changed since I worked there.'

'There'll be no cooking there,' her uncle sniffed. 'People never went there to eat only to ... ' and looked away without finishing his sentence.

They looked at each other, both wondering how living together would work out. 'I can cook for you, Uncle, while I look for a place where I can earn enough money to keep my son to a good school. I had thought of King George V's which teaches in English and a good knowledge of English will get him a good job when he is older.'

'That's true enough but that school is expensive. Too expensive for you.'

She pouted. 'If I can get him a good enough knowledge of English I might ask for a scholarship for him.'

The conversation was boring Deng Bing Yi so he merely said, 'Let me know when you are coming' and left to go back to his garage.

Yap Cheng Wu had long retired as manager of the Yam Yam and his one-time taxi-girl didn't know where he was. That was a shame as he had a wealth of knowledge and might have advised her about her enemy. But, yes, the barman, Kwek Leng Joo. *Maybe he could help me.* In her time working as a taxi-girl in the nightclub, Siu Tse had known about a phone in the manager's office but not downstairs in the bar.

In the garage office was a telephone directory and she looked up the Yam Yam. There it was – *so the place is still open.* Copying each digit on the dial, it rang. A voice she did not recognise answered, saying 'Manager speaking.'

'Excuse me, sir, I am Fong Chui Wan who once worked there. Can I speak to Kwek Leng Joo please?'

'No. He no longer works here. Take this number down and you'll contact him at home if he's in.' She took the number down as it was slowly dictated to her and, thanking her helper, she rang off. Excited, she rang the new number and recognised the voice that answered her.

'Oh Uncle Kwek Leng Joo, this is me, Siu Tse, calling you for help. May I come round and see you, please, oh please?'

Kwek thought she was unduly excited and possibly not quite herself so felt it were better if he could contact her where she was. 'Little Sister, where are you? I can get on my motor scooter and come round and see you.'

She told him and within half an hour he drew up outside her uncle's house. They greeted one another as effusively as Chinese etiquette allowed and shyly she invited him in. Her aunt accepted the guest and offered him a glass of tea, which he gladly accepted, before leaving them alone. They asked after each other, politely probing before the one-time barman asked about her problem.

Siu Tse had bottled everything inside herself ever since she had become pregnant through her Alan, so once she had started her story she went on, and on, and on. 'If I can't trust you, who can I?' she asked in desperation as she ended off.

Kwek Leng Joo stayed silent for a while as he digested what she had said and what he had guessed she had not said. 'Let me see if I have got you correctly. You want to have this Captain Jason Rance killed although you have been told to work with him.'

He looked at her and saw he was correct. 'But if you are known to have killed a man like that you are afraid that the long ears of the Party and the police will be angry and you and your son will suffer. Is that it?' That was good guesswork as she had never analysed either possibility before.

'This is my advice. Find out if he really is a deep-cover agent. If he is, have another long think about what to do; if he is not, do it,' *and be damned* he finished off silently.

She considered that for a while before she answered. 'Who do you know who can tell me if he is a deep-cover agent or not?'

'That is the nub of the problem, isn't it?'

Yes, of course it was.

'I think that there are two people you can ask for a background, for anything suspicious, any clue given to one who is already committed, as I am. I have never met him, wouldn't recognise him were I to see him so I'm no help there.'

'And the two?' she asked, a little breathlessly.

'The two men who have been fresh-ration contractors to the battalion, to 1/12 Gurkha Rifles.'

'Two? I only know of one, Goh Ah Hok.'

'No, there is a second one who worked as the contractor for some time when Goh was away on some family task, I think it was.'

'And who is this second man?'

'A man named Chow Hoong Biu. I don't know where he is but I can find out and let you know. I believe you already know Goh Ah Hok,' he said as he got up to leave.

A bleak 'yes' was all she said until outside the house she thanked him as he got on his motor scooter to go back home.

How to get hold of Chow Hoong Biu was her next problem. From what was known of him but not generally spoken about, was that he was a secret comrade. *He might just be of use if I can get my uncle to help me contact him.* That evening after her uncle had come back from his garage, washed and had his meal he asked her if she was satisfied with what she had learnt earlier on in the day.

'Yes, Uncle, I have the name of one man who can help me.'

'And he is?'

'Chow Hoong Biu, a one-time … ' and she creased her brow as she tried to remember 'fresh-ration contractor of 1/12 GR' but her uncle filled in her mental gap and told her. A shadow crossed his face as he remembered trying to fix the party when the car Captain Rance was to travel in was to be sabotaged but … *No good worrying about that now, it was so long ago.* 'He's a friend of mine and I owe him a drink so stick around while I get him over.' He was as good as his word and after a short talk on the telephone, 'Next Saturday evening he'll be around here.'

Goh Ah Wah and Kwek Leng's catering business was soon flourishing and, like anyone running such a concern where people of a certain type relax and talk about that which is of interest, open or quietly, quietly, subversive. One day someone they had met during the time they were SEPs was Tay Wang Teik, the ebullient Teochew who, they knew, worked in the same place as the man who, they grimly remembered, had threatened to shoot them if they did not come over to his side but were rescued on the brink of being shot by the man they later knew as *Fut Sum Pao*, the Buddha-hearted Leopard – they would never know it had been arranged.

Tay Wang Teik waved at them, winked, ordered two beers and went to sit in a corner booth. Both Goh Ah Wah and Kwek Leng Ming guessed that the Teochew's contact would be someone he didn't want others to know who he had get in touch with so, when a man they did not recognise entered, they paid him no attention. A little later they heard a shout – 'two more beers but cold, cold, cold' – and a giggle. Goh ordered one of his waiters to open two bottles, put them on a tray, take them over to the booth 'but don't open the curtains. Just say "outside" and wait for them to be taken off your tray.'

The visitor was, in fact, only the one-time manager of the Yam Yam nightclub who had been approached by the man who had taken Little Sister on the first leg of an unsuccessful journey to the Central Committee. He had rung up the Teochew, Tay Wang Teik, in the morning and, very softly, said 'remember when I told you I only answered a "me" question from you if one day I asked a "me" question in return?'

'Yes. Is it still valid?'

'Very much so. I want to meet you somewhere safe at half past three this afternoon. Where do you suggest?'

Tay knew one place he could trust, New Hope Restaurant on the Nilai road and told his caller.

Once inside and drinking their beer, Yap said, 'Don't forget, my Teochew friend, "ears only".'

'Understood. Don't worry.'

Twenty minutes later the curtains were pushed back, a man quickly emerged and 'melted' out of the restaurant. The Teochew looked out of the booth and beckoned Goh Ah Wah to join him. 'Bring two more beers,' he counselled.

'Not while I am on duty,' Goh answered and, with one bottle of beer, shortly followed by a cup of coffee, joined Tay Wang Teik in his booth. Putting his mouth close to Goh's ear. Tay softly asked, 'Did you see my guest?'

'Only out of the corner of my eye but I didn't recognise him.'

'I know you well enough to keep an "ears only" matter a secret, don't I?'

'Yes, so long as it doesn't mean any more active service for me.'

'No, it doesn't. Listen well and at the end I'll tell you what I want from you. He is the one-time manager of the Yam Yam nightclub and came to me for advice as he has been approached by Comrade Lin Soong who you may not know: he took Fong Chui Wan as far as he was authorised to meet a courier from the Central Committee.' He was too absorbed in his story to note a start of interest in Goh. 'But the escort from the north was killed or captured and so Fong was brought back. She had hidden in a tree and the story she gave Lin Soong who rescued her was that when hiding in a tree she thought she heard, or dreamt she heard, part of a Chinese song sung to children to make them sleep. She let on that she had only heard it once before, as a girl of, what, sixteen or so, when she was rescued from being raped by a good-looking Englishman who spoke perfect Chinese to her. She doesn't know his name.'

'Strange,' commented his listener. 'I wonder who and where such a man can be, after such a long time.'

'Someone you know well.'

So surprised was Goh that he spilt the coffee from the cup he was raising to his mouth. 'Can't think who you can mean. Tell me.'

Tay's eyes sparkled mischievously. 'The man you know as *Fut Sum Pao*, the Buddha-hearted Leopard! Now, how's that for a coincidence?'

'Tay Wang Teik, you have completely stunned me.'

'Shall I stun you further?'

'Since you've started you might as well finish.'

'Well, Lin Soong asked me if I knew that your *Fut Sum Pao* was a deep-cover Communist.'

Goh shook his head in disbelief *or is it dismay?* he asked himself. 'I would never have thought that and, quite frankly, I don't believe it can be true.'

'Why not?'

'Kwek Leng Ming, me and two others went with him to the Malay-Thai border to bring out a man named, named ... ' and he put his head in his hands as he tried to remember it. 'We called him the emissary; names, names ... got it. Meng Ru. He certainly had to pretend he was a Russian Communist come to cause trouble in newly independent Malaya. Other than that, no. I won't go along with it.'

'It gets more complicated than that,' continued Tay, with a wry grin. 'The girl who was to have been taken to the Central Committee was put in pod by an officer of Captain Rance's battalion. He was on his way when he was killed and the girl thinks your Buddha-hearted Leopard is guilty of killing him. No proof, mind you. Nothing was ever published or announced: you were part of the MRLA then so would not have heard about it in all likelihood.'

'No, nothing about that reached us. This is new to me.'

'Anyway, the girl has made a vow to kill Rance even though Lin Soong told me she was told to cuddle up to him for military information to be used by the comrades.'

Goh, dumbfounded, remained silent.

'I don't believe that for one moment,' added Tay. 'But how did this rumour start? What do the English say? Something about never having smoke if there's no fire. *Was* there a fire?'

'Was there a fire?' echoed Goh, listlessly.

'The reason I have told you this is because you four men put your lives entirely in his hands and he put *his* in *yours*. There is seldom such a strong bond anywhere. You earned your freedom by what you did, didn't you?'

'Yes, there is no doubt about that. I am a free man and delighting in it.'

'Lin Soong risked his life to get me to get Rance's latest news from the girl he called Little Sister. But before I try to contact her to get a message to him – apparently someone up in Betong is asking questions – I want you to ask Major Rance to swear an unbreakable oath, one way or another, which is the truth.'

'How?' Goh asked bleakly.

'I'll contact him, tell him you've started a business and would like him to come and see how you are managing. Can do?'

A slow smile spread over Goh's face. 'Willingly.'

On Jason's return from his visit to Bongsu Helwood's ladang he had to write a report for Higher Authority as well as catching up with the backlog of office work. Remembering his CO's strictures about it being tactful if not evasive, it needed much thought. He was in the middle of it when his telephone rang. He looked up at his clerk and told him to answer it, 'so I am not interrupted.'

The clerk answered it. 'Yes, sir. The OC is here. I'll tell him who is asking for him,' and putting his hand over the mouthpiece, 'from outside, Sabeb. The name sounded like Tay something.'

Jason thanked him as he took the phone. 'Who wants me to fight with the electric speech,' he said in Chinese and was momentarily stuck by the answer, 'Tay Wang Teik this end.' Then it clicked who the caller was and waited for him to continue.

'Pity you don't speak Teochew,' the voice said, 'so it'll have to be in *Kwang Tung Wa* instead.'

'Let's hear what you have to say, *Sinsaang.*'

'Your old friends Goh Ah Wah and Kwek Leng Ming have opened a restaurant, New Hope Restaurant, on the Nilai road, and would welcome you to join them in a celebratory drink.'

'When?'

'At your convenience. How about you picking me up from the Police Station this evening at five o'clock. Your car. Can do?'

And sacrifice my basketball! 'Can do. See you then. I'm busy so I'll ring off.'

It was a happy reunion and the two restaurant owners embraced Jason most effusively, almost to his embarrassment. Telling a couple of their helpers to look after any customers, the two took Jason and Tay to their private quarters at the back. Tay looked at Goh and, with a wink Jason did not see, said, 'I've only time for one beer before I have to go back.'

When he had gone and Jason, not really liking beer had reverted to coffee, Goh looked at him. 'How much so you trust us, *Sinsaang*?'

'As much as you trusted me when I had no soldiers. Why?'

'We have been contacted by someone who has told us that you are a deep-cover Communist ... '

Jason interrupted him with a roar of laughter. 'Oh no, not that rubbish. I won't ask you who told you that rot because I'd want to go and smash him and that would do no one any good, would it.'

'But we just can't believe it, otherwise the nickname we had for you, *Fut Sum Pao*, the Buddha-hearted Leopard, would never have come into our minds. Is there a background to the rumour that you can tell us?'

'Since you ask I'll let you know. Listen to this ... ' and out came the story of what had happened in Calcutta with the Soviet MGB, without mentioned Ah Fat's name, and why. 'So the plan of how best to find out about Soviet influence was successful and I can only suppose that the man I had with me had to say what he did to his own people to keep his own security.'

'You don't want us to talk about it?'

'Better not. Tell you what, to keep you satisfied I'll give you a cast-iron promise it is all nonsense.' And he sought in his mind just what would convince them. '*Yat yin gau ding*', the word is as solid as nine tripods. His listeners knew that he referred to the heavy and solid tripod-shaped brass cooking utensil used in ancient China.

'And we in turn will keep a rock-solid promise, '*Yat nok cheen kam*', a promise is worth one thousand in gold. 'If we were asked we'd get your permission first.'

Jason's mind was still on the alert after that surprise invitation by Tay. 'If it was Tay Wang Teik asking you to clear my name elsewhere I'll be delighted you tell him and then forget the whole subject. I don't believe he would have done that without knowing my real background. I won't be angry if my guess is correct.'

His two guests, with a quick glance at one another, said 'you have guessed correctly.' They solemnly shook hands on it and a wonderfully cooked meal was brought in, which they ate in silence. 'That was delicious. Thank you, thank you,' said Jason, 'the first thanks for the meal and the second for coming clean about that other matter.' And he put his hand over his mouth as a sign of silence.

'You were lucky in the meal,' Kwek Leng Ming said. 'Our chief cook will soon no longer be with us as she is about to be married. Finding good cooks is not easy,' he added chattily. 'We are looking for someone else.'

Major Rance would never know that their choice would be so potentially dangerous for him.

And like an oil slick on water, news that one named Major Jason Rance, correctly or incorrectly pronounced, spread to the various people who had a vestige of interest in the matter. It started off by the Deputy Head of Special Branch, Seremban, talking to the one-time manager of the Yam Yam nightclub, who passed it to his one-time barman who somehow or other never divulged their source, got the message to one named Lin Soong. He, in turn, waited for the next courier from the Central Committee, who arrived when Lin had taken his gunmen squad to visit the next-door equivalent, so, when he returned and was told about it, wrongly presumed that the message had been sent by hand of the returning courier. It died a natural death and had it ever been reported to the Central Committee, either it would not have believed or 'Comrade' Ah Fat would have had to furnish a difficult explanation for what he had previously announced as true.

After Yap Cheng Wu had been told he got on to Little Sister's uncle, Deng Bing Yi, and told him that his niece might be interested in the news – 'Yes, it's true enough. I can vouch for it – it can't make much difference to her now but I did tell her if I found out anything I'd let her know.'

Deng Bing Yi thanked him. 'She has probably forgotten all about it by now. In any case, it is such a long time ago she'll have other things to concern her.' Indeed she had but when her uncle told her the news, Siu Tse's reaction showed him she still had that person very much in mind.

Her uncle had a copy of the daily Chinese-language newspaper in his hand. 'Have you seen this?' he asked her, pointing to one of the small advertisements.

No, she hadn't. He didn't think she had for he had yet to see her take an interest in reading newspapers. *After all, she is not all that literate, is she?*

'What is it?' she asked.

'Oh, the new restaurant on the Nilai road, New Hope Restaurant is its name, is advertising for a live-in cook. You are a good cook and it could be just what you are looking for' – *and get you away from her with your ever-angry son, now practising throwing that knife of his* – 'and the wages look attractive.'

She was immediately interested. 'If I can register my son in a nearby school, that will be even better.'

'I'll take you round there.' He looked at his watch. 'Let's go now. Bring his mark sheet and, if the restaurant owners like you, we can pass the nearest school and get him enrolled.'

The boy was not back from school so the two of them got into the car and drove around to New Hope Restaurant. Her uncle introduced her and told the joint-owners his niece was a good cook and he was sure she could manage even a complicated menu.

They talked about it for a few minutes and it was arranged that she should come for a week's trial, only after which would a decision be made.

'Where is the nearest school for her ten-year-old son, Fong Heng Lit?'

It was, apparently, a little way back towards Seremban. They stopped outside it and, with the lad's papers, went to see the headmaster.

'His mark sheet looks promising but there are no vacancies till the next term, which won't be … ' and he looked at a calendar on the wall, 'for another two months. Bring him around then.'

Once in the car again, she said to her uncle, 'Uncle, if I get the job and if he promises to behave, will you keep him with you until he can enter the new school?'

Her uncle agreed, though not sounding particularly keen about it.

After a week the name of Fong Chui Wan was registered as the cook of New Hope Restaurant.

1/12 GR had been based in Seremban since 1948 and Higher Formation decided it was now time to change over with 2/6 GR, based in Kluang. The official thinking was, apparently, that after a while units became stale so needed a change. Those on the ground did not agree. Certainly men were constantly changing over for one reason or another but there remained a hard core of people who had come to know the ground well enough to know how the local daku moved and worked so by their very presence patrolling and ambushing could keep their offensive activity to a minimum. To lose that precious knowledge and start all over again was damaging to morale and efficiency; in this case both battalions were in two minds about the move.

When the local Europeans learnt about the move they decided to organise a farewell party for the battalion's British officers. A meeting was held one Saturday evening at the local club and it was decided that New Hope Restaurant would be a suitable venue: not too 'stuffy' and known for its good food.

At New Hope Restaurant, Goh Ah Wa summoned his new cook to his office and told her that next Friday evening he wanted a special meal cooked for a special party, given by the local European community. 'One of the guests is a friend of mine. You won't have heard of him but his name is Major Jason Rance.'

Siu Tse's brain turned over a couple of times and she nearly lost her balance. *Finally, a chance for me to get my revenge at long, long last.* 'Don't worry. I'll arrange the very best menu and it will be a surprise to everyone,' and she privately gloated at the surprise.

Rifleman Hemlal Rai was due to go on Nepal leave and a new batman had been detailed to take over from him. The two men went through Jason's wardrobe, Hemlal explaining what clothes were worn when. He pulled back a draw of handkerchiefs and took out one old and blotched, with blue borders. 'I don't know why the Saheb likes this old one when there are so many new ones. He seldom uses it. Lance Corporal Kulbahadur Limbu told me that it was somehow special, no, no details, but it was never to be thrown away.'

Jason came into the room then and saw the two Gurkhas with 'that' handkerchief. 'On Friday night I am going to a party given for the battalion's officers by the local Europeans. Because I've known some of them almost as long as I've had that handkerchief, I'll take it with me. So I won't forget, I'll put it into my grey flannel trouser pocket now.'

There had been a thunderstorm earlier in the afternoon and the rain had eased off by the time Jason got into his car to go to the party. The sun came out as it was still drizzling and Jason thought: *sun and rain together mean either a jackal's wedding or a person's death*. Every time it had almost happened on operations, Jason's company had had a contact and a kill. *And it occurred this morning as well. Twice in the same day has never happened before. Does that bode really bad news? I hope not,* he thought as he drove off.

Towards the end of the meal Jason was sitting with his back to where Siu Tse came out to look at the guests, searching for a man she imagined was medium-sized, balding, slack-jawed, pinched-faced and short-sighted with close-cropped black hair. *He's not there. Have I been tricked?* she thought with dismay. She saw an Englishman turn and her heart somersaulted violently – *surely, oh surely not. It can't be, but that same smile, that same fair hair. No, it's simply not possible*. She watched as Jason took a handkerchief from his pocket to wipe his mouth. *Blue-rimmed, and that spot I could never get clean. It must be him*. She stared, overwhelmed and flabbergasted. *Yeeeees! Shandong P'aau, my saviour, Shandong P'aau, still alive. Bliss!* Her heart filled with warmth and joy as she saw the only person she had ever truly cherished. She hurried forward, eagerly calling out to him, 'Shandong P'aau, Shandong P'aau'. As she did, the lines 'The sun shines its bright light on the hill, Bright Virtue, be good and go back home' rang in her ears.

Jason turned at the sound of her voice and his Chinese name, his mind instantly reverting to that time in the forest with the lovely Chinese girl he had rescued then cuddled and kissed. His heart skipped several beats as he held out his arms to take her as she rushed to him.

Conversation stopped and everyone looked at Siu Tse in astonishment as she ran up to their host and flung her arms round his neck. Jason, momentarily stunned, looked at her and called out her name. 'Siu Tse, we meet again!' And once more, to everybody's surprise, bent over and, oblivious of stares from all around him, turned her to the light to see her better, kissed her then held her at arms' length.

Ten-year-old Fong Heng Lit, stabbing knife in hand, watched

from the kitchen in horror as his mother ran towards the *gwailo*, the foreign devil. The boy's mind was in turmoil at seeing the man he assumed was the one his mother had so long wanted to kill to avenge his own father's death. Heng Lit ran out from the kitchen after his mother, eyes on his *gwailo* target, knife clenched tight. He lunged at the European just as Jason pushed Siu Tse back at arm's length to have a better look at her. Fong Heng Lit could not stop himself as his target was screened by his mother, and the knife bedded deeply in the nape of her neck, penetrating the cervical spine.

Jason was transfixed with horror. Blood splashed on his arms as he held the mortally injured woman. He knew better than to try and remove the knife, doing so would only hasten her death. As he gently lowered Siu Tse to the ground, her body slumped. She was dead. Openly sobbing, Jason got down onto the floor beside her and, ignoring the blood pooling around Siu Tse, gave the one woman he just knew should have been his a final kiss to the forehead.

The next morning, the body of a ten-year-old boy of mixed Chinese and European blood was found floating in a pond a mile up the Nilai road.

By the time a joint funeral had been arranged for the boy and his mother, Jason Rance was back in the jungle, where the embrace of the wild was his only remaining companion in a life of solitude.

JP CROSS
OPERATION
BLACK ROSE

'CROSS SPINS HIS TALE WITH THE EYE
OF INCOMPARABLE EXPERIENCE'
JOHN LE CARRÉ, ON OPERATION JANUS

JP CROSS
OPERATION
JANUS

'NOBODY IS BETTER QUALIFIED TO
TELL THE STORY OF THE GURKHAS'
DEADLY JUNGLE BATTLES AGAINST COMMUNIST
INSURGENCY IN 1950S MALAYA'
JOHN LE CARRÉ

JP CROSS
OPERATION
RED TIDINGS

'NOBODY IS BETTER QUALIFIED
TO TELL THE STORY OF THE GURKHAS'
DEADLY JUNGLE BATTLES AGAINST COMMUNIST
INSURGENCY IN 1950S MALAYA'
JOHN LE CARRÉ

JP CROSS
OPERATION
BLIND SPOT

'CROSS SPINS HIS TALE WITH THE EYE OF
INCOMPARABLE EXPERIENCE'
JOHN LE CARRÉ, ON OPERATION JANUS

JP CROSS
OPERATION
STEALTH

'CROSS SPINS HIS TALE WITH THE EYE
OF INCOMPARABLE EXPERIENCE'
JOHN LE CARRÉ, ON OPERATION JANUS

JP CROSS
OPERATION
FOUR RINGS

'CROSS SPINS HIS TALE WITH THE EYE
OF INCOMPARABLE EXPERIENCE'
JOHN LE CARRÉ, ON OPERATION JANUS

JP CROSS
OPERATION
BLOWPIPE

'NOBODY IS BETTER QUALIFIED
TO TELL THE STORY OF THE GURKHAS'
DEADLY BATTLES AGAINST COMMUNIST
INSURGENCY IN 1950S MALAYA' JOHN LE CARRÉ

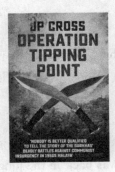

JP CROSS
OPERATION
TIPPING
POINT

'NOBODY IS BETTER QUALIFIED
TO TELL THE STORY OF THE GURKHAS'
DEADLY BATTLES AGAINST COMMUNIST
INSURGENCY IN 1950S MALAYA'

JP CROSS
OPERATION
HUNTER

'NOBODY IS BETTER QUALIFIED
TO TELL THE STORY OF THE GURKHAS'
DEADLY BATTLES AGAINST COMMUNIST
INSURGENCY IN 1950S MALAYA'